Maid of
WONDER

Also by
Jennifer McGowan

Maid of Secrets

Maid of Deception

A Thief Before Christmas

Maid of Wonder

JENNIFER McGOWAN

SIMON & SCHUSTER BFYR

New York London Toronto Sydney New Delhi

An imprint of Simon & Schuster Children's Publishing Division
1230 Avenue of the Americas, New York, New York 10020

For information about special discounts for bulk purchases, please contact Simon & Schuster Special Sales at 1-866-506-1949 or business@simonandschuster.com.

The Simon & Schuster Speakers Bureau can bring authors to your live event. For more information or to book an event, contact the Simon & Schuster Speakers Bureau at 1-866-248-3049 or visit our website at www.simonspeakers.com.

Book design by Lucy Ruth Cummins
The text for this book is set in ArrusBT Std.
Manufactured in the United States of America
2 4 6 8 10 9 7 5 3 1

Library of Congress Cataloging-in-Publication Data
McGowan, Jennifer.
Maid of wonder / Jennifer McGowan. — First edition.
pages cm. — (Maids of Honor)
Summary: In 1559 England, Sophia Dee, a member of the Maids of Honor, Queen Elizabeth I's secret all-female guard, is pitted against some of Europe's most celebrated mystics, including Nostradamus, in a race to uncover the answer to a deadly prophecy.
ISBN 978-1-4814-1826-3 (hardcover : alk. paper) — ISBN 978-1-4814-1828-7 (eBook)
[1. Courts and courtiers—Fiction. 2. Spies—Fiction. 3. Elizabeth I, Queen of England, 1533–1603—Fiction. 4. Sex role—Fiction. 5. Psychic ability—Fiction. 6. Prophecies—Fiction. 7. Great Britain—History—Elizabeth, 1558–1603—Fiction.] I. Title.
PZ7.M4784867Mb 2015
[Fic]—dc23
2014046127

For my nieces, Abigail and Danielle.
May your lives be filled with wonder.

ACKNOWLEDGMENTS

Writing *Maid of Wonder* was a true gift, as it allowed me to marry up my love of all things magical with my love for Elizabethan history. Many thanks go to my agent, Alexandra Machinist, for taking a chance on the Maids of Honor. It has been a wonderful journey! Thank you also to my editor, Christian Trimmer, for his profound insights and guidance, and to Catherine Laudone, assistant editor extraordinaire, for her patience in answering my never-ending questions. I am also sincerely grateful for copyeditor Bara MacNeill, who not only kept me in line with dates, word choices, and *math*, but who honored me with her thorough and careful review of my work. Any errors are, of course, my own.

Last but never least, thank you to John Dee for his fascination with angelic communication, and to the practitioners of magic and mysticism throughout the ages—the alchemists and astrologers, seers and psychics. This is Sophia's story, and that makes it your story as well. Thank you for the inspiration.

CHAPTER ONE

OCTOBER 1559
WINDSOR, ENGLAND

Death always starts as a whisper.

The dark angel hovers just at the edge of the glade, cloaked in shadows. But its voice is clear enough, the undertone so grim, so depressing, the very air around me seems to wilt a little at its passage.

Back on my own plane, amidst Queen Elizabeth's chattering court at Windsor Castle, I would not have heard its dire prediction so well. There, the angels' voices are no more than a puff of wind, the rustle of a playful breeze. Too quiet to be understood but impossible to ignore; an endlessly taunting conversation, just out of reach.

But here in this place that is more their world than mine, here I perceive the angels all too well. Here they shout and clamor; they demand and scoff. Here they insist and wail and rage.

Still, when they speak of death, even the angels are careful to keep their voices low. As if they understood that this is information not made for man to hear.

Man—or in this case, woman.

Death comes to Windsor, the specter murmurs again.

I turn toward it more fully, taking its measure through the gloom of this bleak hollow that serves as our meeting place. For I know this dark angel, and it knows me.

I have dreamed of it since before I could speak, terrifying nightmares that accompanied my loneliest nights and most desolate days. Throughout my childhood I feared it with the whole of my being. But since I have begun entering its realm more boldly these past few weeks, something fundamental has shifted between this grim specter and myself. I have watched it drift closer and closer to where I stand, surrounded by the other angels. As if it cannot stay away from me, despite its clear aversion to the other spirits who grace this quiet space.

For it is not like them.

It does not gown itself in blue-white light, almost too beautiful to behold. Sparkling wings do not flutter around its broad shoulders, displacing the eerie mists of this realm. It does not even style itself as a man or woman, like all the other angels do. Instead, it is a creature of shadow and fire, of pain and loss and despair. Across the hollow it stands, hunched and cowled in its heavy robes, the faintest hint of yellow flame emanating from its hooded head. It bends that hood toward me now, and I feel the blackness of its stare all the way to my physical self. Dread and deep foreboding lance through me, though my physical form remains hidden away, seated on a stone bench in a quiet glade much like this, just inside the edge of Windsor Forest.

But while my body rests safely in that small wooded clearing, my spirit is here, in the angelic realm. And in this place of dreaming, my spirit is strong. Here, I need not mask my oddness, desperate to remain unnoticed. Here I need not cower or shrink.

Here I need only one thing.

Answers.

"*Who* will die at Windsor? Can you give me a name? Or has this shade already crossed over?" I glance into the murk surrounding me, feeling the gaze of some poor departed soul trapped there, who is even now peering at me from the gloom. Its attention seems almost too strong to be one of the dead, too focused and intent, but I have never encountered any creature in this spectral realm that was neither angel nor shade. Perhaps this soul died recently . . . or reluctantly.

A chill slips along my skin. When I was very young, I believed that the angels who whispered to me were people who had passed away, still longing to reach the ones they'd left behind. But I have since come to understand that the dead do not speak in this shadowed realm. The souls of the departed can linger here, true. But they merely wander silently, caught between the world they've left and the world they fear to enter.

I have always pitied those grey shades. Recently, I have come to understand them as well.

For I am Sophia Dee, the much-remarked-upon niece of the most learned man in England. I am the weird girl, with nightmares and headaches and strange visions that assault me at awkward times. The girl who hears whispers when no one is talking, and who sees shadows in the full light of day. But despite all these things, I was also always the girl who knew her place in the world—who at least was certain of her past, if not her future.

No longer.

Because, as I have recently learned, I am not merely Sophia Dee, quiet and strange; the youngest member of the select group of maids chosen to spy for the Queen. I am also Sophia Manchester, the stolen-away child of a wealthy, loving father and a long-dead mother. The girl of pure potential, a symbol and a prize. The soon-to-be mystical warrior, whose power shall lie not in my sword, but in the secrets I will one day snatch from the angels' perfect lips.

And I will show them all.

I will be the seer the Queen believes that I can be. I will earn my title as a Maid of Honor, standing shoulder to shoulder with the other girls who make up our secret company: a thief, an assassin, a genius, and a beguiler. I will see the future so well and so clearly that I will prove to be Elizabeth's most valued asset, worthy of my place in her service. I *will* belong once more within the world of man, even as I learn to walk ever further into the realm of angels. And I will show them all.

Finally.

"Answer my questions, else I will leave!" Most of the angels shrink away from my harsh words, but the grim specter seems to embrace my anger. To revel in it. The wisps of flame, which were at first barely visible at the edge of its cowl, now seem to brighten as my irritation sharpens, and the dark angel's body becomes more solid in its cloak of dun-colored wool.

Emboldened, I take a long step forward, away from the bench that serves as my grounding point within this dreaming plane. The bench is made of pure obsidian, the same material as the small scrying stone I carry around my neck. When I first saw the obsidian bench in this glade, I knew its purpose immediately. It is my touchstone, the way back to my own plane. As long as I can see that bench, touch it, I will always find my way home.

Accordingly, I know I should never lose sight of this bench, though I am sorely tempted. I long to race into the angelic plane without restriction, to learn all its secrets. I dare not, of course . . . and yet I cannot help but wonder what lies beyond this misty glade.

Worse, the specter seems to sense my unspoken yearning. It watches across the open space between us, its silence now a mockery. It recognizes that I am linked to the obsidian bench, as surely as if I were holding on to my mother's hand, a hand I can no longer remember. The dark angel stands there, testing me, and I take another step forward, away from safety. Away from the certainty that I can leave the spectral plane at any moment, the certainty that I am in control.

I am no fool, mind you. But this angel spoke of *death*. And this is information I must have. My eyes never leaving the grim specter, I step forward yet again. I have never been so far into the center of the glade as this.

Then it deigns to speak, and my heart shrivels within me.

Though I see it plainly across the clearing, the dark angel is *also* at my side, bent close to my right ear, its fiery breath hot upon my neck.

Death plays your Queen in a game without end, it whispers. *It circles and crosses, then strikes once again.*

"No! No riddles," I demand, grateful for the spark of anger that drowns out my fear. "Tell me plainly what I must know."

They do this, the beings in this place. They speak in rhymes and twisted verse. I am certain their craftiness is deliberate, to keep me here as I struggle to understand them. But I have no patience for such games this day, not if the Queen is truly in danger. "Elizabeth herself will be attacked?" I ask. "But when? How?"

Across the glade, yellow flames blaze around the angel's hood, licking along the rough wool. Suddenly there is a hiss of words in my left ear, as swift as a murderer's knife. *The death you don't seek is the one you should fear. It aims for the blind, but catches the seer.*

"Stop that!" I jump away, but there is nothing beside me. I look back to where the specter hovers. "I need actual answers!"

It is no use. My dark angel seems done with me, shifting away into the gloom. I know better than to follow it. Instead, I withdraw as well, stepping backward until the obsidian bench grazes the backs of my legs. I sit down firmly, resolutely, and stare out at the specter's retreating form. If its words are worthless, then they are worthless. I will not drive myself to madness chasing it through the shadows.

Not today, anyway.

At the last moment, the dark angel turns to me. Its final words tease at my mind like a faint, mournful cry:

Follow the doves.

And it is gone.

Follow the doves? I groan inwardly. That's like telling me to chase the wind. I close my eyes and allow myself to leave this realm of mists and misdirection.

I feel a familiar terror clawing at me as I resurface in the center of a brightly lit forest clearing, my lungs straining for breath, my hands clenched, my jaw tight—

I open my eyes. Around me, as always, I see naught but my charming glade tucked up against the eastern walls of Windsor Castle. It is a fine October day, and the leaves are ablaze with color. Hastily I tuck my obsidian scrying stone and its chain back into my bodice, smoothing down my simple dress. I draw in several steadying breaths, reminding myself that I am *awake*, I am *alone*. I am, for now anyway, *safe*. Gradually my heart stops its thundering, and I slump on my little stone bench. I prefer this location in the depths of summer, but I cannot deny its beauty even today, with the sun dipping low in the sky, and . . .

I frown, peering upward. How has the sun moved so far, in truth? What time is it?

A distant peal of bells shatters the silence, and I move quickly toward the edge of the clearing. The bells strike one, and I gather up my skirts, preparing to run.

The bells churn on. Two, three. I am running now, realizing that I have been absent for hours. Hours when I was supposed to have been bent to my tasks for the Queen, or for one of her ladies. Hours when I was supposed to have been studying.

Four. Then nothing further. Four then, but not five. I can still make the end of my last class!

I dash through the forest till my breathing is ragged and my lungs ache. *Death plays your Queen,* the dark angel said, *in a game without end.* Does that mean there are multiple threats to Her Grace? If so, from what quarter? And why can't these messages ever make sense?

My lungs almost bursting with the effort, I reach the King's Gate and do not bother slowing down, turning the corner and rushing into the Lower Ward. With the coming of harvest season, it seems the castle has flung open its doors to travelers far and wide—they are all here, and they have money to spend. I dart in and out of the closely packed carts, desperate to get through. Rounding a corner too quickly, I hear a startled shriek but cannot stop. I barrel into a woman whose cage goes flying, setting free—

A small flock of doves.

CHAPTER TWO

"Look 'ere! Wot's this!" The woman's caterwauling sounds far too loud in my ears, and my hands fly to my pouches, scrabbling for coins. Nothing soothes the affronted like shillings. I've learned to carry money with me at all times, as I am constantly running into everyone, from goodwives to guards.

"I'm so sorry!" I begin, still fumbling with my skirts, but the woman is already speaking over me.

"Ye've released all my doves, you silly chit! I'll never—Ah!"

She chokes off her own words so sharply that I glance up at her. The old woman is suddenly as pale as death, her mouth agape. I turn to see what has caught her up so completely. Then I stare too.

Her flock of doves hasn't scattered to the sky as we both expected it to do. Instead, the birds are racing through the market stalls, weaving and bobbing and diving around townsfolk and farmers, nobles and serfs. I grow dizzy trying to follow their flight, and then I notice something else. The birds are *trying* to escape, to soar up into freedom, but they just . . . can't. An invisible force is somehow holding them back, trapping them within the circle of carts in the Lower Ward.

I see other shadows among the carts then, skimming and darting like half-remembered dreams. The angels? Are they yet with me? I purse my lips, trying to focus. I need to see what's happening here. *I need to see!*

I tilt my head, and the world around me shifts, signaling that I have breached the spectral plane. I can see more when I am grasping the obsidian stone, but for now this half trance will do. Through the prism of my altered vision, the ward is transformed from a raucous collection of hucksters and buyers and steaming meat pies into a crush of carts that seem hemmed in by a malevolent force—everything trapped, frozen in place. The doves that I startled cannot escape this invisible force either. They are beaten back every time they reach the edge of the carts.

Through the frantic weaving of the doves, I see something else as well—ravens. Several of the large glossy birds are perched atop the outermost stalls of the market day crowd, their beady eyes locked on the frenzied white doves. The carts the ravens have chosen are all prosperous, large, and overflowing, with grinning, gap-toothed women out in front. When I focus on the women, however, a chill clutches at my heart. I know one of them.

It's Mistress Maude.

As round as an apple, with steel-grey hair and a loud, boisterous manner, Maude is an herb mistress in the town of Windsor, renowned for her true love tinctures and honesty teas. But of late, my fellow spies and I suspect that she brews far more than harmless potions in her cottage workroom. I, for one, came away from her market stall in Windsortown but weeks ago *convinced* she was a poisoner. So far, however, I have no proof, only my suspicions. Which is hardly enough to call in the magistrates.

But seeing Mistress Maude here, in the Lower Ward of Windsor Castle, strikes me as important. And important in a very bad way. I glance from her to the women standing next to the other carts where the ravens have perched. Their presence feels dark, almost ominous. What is their purpose here?

"'Ave a care!" The startled voice of the dove seller cuts across my half trance, and I snap back to the present moment, just as we're both surrounded by frantically flapping doves. The birds—quite literally—have come home to roost, landing with a flurry of wings at the old woman's feet.

"God's breath," she says, her voice awed. "I've never seen the like."

Stupefied, she sets her cage upon the ground and opens it, and the birds walk, flop, and hop in, as docile as hens at feeding time. We both stare at the cage, then at each other. When have wild birds ever acted this way?

"Ho there, Miss Sophia!"

The booming voice nearly scares me out of my skin, and I spin round in alarm, recognizing the speaker immediately. The thick, burly man is one of the nicest members of the Queen's guard, but he is still a guard. I must always remember that.

"Master Seton!" I manage. "You startled me."

"Not 'alf as much as you just startled that poor goodwife,

I wager." Seton chuckles and moves his hand over my hair. At the light brush of his weathered fingers, a few white feathers drift down past my face. "Shouldn't you be in the Upper Ward?"

I try to quell my nerves. Of late, it seems as though every guard in the castle knows my business. Has the Queen ordered that I be watched? I know Elizabeth is eager for me to show signs of my skills, but surely she hasn't grown so impatient that she tracks my every move. "I was getting some air."

"Outside the walls? Good Windsor air does not suit you?" Seton draws in a deep breath, his barrel chest expanding to its full bulk, and I cannot help but laugh. I do like Seton, no matter that he treats me not as a young woman of the court, but as if I were his own grandniece, always underfoot. I glance past him and see his mare tethered away from the other mounts, and I blink in surprise. Sitting on the horse's back, right at the crest of the saddle, is another blasted dove. "Since when does Ladysweet give shelter to birds?"

Seton glances over as well, and an indulgent smile creases his face. "She's feeling poorly today." He shrugs. "Perhaps the wee thing will lift her spirits."

Only then do I note the mare's drooping head and tired eyes. I am well acquainted with this horse, as I try to sneak her an apple more days than not. She's normally as lively as a foal in the springtime, but not today.

"What ails her?" I move toward the horse, noting her unusually full belly beneath the loosened saddle straps. As I approach, the dove startles. It flies over my shoulder to where I suspect it will rejoin its fellows.

"A touch of the megrims, I warrant," Seton says. "She was 'appy enough when we started the day, but she's been off since we opened the ward to the carts."

I frown, patting Ladysweet's sweaty neck. She snuffles at me, and I can almost taste the wave of despair coming off her, thick and murky. "What's wrong, sweetheart?" I move around to look into her eyes. There's something there, behind the large brown orbs, that speaks of pain and yet more sorrow. But pain from what? Seton takes almost obsessively good care of the mare; her coat is glossy, her hooves well shod. Suddenly Ladysweet rocks her head forward, and my hand slips to her chin. It's a testament to my affection for the horse that I don't wince as she wetly smears grass and saliva into my palm.

"That's quite disgusting, Ladysweet," I say. I glance down at my hand as I prepare to shake it dry . . . then pause. There's something odd about this chewed-up mixture of grass that the horse hasn't quite seen fit to swallow. A sprinkling of short, dark leaves, a few seeds, and a sliver of red, like the skin of a cherry but smaller—far smaller.

Oh, no.

I act without caution, once more slipping over the precipice between this world and the next. I glance up at Ladysweet again. Now in her dark eyes I can observe far more. I can see her trotting into the Lower Ward, having been tied up too loosely by her kind owner. I can see her greedy mouth as she nips up the falling treasures from one cart, then another—and finally from Maude's cart, which trails boughs of yew.

Lovely, *deadly* yew.

I close my eyes, understanding her pain at last. "This is not going to be easy," I murmur, "but you must do this." The horse nickers wearily at my words, and my Sight expands, my heart jumping in fear to match the rapid beating of her own. Even if she has ingested only a few of the seeds, yew poisoning almost always leads to a quick and horrible death. I squint at the other guards' mounts. Some of them are already listing. This is not an accident, I am certain. These horses were deliberately poisoned.

But why?

Will Seton steps to my side. "Are you . . . well, Miss Sophia?" he asks, in that tone I have heard too often, when I do not mask my oddness quickly enough. But I don't have time for the guard's delicate sensibilities. Not now, with Ladysweet so close to death.

"Get water and honeycake, or send a page to do so," I snap. "In but a few moments, when she works up her strength, Ladysweet will empty her stomach quite violently and long. When the fluid she purges is naught more than water, provide her with a quarter cake each hour, no more, and a quarter bucket of water. She will live, I swear it, but only if you do this and do it quickly." I shudder, seeing the mare's future painted before me in whisper-thin strokes, unsure of whether I can trust this image in my mind. Still, for Seton, I speak with calm assurance. "She will live."

"What're you talking about?" Seton's voice is harsh and filled with fear. "What's wrong with her?" He reaches out and pulls me around to face him, and I do not flinch, though I sense his shock as he takes in my appearance. My eyes—it's always my eyes that are affected most when I draw upon the Sight.

"Yew," I say, and he visibly recoils, whether at the word or my face, I am not sure. Our time together is at an end, however. Ladysweet gives a keening cry, and her head jerks wildly.

"God's teeth!" Seton curses. I step aside as he lunges for his beloved horse, and I swing my Sight-widened gaze back across the market stalls. Once more I sense that the carts are hemmed in by a dark force, only now I also see a thick, black trail of energy that knifes through the gathered carts, a pathway of spite and sorrow that seems woven together by the devil's hand. I follow the coarse line to where it reaches the far edge of the carts, deep inside the Lower Ward.

But the trail does not stop.

It continues on, this spew of filth and darkness, roiling across the grassy field in front of Saint George's Chapel, on up through the Middle Ward. It curves around the Round Tower and flows toward the Norman Gate and the Upper Ward of Windsor Castle, dense, black, and ugly— and on an unmistakable trajectory for . . .

The Queen.

CHAPTER THREE

I am running again, though I can hear another guard crying out in alarm as his horse suddenly buckles beside him, trembling and thrashing.

Follow the doves, the dark angel said. The doves led me to Ladysweet, and Ladysweet may die, in truth. But is that the death predicted to come to Windsor? Surely not!

So why tell me to follow the doves?

I can only pray that death has not come for the Queen so quickly. I run yet faster, hiking up my skirts, my Sight dimming as my exertion grounds me more firmly on this plane. But I can still see the stain of evil as I race through the Norman Gate and enter the Upper Ward.

I burst into the castle, past startled guards, but the familiar gloom of Windsor's corridors provides none of its usual balm. Instead I feel trapped, the dank air too heavy for my lungs.

I do not slow until I reach the Presence Chamber. I enter the wide doors, also flanked by guards, but even as I cross the threshold, I sense I am too late.

Far to the front of the room, a frail old woman is on her

knees before the elegantly gowned Elizabeth. The Queen herself, her crown glittering in the waning light, has descended from her dais and leans forward as if to hear the crone more clearly. And surrounding them the thick cord of darkness suddenly tightens, like a snake eating its own tail.

"No!" I gasp, though no one hears my cry. My feet are rooted to the rush-covered floor, and I can barely breathe. I force myself to open more fully to the Sight, and the words that tumble toward me are as dire as the ancient woman who speaks them:

"A royal house defeated,
disaster unforeseen.
Death comes to Windsor
to court the maiden Queen."

Elizabeth jerks back as if she's been slapped. *Death comes to Windsor*—these are the exact words of the dark angel. But the rest of the prophecy is terrible and new. A phalanx of guards immediately presses forward, surrounding the old woman as Elizabeth is hauled back by the strong arms of her advisors, Sir William Cecil and Sir Francis Walsingham. The Queen's advisors take charge, and Walsingham's sharp, imperious command fills the space. A pair of guards sweeps forward to accost the old woman.

But she will have nothing more to say. As I take one last look before quelling my Sight, I can see the thick knot of evil drifting away from the old woman, like smoke on a fitful breeze, as she crumples to the ground.

She is dead.

Instead of apprehending her, the guards change course smoothly, one of them lifting her in his arms, the other clearing the way. It's not common for villagers to drop dead while in audience with the Queen, but that doesn't mean the guards aren't prepared for it. They walk by me, carrying the old woman, and I step into their wake—only to be turned back by a firm hand.

"Why are you here?" Cecil growls as Walsingham hurries by us, supporting the Queen. Only the tips of Elizabeth's gilded crown are visible as more guards gather close, ushering her back to her Privy Chamber. "Shouldn't you be with your fellow maids?"

"I, ah, sensed that something was happening here and slipped in but a moment ago," I say, not missing Cecil's sharp glance. This is a dangerous game, to indicate that my Sight is manifesting. But it is no more dangerous than admitting to Cecil that I disobeyed the Queen's command and wandered off while I should have been bent to my studies. I rush on. "Who was the old woman? And how did she gain entrance?"

"She came in after the last of the commoners left. None of these fools noticed her." Cecil's voice conveys his disgust, though I am not surprised. The elderly are often overlooked, and if the woman was dressed in simple clothing, who was to say she was not some servant or another, sent here to carry out the scraps of the last meal? "She had to have traveled past the front doors in the thick of the petitioners, then waited until the day was done." He scowls. "The Queen's audience should have ended a half hour ago."

"So she simply approached the Queen?"

"Called her out!" Cecil says. "Said she had news, important news, from none other than Mother Shipton." His face registers yet more disgust. "And at that, of course, Elizabeth all but leaped off her throne, the better to hear the creature."

"Mother Shipton," I murmur. "Oh, no."

"Oh, yes." Cecil rubs his hand over his eyes as we step aside to make way for another wave of guards.

Old Mother Shipton is quite possibly the most notorious woman in all of England, though she generally keeps to her own tiny cottage far to the north. Born in a cave as her mother was dying, she grew up to possess two singular traits: extreme ugliness and, by all accounts, the Sight. Unlike most women with the gift, however, she has used it openly and to great effect. She has become so powerful that *no one* dares cross her, not even the Church. Her mystical portents have been frightening both commoners and kings for the past fifty years, particularly when she correctly predicted the downfall of old King Henry's chief minister, Thomas Cromwell, before I was even born.

Now she is famous throughout the land. Not even the French prophet Michel de Nostredame is more renowned than Mother Shipton, though at least Nostradamus can claim an actual medical education to his name. Mother Shipton merely snatches her prophecies out of smoke.

Still, this is the first I've heard of the ancient seer speaking of Elizabeth.

I tilt my head, lost to my own thoughts. Shouldn't I have divined that Mother Shipton had targeted the Queen? Couldn't the dark angel have said *Mother Shipton is sending an old woman to disturb the Queen with a terrible prophecy,* instead of *Follow the doves?* I mean, yes, the specter did speak the words "death comes to Windsor" but not the other three lines, which are equally important! And nowhere in Mother Shipton's prophecy is there any mention of *doves*.

None of it makes any sense. As usual.

Cecil sighs heavily, recalling my attention. "Fortunately for us all, the old hag's words were loud enough for only Elizabeth to hear. To the court this was naught but an odd disruption to an otherwise ordinary day." He grimaces, and I don't even try to explain that I also heard the old woman's prediction with my Sight-enhanced senses. "To the Queen, however—"

"Sir William!"

We're both startled by the arrival of a new young guard, whose relief is clear when he sees me. "And Miss Dee. The Queen sent me to collect you both." He scowls at me. "You were not with the other maids."

"I needed some air," I protest again, praying the man doesn't ask any questions of his fellow guards who were in the Lower Ward. I'm reminded of that scene—wild-eyed Sophia Dee, covered in dove feathers, racing away from a small herd of soon-to-be-dying horses. That should add to my sterling reputation as the oddest girl at Windsor.

Before the guard can say anything else, Cecil cuts in, directing him to take us to the Queen. And as we pass through the double doors into the Privy Chamber, I at last see something to gladden my heart this day.

The Queen is seated upon her throne, her back straight, her color quite regained.

Walsingham stands at her side, looking like he has eaten something bad, which is his natural look.

But it is the four young women now ranged around the Queen who truly comfort me. The Maids of Honor are my family, though they do not know it. The witty, resourceful Meg Fellowes, the quickest thinker of our group; the lovely, sharp-tongued Beatrice Knowles, whose cool exterior cannot quite mask her gracious heart; the impossibly intelligent Anna Burgher, who sees windows where the rest of us see walls; and the grey-eyed, grey-souled Jane Morgan, who has stared death in the face one too many times, yet lived to fight again. Thief and beguiler, genius and assassin. And finally, myself—the seer. I am the youngest of these women, and yet the oldest, too. The maid who has seen too much.

And Elizabeth has called us here, with her most trusted advisors and no others. Not even the guards remain inside the room once Cecil and I arrive. From her height upon the dais, Elizabeth gazes at me without expression as I join my fellow spies, while Cecil mounts the short steps to stand beside her. I straighten carefully under her regard, trying to look useful without betraying my secrets.

For I am the keeper of words that cannot be spoken, of visions that cannot be shared. From the crashing, jumbled nightmares of my youth to my more recent, saner forays into the angelic realm, I have chronicled the rushing tide of both the past and future—loves, losses, deaths. Wars won and lost. I have witnessed more than most can imagine. And more than I can ever reveal.

Because though my gift is grand, it is also flawed. I don't

see merely one future for a person. I see two. Sometimes more. And until I can say with certainty that yes, *this* is the true future that will pass, then I dare not say anything at all.

My Sight remains both a weapon and a weakness, and I must guard it at any cost.

Elizabeth waits another long, measured moment. Then she speaks. And given my weapon—and my weakness—her accusation cuts me to the bone.

"You have all failed me," she hisses, her voice heavy with outrage. Her gaze sweeps along the line of maids, then fixes on Cecil and Walsingham. "You, who are my chief advisors, my closest counselors. You have been put to the test, and you have failed."

Cecil stiffens, indignant. "That old woman was part of the petitioner group, Your Majesty," he protests. "You would rather us keep your people at a distance?"

"No!" Elizabeth says. "But I would rather not hear of a death in my own castle from a dying peasant at my feet, but from the people I feed and clothe and house!" She curls her hands into fists, her body rigid on her throne. "She presaged a death, Cecil. And not just any death, but one that courts *me*—"

"She was an old woman breathing her last," Walsingham cuts in, speaking in reasonable tones. "You cannot place any import in her words."

"She received a vision from *Mother Shipton*," Elizabeth retorts. "A vision that, despite the old woman's failing health, brought her to my castle in supplication and warning, that I might be prepared. Would that those closer to me have such a care about my person!"

Cecil sniffs. "I hardly think—"

"Do you not understand? I do not need your thoughts!" The Queen's face is white once more, and I realize she is well and truly filled with fury. Fury, and perhaps a little fear. "If Mother Shipton is presaging a death in my house, do you think this one old woman in Windsortown is the only one who has heard about it? Do you not suspect that news such as this will travel far and wide, giving rise to suspicions about the stability of my throne? And, worse, if it *is* myself who is predicted to die, do you not imagine that my enemies might think this is an opportune time to strike? A time 'blessed by the heavens'?"

She slumps back against thickly embroidered cushions. "Everything I have done this year is to convince my people that their kingdom is safe and secure. I have worked for tolerance. I have endeavored to heal the wounds of faith wrenched open by my sister. I am securing our borders and making sure the French do not gain a foothold in the north. But I cannot do any of these things if I am dead, Cecil. And I will not be a mere note in the annals of history. I will not!"

I open my mouth to protest, but the words will not come. I do not trust my Sight so much that I would counsel my Queen that she will live to a ripe old age, though I have seen that she does, over and over again. For if in telling her this, I put her at risk, then it is not merely my judgment that will be held accountable, but my life.

And, far worse: if Elizabeth were to die as a result of my smug boldness, the kingdom would be ruined.

Such is my constant dilemma:

Speak, and risk everything.

Stay silent, and risk everything.

"I demand a convocation," Elizabeth declares. "If the simplest goodwife of my kingdom can give me such information willingly, freely, and on her deathbed, then surely the greatest minds at my disposal can shed light on the full meaning of her words. I want those minds here, within the fortnight, that they may discern this prophecy and expose every subtlety of the old woman's message."

"A convocation?" Walsingham's voice is steady, but the concern in his tone is plain. "Here at Windsor Castle? But a gathering of strangers will only increase any risk to you, Your Grace, not diminish it."

"The risk is already too high!" Elizabeth fairly spits the words. "Until we root out the truth of this prediction, Walsingham, my court is not safe. I am not safe."

"According to a woman about to die," he observes. "A woman with nothing to lose."

Elizabeth glares at him. "And nothing to gain, either."

This is not true, I know in an instant. The old woman certainly could not have been promised gold or goods for herself, as close to death as she was. But there are many ways to repay a service such as she performed. Who would need to send a messenger like this, with such terrible words for the Queen?

In my mind's eye I see Mistress Maude again, grinning in the Lower Ward. Then, beyond her, hunched in a shawl, I see another bent form, her body twisted with age, her face gnarled and as ancient as time itself.

"Why not ask Mother Shipton to explain her prophecy?" I am startled to realize that I am the one speaking, and all eyes in the room quickly shift to me. It is not my way to assert myself, but now that I have begun, I must finish. "Can we not send a brace of guards to escort her here, or at the very least petition her to clarify the prediction?"

"Mmm," Beatrice offers in a tempering voice. "That would seem ideal, Sophia, but from what I have heard, Mother Shipton is not famed for her gentle nature."

I grimace, recalling the same dozen or so stories, handed down through the years, of the old woman's harsh treatment of those who sought her out. "But mayhap if the men didn't offend—"

"Enough!" The Queen's sharp word cuts across the room. "I will send guards, of course, and with strict instructions not to inflame the woman. They will withdraw the moment they feel anything is amiss. I have no interest in having more curses thrown down on my head. But in the meantime I will seek my own answers." She scowls at me, and I sense the danger in her glance. "Consider this your chance to prove yourself, Sophia. It is beyond time that you served me to your fullest ability, so that all may know that my strength extends beyond the might of my men."

"Your G-Grace?" I stammer.

The Queen draws herself up, lifting her chin. And in that moment I see her both for who she is now and for who she will become. Tall, with a bearing she has perfected over long and careful years, Elizabeth is strikingly beautiful, with flowing red hair, fair skin, an aristocratic nose, and a firm jaw.

However, it is not her lovely features that will beguile the generations to come, but the legacy of her strength. Her soul shines so brightly, it will be honored evermore.

"The greatest minds of our age will be summoned to Windsor in the coming days," Elizabeth announces, "put to a simple task. And you, my own Maid of Honor, shall be put to that task as well. I pledge you against mystic and mathematician, alchemist and sage. Because one of you, by God, *will* tell me what I seek." She nods, warming to the picture her vivid imagination is painting for her. "These few most worthy souls will gather, and each shall be asked, who will die next at Windsor? And when, and how?"

She leans forward then, intent. "And should anyone learn of this fell prophecy, they shall also learn that England's Queen was not caught unprepared. That she is neither weak nor foolish. If it is a death that we can prevent for the good of the people, then by my troth we shall prevent that death." She grimaces. "But if it is a death that is in accordance with God's will, a course so set in the stars that man has no place diverting it, then we shall mourn the passage of the individual's soul and bury him or her with all due honor. And either way, this nonsense will be done."

A long silence follows her words.

Finally, Cecil, as if seeing no advantage to arguing, bows to Elizabeth. "Of course, Your Grace. We will begin at once, but quietly," he says. "There is no need for word of this to get out. Who shall we bring together? And how long shall we bid them tarry within the walls of Windsor?"

Elizabeth taps her chin with a long finger. "The list of

able men is short enough," she says. "And their answers will be shorter. We will not need much time." She smiles then, though there is no warmth in it, and turns once more to me. "Would that my own maid succeed where they cannot."

I feel the weight of her stare, the awesome responsibility she is laying at my feet.

But it is the next words of Queen Elizabeth Regnant, Gloriana most high, that inscribe themselves into my very bones:

"I do not pretend I am greater than the Almighty, to believe I can stop a death that He has sanctioned," she says. "But though death may come to Windsor, it shall not come for me. I defy God, the heavens, and the devil himself to take me from this throne."

CHAPTER FOUR

That night, well after the castle has sought its rest, my fellow spies and I sit upon our pallets, unable to sleep. In less than a fortnight I must pit myself against the most revered sages in Christendom, to name which soul at Windsor has been marked for an untimely death. And though this burden lies squarely upon my shoulders, it is one that all the other maids wish to help me carry.

"Sophia, you must take care," Beatrice says, sensing my distress as she watches me from across the room. "You can see only what you see, as it is revealed to you. If you push too hard, you'll get sick again."

I smile ruefully. She speaks of an experience I cannot recall, a frenzied dash through the grounds of her ancestral home a few weeks ago, where I ended up in a wild group of Travelers, Egyptians who were illegally living on Beatrice's family estate. There, while I was quite out of my mind with delirium, I was given the obsidian stone that now dangles from a chain around my neck. Since I've had the stone to ground me, I haven't fainted dead away while trying to invoke the Sight. My eyes become glassy and grey, it is true, but that is an easy enough thing to hide. Usually.

Still, Beatrice is correct. I have already begun to sense a curious pain that builds inside me when I stay too long within the angelic realm, when I demand answers that the angels are unwilling to give. It is almost as if my brain grows too big for my skull and, desperate for relief, tries to push its way free. That cannot end well.

"And you do have time," Meg says. "It will be another several days more before these few 'great minds' gather and you must produce the victim's name. Perhaps it will come to you before they descend on our doorstep, and we can send them cheerfully on their way."

"Perhaps," I agree, but I have my doubts. I asked the dark angel who would die at Windsor, and received only riddles in response. There is nothing to suggest its answer will change merely because my need is great.

After the Queen's proclamation, my fellow spies and I were summoned to Cecil's chambers and given a new, intriguing task. It appears that both of Elizabeth's advisors suspect that, along with the Queen's invited guests, a raft of hangers-on and villains will descend upon Windsor once they hear whispers of this convocation, frauds fully prepared to predict a dire murder they will then attempt to bring about in return for both the Queen's gold and her favor. It has fallen to the Maids of Honor to keep track of this score of strangers who are expected at the castle, that we might ensure that each of them is watched at all times. Accordingly, Anna and Meg must sharpen their wits, Beatrice must sharpen her wiles, and Jane must sharpen her knives.

And I must sharpen my Sight, that I might see what must be seen—with confidence—in time to prevent disaster.

"It's Maude who has me worried in all this," Anna muses from her pallet. She is working another of the puzzle boxes given to the Queen by my "uncle" John Dee, gifts of which Elizabeth has long since tired. Anna has solved each of them at least a dozen times, and now she has taken to doing so with her eyes closed. She speaks thusly, her face as serene as if she were sleeping, yet her voice is clear and strong. "You say she was standing at one of the carts that was topped with ravens and trailing boughs of yew. What service is it to her to kill the Queen's horses, though? Yes, we suspect her of brewing poison, but her focus seems primarily to be on her teas, tonics, and potions. Even Jane here has toyed with her wares."

"Which failed," Jane says flatly. It is all I can do to hide my grin as Beatrice mischievously catches my eye. When last we were in Windsortown at the herb mistress's stall, Maude gave us a potion to try, which Beatrice boldly presented to Jane as a tonic to ward away men. In fact, it was some kind of love tea, and in the wake of applying it liberally to her person, our resident assassin has never been more popular with the guards. "Once I get my hands on—"

"Nevertheless," Beatrice cuts in smoothly, "Anna is correct. Maude has hidden her darker nature well to date, but her presence in the Lower Ward today cannot be an accident." She glances at me again. "You say her cart was part of this strange oppression? That kept everyone trapped together in the Lower Ward?"

"It was like this," I say, picking up one of the pencils we are constantly stealing from Cecil's office chamber. I move to the wall, not wanting to waste precious parchment, and draw the scene I saw so clearly within the Lower Ward. "There were five carts, scattered around the edges of the Lower Ward, which would be nothing terribly surprising, except that when I viewed them with my Sight, they all seemed positioned to hem everyone in, with Maude at a place of power, farthest out into the Lower Ward." I mark the locations of the carts, underlining Maude's. "And then, through the center of it all, leading away from the King's Gate and on up through the Lower Ward, there was this . . . thick trail of energy, dark and horrible. I felt quite clearly that this line marked the passage of—well, of evil."

"You can't get more cursed than that," Jane says from her corner. Having been born in Wales, she is more familiar than the rest of us with the old ways. "An' now the old woman who spoke to the Queen is dead for her troubles, which is eviler still."

"Unless she was just that!" Meg stirs in protest. "An old woman, weak of body and confused of mind." Meg grew up on the streets with her traveling theatre troupe, and is ever defending the common soul to those of us more used to life inside of walls than out. "Nobody among the courtiers recognized this goodwife, and we've not yet had a chance to ask the villagers of Windsor."

"You'll get no answers there." Jane shakes her head. "Those people aren't fools. That old woman scared the Queen; not even Cecil and Walsingham deny it. Her own family would disavow her rather than be called into question by the Queen's men."

Meg frowns in the gloom, but we all know Jane is right. Elizabeth is both infuriated and frightened, and that spells danger to any who might be held accountable. But there is something more to this we are not seeing, I am sure of it. *Follow the doves,* the dark angel told me. *Follow the doves.*

"We must go to Windsor and see for ourselves," I say, wondering if I can find the dove seller again, or if she has done what her own birds could not, and flown away. "Surely there must be something there that will shed some light on these riddles."

"And there are three riddles, yes?" Anna asks, opening her eyes to focus on this new subject. "The first, most simple: follow the doves. Well, you did that."

"But they went nowhere." I sigh. "Just round and round the Lower Ward, and then back to their owner."

"And to Seton's horse," Jane says. "For which I'm sure he's grateful."

We pause, considering today's tragedy in the Lower Ward. Seton's horse alone survived the poisoned yew. More intriguing, the collapse of the other guards' steeds, even as the old woman was dying on the rushes of the Presence Chamber, sent all of the Lower Ward into scattered flight, villagers racing to get their carts out of the castle before anyone could blame them for the anguished screams of the horses. By the time the chamber guards reached the Lower Ward to question any villagers who might have seen the old woman as she'd entered Windsor Castle, the place was deserted.

So, I was correct. The horses *were* poisoned deliberately. Their violent illness and death created the distraction needed for Maude and her fellow goodwives to slip away from Windsor unseen.

Guards have been dispatched to the town, of course, to see if they can track down any carts adorned with yew, but not even the Queen's men believe they'll find the stall-keepers who brought such a deadly poison inside the castle walls. And I can't point the guards to anyone, save Maude. Worse, I did not see the yew trailing from the herb mistress's cart with my own eyes. I saw it with my Sight, which oftentimes sees both past and present as one. More than likely, Maude hid away the yew once the horses had nipped its deadly branches, and now it is long gone.

"Leave off the doves," I say. "The other predictions are more important. 'Death plays your Queen in a game without end. It circles and crosses, then strikes once again.' What can that mean? Will the Queen be attacked during some sort of dance?"

"Or a country game," muses Meg. "But some sort of entertainment, surely." She glances up. "The only festival we have coming up is Samhain, but that is nearly a fortnight away."

"And Mother Shipton's prophecy seems more imminent as well," I say. "'A royal house defeated, disaster unforeseen. Death comes to Windsor to court the maiden Queen.' The part about death coming to Windsor, I . . . I saw that too, today. When I was scrying."

I have not told my fellow spies that I can actually speak with angels. They have seen only that I fall into a sort of trance where I receive visions and messages. The idea of a true conversation with angels is too odd, verily, for anyone who hasn't done it. It's odd even for me, and I have.

"Ha! Scrying. I knew that was where you were off to." Jane's words ring with satisfaction. "Next time I'm coming with you. I've had enough of languages and books."

"Were you scrying outside the walls, Sophia?" Beatrice asks, but I wave off her concerns. She is always so worried about me!

"I was very careful. But don't you see? The words I received in the angelic realm were exactly the same as those the old woman used in her prediction to the Queen. That *has* to mean the angels are finally giving me something I can use—actual information, instead of messages that are little more than a rhyme wrapped in a riddle strung together with a cipher." I sigh. "What I could really use, though, is a *name*. Then my Sight would at last be an asset to the Crown."

"Be careful what you wish for," Beatrice says gloomily, and her words set a pall upon the group. I grimace, grateful for the long shadows in the room that hide my frustration. She means well, they all do, but this is exactly why I haven't told them of the final prediction I received today, that the death I should actually be worrying about is one that befalls a "seer." They would simply assume the seer is me and try to keep me safe.

But I know the truth of it. None of us will be safe until we know where death will strike next at Windsor.

And perhaps not even then.

CHAPTER FIVE

The following several days pass in a blur of activity, as I feel every day will until the Queen learns the name of the poor soul predicted to die in her court. The servants prepare rooms for the men of science that Elizabeth has invited to solve Mother Shipton's prophecy, and the Queen is using the occasion to turn the Visitors Apartments inside out. As we expected, additional metaphysicians and arcane scholars have also somehow learned of the mysterious prediction spoken to the Queen and have journeyed to Windsor Castle to pledge their assistance. With his usual skill and diplomacy, Cecil has turned them all away, none of them the wiser that their suspicions are well grounded.

While they remained under our roof, however, the Maids of Honor performed our task of following them around, listening to their conversations, and reporting on their activities. Anna, most of all, has enjoyed this work; talking with the scientists for long hours about recent discoveries in science and alchemy has been a true thrill for her.

As for me, I cannot focus. Even this morning, when I am

supposed to be in class with my fellow maids, I tarry in the shadows of the great kitchens, grateful to be alone, if only for a moment. Elsewhere in the castle, and everywhere I look, I see a guard, or Cecil or Walsingham, staring at me from across the room. I cannot escape to scry in the forest, and my dreams have been blank canvases, despite my impassioned nightly prayers that the explanation of Mother Shipton's dread prophecy might grace my sleeping mind.

It is almost as if the more desperate I am for answers, the more I am forsaken. It is likely to drive me mad.

Since I have received no grand revelation, however, I've been forced to join my fellow spies in our daily classes . . . though I constantly am late. Like now. I cannot claim any good reason for my tardiness this morning either, other than that I closeted myself away in the eaves of Saint George's Chapel, peering out over the Lower Ward as I watched the arrival of the first learned man Elizabeth has called to Windsor Castle to solve her dilemma. John Dee—astrologer, scientist, metaphysician, alchemist . . . kidnapper, criminal.

Villain.

The sage now considered the greatest mind in Europe has not always been so distinguished. Not twelve years ago, certainly, when he stole me from my family, kidnapping me and hiding me away to wait until the day when I would help him achieve greater mystical accomplishments than he apparently believed he ever could on his own.

I discovered this treachery only recently, when Jane and Meg stumbled across documents earlier this summer that revealed that the man who was my betrothed—Lord

Brighton—was actually my long-lost *father*, a man John Dee had told me was dead. My father somehow discovered my existence and traveled to Windsor Castle, duping the Queen into believing he wanted to marry me, in order to keep me from being married to anyone *else* until he could devise a way for me to escape the castle.

It was a dangerous game. If my father's ruse had been discovered, he would have been charged with treason. Fortunately, I convinced him that I could fight my own battles, and Beatrice used her wiles to persuade the Queen to encourage my father's engagement to another, far more suitable woman of the court—thus keeping him safely out of harm's way.

But now John Dee is here once more; now I will have to face him, with the knowledge of what he did to me so long ago. Now I will have to nod and curtsy and look into the eyes of the man who took everything away from me . . . and all I will be allowed to do is smile.

For after all, it was by John Dee's own hand that I was brought to serve the Queen barely a year ago, with whispered assurances to Her Grace that I would one day blossom with the Sight. But Dee doesn't know that, in fact, I *have* begun to gain control of my Sight—just as he doesn't know that I am aware of his villainy. There is much he doesn't know.

I need to keep it that way.

"Sophia? Sophia!"

I jerk to attention, only to see Anna peering at me from the top of the stairs at the far end of Windsor Castle's enormous kitchens, where my feet have taken me, despite my mind's insistence on wandering.

"I've been sent to fetch you." Anna purses her lips, blowing a curl of red hair away from her face. "We've been waiting this half hour! Have you been here all this time?"

"A half hour?" I am aghast. Even under castle watch I cannot seem to keep track of time. "I'm so sorry. I—"

"Well, be sorry with your feet." She grins at me. "It's poisons, and I canna wait to get back to them, I tell you plain!" She whirls and clatters back down the stairs toward the cellar chamber, and I come more slowly behind.

Anna has a passion for knowledge of any stripe, be it of poisons or princes or Ptolemy. She seems born to ask questions that have no answers, to crack open every dusty book, pry apart every locked chest. I have seen visions of nearly all my fellow spies at one time or another, but Anna's future remains murky to me.

Now, as I near the lower level, I hear voices and am relieved that Meg is in class. She can recite any lesson from memory, no matter how lengthy, and she is cunning besides. She will remember the important bits of today's class more clearly than even Anna, for whom every aspect of every discussion is interesting.

Anna dashes ahead of me to join my fellow spies, and as laughter breaks out among them, I glance up, missing the end of the stair entirely. I stumble forward and catch myself against the rough wall. Instinctively I reach for my necklace.

When my fingers touch the stone's cool surface, the scene around me snaps and flutters, like a sheet caught up in a stiff breeze. Instead of thick cellar walls, I see a man in a beautifully appointed bed, draped with luxurious coverlets.

A crown rests on his head, and a mantle of purple drapes his shoulders. In his lax grasp a gold scepter lies awkwardly across his legs. He is not old, but he looks as if he has been terribly ill, his face lined and gaunt. Beside him sits a weeping young woman, pretty and blond, the swell at her abdomen indicating she is heavily pregnant. I look more closely at the man and recoil, wishing the image away.

He is dead. His sightless eyes are fixed on some far-off horizon he will never reach. His mouth gapes open, and blood trickles from the corner. Only, the man's blood is not red but a rich purple, the color of his cloak. The color of kings.

The faintest whisper curls around me. *Death comes to Windsor.*

I jerk away from the wall, both hands to my face, my breath catching in my throat. Who is this man? Is he already dead, or is his death something I'm supposed to prevent? And the scepter and crown—there is no mistaking *that* implication, but are those riches allegorical, or is a true king about to breathe his last? He looked like no king currently enthroned across the Continent, but I have only painted miniatures to go by. Those are no real indication of anyone's actual appearance but, rather, are an artist's oft-desperate portrayal of the subject's best features.

Forcing my breathing to slow, my heart to stop pounding, I step into the cellar chamber as quietly as possible . . . though, of course I am noted. The head cook of Windsor doesn't stop her lecture, but her glance flies to me, then slides away in fright. I am certain that if her hands were not holding up a bunch of wild lettuce, she would cross herself.

Among the servants of Windsor Castle, there are two decided reactions to me. The first is that of Will Seton: indulgent protection, as if I were a fey bird hopping along a tree branch. The second is that of this woman and so many of the servants: fear and mistrust. I have done naught to deserve such a reaction, I swear. Yes, I flinch at shadows that no one else can see. Yes, I mutter under my breath while standing alone. And yes, I am the supposed niece of the most celebrated astrologer in England—and a seer in my own right. But still.

Fortunately, the cook, who is also the royal herb mistress, does not hesitate, but plunges on with her lesson. We have long studied obscure poisons from all over, from Italy to the Netherlands, learning in detail who poisoned whom and with what from the ancient times on. But today our interest is much more homespun. We seek to understand what the local cunning folk might be able to pull from the ground or the trees, or to purchase at market day, for these are our greatest threats. We also wish to understand what tinctures and tonics lie within our own storerooms, and what they are used for at Windsor Castle.

The herb mistress details the contents of the royal larder, and I mark her words as I ease into a seat beside Jane. As usual, Jane is polishing the hilt of her blade, this one a short, vicious-looking dagger recently come to England from the Alhambra of Spain. Caring for her weapons collection soothes Jane unlike anything else, which is all one really needs to know about our resident assassin.

Now she grins and points to the front of the room with her knife. "Sleeping potions," she mouths, and I nod. The courtiers are besotted with such remedies, the endless round of festivals and parties exhausting them to the point where they crave a peaceful sleep they can never seem to find.

"Coriander, lemon balm, sweet cicely, rose petals," the herb mistress intones, causing Anna to draw in a breath.

"Rather a lot for one tincture, is it not?" she asks.

"And saffron as well," the woman says triumphantly. "To be mixed with equal parts sugar and wine. We used it just last night for the Queen, and it worked like a charm. If you'll wait a moment, I'll prepare it for you all, that you might recognize the taste." She bends over the table, measuring drops from several vials into five empty cups.

Jane snorts beside me. "I'm not drinking that swill."

"I fail to see how this helps us." Meg sits forward on the edge of her chair, a frown marring her face. "We need to leave off sleeping potions and return to poisons. That is the danger here." She shakes her head. "And if we can ever break free of this accursed castle, we need to get to Windsortown and see what Maude is cooking up in that cottage of hers."

"Everyone, please take a taste." The herb mistress's command drowns out Meg's quiet words.

Reluctantly the five of us move forward and lift up the tiny glass cups. I wrinkle my nose at the overly sweet scent. "This smells like a pomander, not something to drink."

"You canna know until you try it," Anna says, and she shrugs and tosses hers back. Jane has already dumped hers out onto the rushes, and Beatrice and Meg are eyeing their glasses with bemusement, as if the liquid might reveal its secrets solely under the weight of their stares.

"Now we shall discuss the Crown's cures for poisons, though, God bless her, this is not a concern for our Elizabeth."

That brings us all up short. "Not a concern?" Anna asks, her head tilting. "Whyever not?"

The woman chortles. "Well, she has the horn, of course."

All of our faces remain blank, and our instructor immediately realizes her mistake. "Let's carry on," she says briskly.

"No, wait. *What* horn?" Anna asks. "Do you mean an animal horn, like a stag's?"

"'Tis nothing at all. I assumed you knew," the herb mistress responds, clearly distressed. She has information we do not, which is not unusual. Servants possess a deep ocean of knowledge, while the rest of us barely skim the surface of the sea. But now she has let her secret slip, and she doesn't know how to act. We rank higher than she does, but if she is not supposed to share the information with anyone of any station, I understand her fright. The politics of Windsor are not for the faint of heart.

"Mistress Frances," Beatrice speaks up, her voice as gentle and full as an opening rose. "You have been *so* kind to share with us the strengths of the kitchens of Windsor in protecting our Queen. She is truly blessed to have a mistress such as you caring for her needs. You are to be commended, and I shall tell her so myself."

I bite my lip. The Queen and Beatrice would sooner throw daggers at each other than speak, though they have seemed to come to some compromise over the past weeks.

The herb mistress's eyes flare at the unexpected flattery. "In truth?"

"In truth," Beatrice says firmly. "But we have been sent here by Her Grace such that we may understand the full arsenal of Windsor's protections, and you have already so admirably explained the wide range of poisons we should fear."

I lift my brows. I clearly missed this part, but Meg is helpful enough to supply the list, most likely for my benefit. "Aconite, yew, caustic lime, bitter almonds, and—this is a nice touch, I'll say—powdered *glass*. And don't forget the arsenic, with a little honey to ensure it all goes down smoothly. Makes pills the size of walnuts, but with enough wine to dissolve them, you could fell a household in no time at all."

"But not *this* household!" the herb mistress insists. "The Queen's food is all tasted by willing agents, her gloves and handkerchiefs switched out repeatedly to ensure no poison might touch her fair skin. And then—and then there are the antidotes she stirs into her nightly sleeping draught."

"Coriander, lemon balm, saffron, and rose," Meg supplies helpfully. She rather enjoys the repetition of others' words, as it helps her learn without her ever needing to write her lessons down. She gives the herb mistress a wink. "Stirred, unless I miss my guess, by this mysterious horn?"

"It's a unicorn's horn!" Anna declares with sudden certainty.

"A *what*?" Jane's surprise is palpable, as is her disdain. I nudge her side, and she glances down at me, confused, before she seems to recover herself. She clearly does not believe in the existence of unicorns, but many among the court of Queen Elizabeth do. Including Elizabeth herself. The Queen's complex web of superstitious beliefs is something I have been tangled in far more than the rest of our company.

"Where came she by such a treasure?" asks Beatrice, who by her tone clearly does not possess such a singular prize in her family coffers. Whether real or not, the horn of a unicorn is believed to have the powers of healing and purification. "Unicorn's horns are rare indeed. And to think, our Queen has had one all this time."

The herb mistress is blushing, but she cannot keep herself from sharing the full secret, especially as it is all but out anyway. "It—it is broken, I'm afraid. She has but a remnant of it, a gift from a distant cousin. But she does set great store by it, until she is able to find a complete one."

"Well, it's clearly worked so far," Jane observes. Her words are a touch too dry, and this earns her another nudge from me. She rolls her eyes. "What? She hasn't died of poisoning, right? So the horn must be the reason why."

"Jane," Beatrice warns, as Meg starts coughing loudly.

"Hmm." Anna taps her lips. "It is enough that she feels more secure with it, no matter its origin," she says. "But in the, ah, unhappy absence of this horn, what do we have in the way of antidotes?"

And with that the herb mistress is off again, discoursing on the relative merits of common rue versus ginger, horehound, mugwort, and oak, which all make up remedies easily prepared within the castle. By the end of the session, we well understand that the cooks at Windsor can assemble the antidotes to *any* poison, and stand at the ready to defend the Crown as needed. Along with our unicorn horn.

We finish out the lesson in good spirits. The herb mistress is well schooled, and under Beatrice's careful guidance the talk shifts all too quickly to which potions and posies work best for such practical needs as a clear complexion or a rosy glow. Jane's irritation grows with every request, until she begins to eye the door.

Almost as if Jane ordered it, a sharp rap sounds on the heavy wood.

The door opens to reveal a young male servant whose eyes, predictably, are only for the lovely Beatrice, though the message is for us all, save the herb mistress. "If you please, you've been summoned."

"To the Queen? You cannot be serious." Beatrice groans.

"No, my lady." The boy draws in a long, noisy breath, puffing himself up. "It is Sir William Cecil who requests your presence. Please, if you will. He said to come at once."

CHAPTER SIX

Sir William Cecil sits in his darkened chambers, peering down at stacks of parchment illuminated by the flame of a single candle. He is ever stingy in the use of light, and I've always wondered at it. He's considered a visionary, both he and Walsingham, the Queen's most valued advisors. Why not actually break out a few candles to see those visions more clearly?

He pays no attention to us as we arrive and arrange ourselves in a line before his desk. It is only when Beatrice begins to tap her foot that he appears to take notice. Even then he does not speak, but merely lifts his head to peer at us.

Well, at *me*, I should say. He is peering at me.

I try to remember to show naught but wide-eyed innocence, though I confess the act is wearing a bit thin.

"The few men of science and astrology who have heard the whispers about the Queen's summons have come and gone. None of them knew anything about Mother Shipton's prediction, nor did they offer up any prophecies or warnings remotely similar," he says, his gaze never leaving me. "But now, with the arrival of John Dee and his company, the game has changed, and we can be done with the pretenders. Still, Dee apparently feels the need to impress Elizabeth immediately, and he is unwilling to wait until their private audience. The Queen, of course, is delighted to be impressed." Cecil's weary voice betrays his fatigue. Clearly, whatever Dee has planned for Elizabeth has already caused him grief. "After the welcoming feast this evening, Dee will perform an astrological wonder for the Queen and her members of court. You will all be in attendance for this spectacle, and do what you can to ensure its success. The Queen has been much strained by her worry over Mother Shipton's premonition, and has need for the distraction."

I consider this. I know Dee must be eager to provide the Queen with the answer she seeks. As one of the most celebrated thinkers in the kingdom, and an avowed student of angelic conversations, astrology, and the arcane, who better to shed light on the mysterious prophecy of Mother Shipton? All eyes will be upon him to reveal who is to die at Windsor Castle.

When he does, *if* he does, he will be richly rewarded, too. Secure in the belief that she has a true prophet in her service, the Queen will spare no expense to support Dee's work. This spectacle that he is presenting, then, must be to lay the foundation for his great revelation to the Queen. To show that Dee can not only serve as the Queen's link to the angelic realm, but he can delight her with scientific marvels as well.

And as for me?

It suddenly occurs to me that perhaps two seers for the Crown is one too many.

"Sophia, are you aware of what your uncle is preparing?" Cecil asks, drawing my attention back to him. "This 'astrological wonder' that requires every candle in the castle to be brought to the Presence Chamber?"

"No, Sir William," I say sincerely. "I am not in communication with my—my uncle. I have not seen him these past several months."

"You would do well to nurture that relationship anew, then," he says. "Your uncle is a valued member of this court, and an advisor of no small standing to the Queen. He has also traveled extensively of late, and his studies have been much remarked-upon by those courtiers with whom he is friendly. We need to understand not only what he knows but who he has talked with, where he has been, and what he's been doing." He taps his papers. "He mentioned his alchemical studies in particular, during his audience with the Queen but a bare half hour ago. Has he gotten any closer to finding the Philosopher's Stone?"

Beside me Anna huffs in derision. "You really think Dee wouldn't run to the Queen immediately if he'd found a way to transmute lead into gold? His future would be assured."

Cecil shrugs. "He has been traveling on the Continent, and the Queen is not the only monarch with money." He refocuses on me. "What has he told you?"

I raise a brow. "Sir William, I am but John Dee's niece and ward, not his trusted colleague. Our relationship was never that close, nor will it likely be so now, given my current position within the Queen's household." I offer him an apologetic smile, though in truth I could not care less whether I ever see Dee again. "I am afraid he has no interest in speaking with me."

He waves off my words. "Happily, it appears you are wrong. He is currently asking for you, in fact, to join him and the Queen."

That does alarm me, but Cecil continues. "As to the rest of you, Dee has brought a small army of his associates to the castle, claiming them as apprentices to his studies." Cecil's tone belies his skepticism. "More likely, he promised them the Queen's food and hospitality in exchange for their service."

"What sort of service?" Anna asks. "Are they to help him divine the truth about Mother Shipton's prophecy? Or simply to aid him in tonight's spectacle?"

"That, or perhaps their duties are simpler still," Jane mutters. "How hard is it for one of them to murder a courtier in his bed, so that Dee wins the Queen's challenge with one quick cut?"

"Exactly so," Cecil says. "However, Dee has vouched quite loudly and long for his associates. Since the Queen is presently transported with the idea of Dee's 'wonder,' she is inclined to trust him. And, of course, *we* trust him."

Beatrice speaks now, her words wry. "But we don't trust whatever he drags in with him."

"We do not." Cecil stands. "Sophia? Please attend me. The rest of you, please return to your studies. Tonight, dress for a formal dance. It would not do for Dee's cohort to suspect you have any interest in them, save to be entertained. And, Meg." Cecil levies a glance to my right. "Stay near Dee himself, and follow any conversations he may have. We will want a full account."

"Of course, Sir William," Meg says, sinking into a quick curtsy. She does that, quite often without provocation.

My four colleagues file out of Cecil's office as he rounds his desk, his long face going even longer as he studies me. "You have had no conversation with your uncle, you say?"

"None whatever," I reply. "I have not spoken to him since dispatching him a letter last spring regarding my betrothal to Lord Brighton." I shrug. "He was already on the Continent and sent his blessings, nothing more."

"Hmm." He gestures for me to precede him to the doorway, his voice dropping to a low murmur. "And yet he insists that he has knowledge of your developing abilities. How can this be?"

I stiffen in surprise. "I do not know, my lord," I say. "I have had neither reason nor occasion to share any developments of that nature with Dee or anyone else. There is nothing new to report on that topic."

Once again, I must tread carefully. Cecil and Walsingham know I have gained some measure of the Sight. But they believe, as I want them to, that I still have no control over what I see.

They do not know I have begun using an obsidian scrying stone to focus and hone my visions. They do not know I have begun to speak with the angels more regularly. And they certainly do not know that I, too, have been told that death shall come to Windsor.

Speaking of that . . . "Sir William," I say as we enter the

corridor, "can you recall any current monarchs who are on their deathbeds? Young men, perhaps younger than thirty, but frail and apparently sickly?"

He frowns at me. "No. The lot of them are depressingly hale and hearty at the moment. And most of them quite a bit older than thirty years." He hesitates. "Why?"

"And none of them are here, now, correct? Visiting the Queen?"

"Sophia, what is it?" Cecil's words are sharp. "What have you seen?"

Dread pools in my stomach. If there are no monarchs at Windsor other than the Queen, then my vision makes no sense. The scepter and purple sash were clear indications of royalty. I am not mistaken there. Which means I am once again seeing a future that will never be.

"I've seen nothing," I say, and even to my ears it is not enough. "Yet. Nothing certain, anyway."

I feel Cecil's cold glance, his disappointment evident. Along with Walsingham, he has spent the better part of a year training me to be a spy, after all. Is it any wonder that he's also eager to see some benefit to all his work? "Tell me immediately, the moment you do see something."

"Yes, Sir William," I say, not needing to feign the meekness in my tone. I clench my hands into fists as we continue to walk in silence. *Why can't the angels show me anything of use!* And how is it Dee can claim to know anything about my abilities? In the decade and more I lived with him, he never gave any indication that he knew I had the Sight; and in truth he presented me to the Queen a year ago as someone who only "might" one day develop such a gift. So how has he learned about me now?

Cecil abruptly stops as we reach the Queen's Privy Chamber, gesturing for me to precede him into the small, private space. I am unsurprised to see Walsingham standing at his ease near the door, while John Dee and the Queen sit in cushioned chairs at the base of the stairs leading up to Elizabeth's throne. I've seen this air of comfort before, between the Queen and Dee; unlike her manner with nearly everyone else in the court, she does not put on airs when it comes to her former tutor. She appreciates his mind and his insights. Upon being told she was to be the new Queen, she even summoned Dee to provide her with an astrological reading to set the date for her coronation, to ensure the stars would bless her new reign. Being highly educated herself, Elizabeth also adores Dee's tales of travels and books. And, perhaps most important, she is quite certain of his loyalty to her.

Which makes Dee's suggestion that he has evidence of my skills all the more dangerous.

As we approach, Dee stands and bows gallantly to me, allowing me to pause and sink into a curtsy. He looks like he ever does. Now in his early thirties, he is, I suppose, an attractive man. Slender of build, his short brown hair and beard are both trimmed to accent a long, intelligent face. He dresses as a scholar, his cloak thrown back to reveal a modestly cut doublet and trunk hose, his skin pale against the white refinement of his neck ruff and his ever-present dark cap. Dee's dark, searching eyes are his best feature, and they rest upon me, alight with interest. "You look well, my niece."

"I am well, my lord, thank you," I murmur. I am no more his niece than he is the Queen of England, but he apparently does not suspect that I have learned of his villainy. Instead, I must merely content myself with staring at him, as if I could pierce him with silent daggers.

"Sophia, pray, join us." The Queen speaks into our awkward silence with something approaching relish in her tone. I arrange myself and my wide skirts upon the bench to the Queen's right. Cecil himself remains standing, slightly behind me, watching Dee. Clearly he cares more about Dee's reactions to our coming conversation than my own. "Your uncle here believes you might have some news for our ears alone."

"I cannot imagine what that would be." I furrow my brow. "Other than my broken betrothal, but surely that is not news?"

"Not that, child, no," Dee says, his manner suddenly ill at ease, almost as if I have embarrassed him. "I have reason to understand that you might be having, ah, disturbed dreams of late," he says. "Would you share those experiences with us?"

"Disturbed dreams?" I shake my head. "My lord, I am blessed with gentle sleep as—" I stop short of saying "as ever," for that would be a patent lie. He was there for all those childhood nightmares, after all. "As any would be, in the care of the Queen."

"But others have seen you, on the plane of shadows," he says abruptly, leaning forward. "Have seen you and told me the tale of your distress."

I draw back, and even the Queen shows alarm. "My lord?" I ask.

Dee's words are as sharp as a slap. "What do the angels say to you, Sophia? What secrets have they shared?"

"You are mistaken." I clasp my hands together, fully unnerved. *How can he know all of this?* "I have never been to this 'plane of shadows' or seen these angels. I do not speak to them."

"She would have told me if she had," the Queen observes. Her gaze narrows upon me, as if she, too, is assessing my ability to lie in the face of Dee's questions. "She is a Maid of Honor."

"A what?" Dee sits up straight, his head turning to the Queen as if he's only just realized that she shares space with him. His eyes are clear once more, but in that clarity there is a craftiness that wasn't there before. "Of course, Your Grace. I did not mean to imply otherwise. Sophia is blessed to have your patronage, as am I." Even as he speaks the words, I feel the malevolence simmering beneath them. "It is just disappointing. I believed she would soon come into her gifts, else I would never have agreed to your kind offer for her to reside in your household, eating your food and enjoying your goodwill. Certainly by this late date, her skills should have manifested. Indeed, the angels have advised that it is so. But it appears I am mistaken." He shrugs. "It appears we must still . . . wait."

A chill slides through me. Dee damns me with his words, as he is well aware. The Queen is not known for her patience, and she *has* been sheltering me for nearly a year, without results. Dee has now reminded her of that, and I sense Elizabeth's dark eyes on me as she allows his words to settle around us.

"The wait will not be for long, in any event," she says after a long moment. "The test is at hand. There is no better time for Sophia to come into her own than at this present hour, when our need is great."

Is her voice harder now, or is it my imagination?

The Queen continues with a considering lilt to her tone. "And if she does *not* come into her own, then we will simply find some other way for her to serve the Crown."

It is not my imagination.

CHAPTER SEVEN

The day is waning as we process into the Presence Chamber for the evening feast, Dee on the Queen's arm. Walsingham and Cecil follow behind them, and I find myself alone, walking in their wake. Fury still knots my stomach, though hours have passed since my audience with the Queen and my "uncle."

How dare John Dee turn Elizabeth against me so quickly and so well! And how dare *she* take his side! He has not been at her beck and call for the past year, jumping at her every command. He has been traveling on the Continent, learning all that he might learn. He has been writing and studying and sharing his work with like minds. He has been *free*. And now he has returned and seeks to destroy my life, without so much as a thought.

He stole me away from my parents when I was only three years old. Apparently, he seeks to steal me away from Queen Elizabeth too.

A dark emotion stirs within me as I think of everything I have suffered at this man's hands. A wild, almost violent urgency fills me up and seems to pulse in my very veins. It lurks beneath the surface of my skin, eager to be set free.

I will show them all.

I sense a courtier move up beside me, taking my arm in his. Some nobleman taking pity on me, perhaps, or a lesser lord sent to make the numbers even. It does not matter; it cannot matter. I have larger concerns.

"You should not be so distressed, my lady." The voice floats over me like velvet, rich and soft.

I turn to face the young man, schooling my expression into guileless confusion. "'Tis just Sophia," I say, and then I stop. In truth, I would fall down, were the courtier's hold on me not so strong. Looking into his eyes is like gazing into the endless and open sea, its waters glittering as if lit by an unseen sun.

"Do I know you?" I ask baldly, and something has gone quite wrong with my voice, as if I've used up all my allotment of air for the day. But really, I can be forgiven. This young man is like nobody else I've seen, and yet he is so distressingly *familiar*, I feel I must have met him before. He is tall, with a slender, aristocratic build. He is richly dressed, from his expensive doublet and trunk hose to his luxurious midnight-blue cape. But it is the young man's face that stops me short—fair and sculpted, as if it were carved out of palest marble, with a full, smiling mouth, sharply edged cheekbones, raven-black brows, and those eerie light eyes. Surely I have seen this face before!

Suddenly I realize the young courtier hasn't responded to my sharp question, and I feel the blush crawl up my neck. "F-forgive me," I stammer. "That was terribly rude. Allow me to introduce myself, good sir. My name is—"

"Sophia Manchester, yes. It is my absolute pleasure to meet you at last."

I cannot help but recoil at his use of my true birth name, which even *I* didn't know until a few months ago. "Nay, you are mistaken!" I say, shaking my head. "My name is Sophia *Dee*. Plain, simple Sophia Dee."

"Of course." He offers me an inscrutable smile, and I find myself torn in two with a soul-deep recognition of this young man. "My mistake," he continues. "So, then, what brings you to Windsor Castle, plain, simple Sophia Dee?" His smile broadens. "Besides your uncle, that is. Such a good man, to look after you when there was no one else to take you in. And such a terrible tragedy you endured when you were, what? But three years old?"

I stiffen, all pretense of politeness gone. "Indeed, sir." I stand back from him, pleased to hear the steel in my voice. "And who are you, that you know so much about me, when I have not even your name to rely upon?"

"Marcus Quinn, at your service." He sketches me a short bow, and his face catches the light. He is younger than I realized, perhaps only seventeen, for all his confident manner. "And forgive my boldness. It has just been so long that I have wished to meet you in person. So very long, it seems."

He takes my arm once more, and we continue walking even as I frown. "So we do not know each other?"

"You believe we've met?"

"No! No, I would have remembered," I say. Some fey spirit spills new words from my tongue. "And yet—"

"And yet," Quinn murmurs, his voice like warm honey. "Perhaps you do remember something."

His words are soft, but he gives me no more time to think, stopping abruptly. "Ah!" he says, as I blink up at him, confused. "It seems we have arrived."

We stand at a secondary table in the long rows of diners gathered for the banquet. He eases me onto my bench with an elegant hand, and as he does so, I feel something brush against my palm. I draw my hand back, startled, and realize I am clutching a soft-petaled autumn rose.

I hold it up, vaguely aware I should draw out this "Marcus Quinn" with Beatrice's sly skill, but my mind is still staggering around like a drunken farmer, and my words are more challenging than coy. "You are a magician, then?" I ask.

"Only for you, Lady Sophia," Marcus Quinn says quietly, his eyes locking with mine. Then he steps away, but I swear he keeps speaking, his words floating back to me over the clash of knives, cups, and trenchers. "Only for you."

I turn round to my fellow diners, lifting the flower to catch its scent. *Marcus Quinn.* The name is not at all familiar to me. He was not on any of the lists Cecil and Walsingham gave us to memorize. Who *is* this young man?

And how in God's name does he know so much about me?

Unfortunately, Quinn is seated several tables away from me, so I cannot pursue these questions, though I am desperate to do so. Dinner passes without fanfare. Then the Queen orders the tables pulled back, and the servants scramble to rid the surfaces of food while leaving the cups and tankards standing within easy reach of the courtiers. By common accord the feasters have all stood, gathering in a loose circle around the Queen, her advisors, and Dee. Now the room is full dark, save for the candles burning on the tables.

Jane moves into position at my side. "What would the court do, were we not so 'entertained' on a nightly basis?" she asks.

I smile. "Expire from boredom?"

"At least that would be something different."

At a sign from one of Dee's men, the candles on the tables are extinguished. I feel Jane stiffen beside me. We have guards by every table, but even they cannot see in the dark.

Dee's men apparently have no such issues. At the first rustle of their feet, we crane our necks toward the entrance of the Presence Chamber. Jane slips away from my side. Gradually I sense more than see four heavy-shouldered men move into the center of the room.

Dee's voice suddenly rings out over the assembly. "Except those in service to the Queen, I beg of you, for full effect, to shield your eyes a moment, until you see the heavens presented to you in full glory!"

By my rough estimation, as the first candle in the center of the room flares to life, about half the throng does as Dee asks. The rest of us strain to see more as he lights fully twenty candles in the center of what looks to be a large spherical cage, with a long slender rod bisecting it at an angle. The cage is set upon a pedestal, and when the lights are all set, it looks almost like a chandelier that has been brought down to the rush-strewn floor for cleaning. Only this chandelier is not intended to ever be raised. Instead, four more of Dee's men step forward with what look like a pair of enormous earthen bowls, each four feet across, the thin basins pricked full of holes. As we watch, his men fit the two sides of these bowls together over the cage of flame—

And the walls and ceiling of the Presence Hall suddenly become painted with all the stars in the night's sky.

"Oh!" It is the Queen, purely delighted. "What manner of presentation is this?"

"I cannot give you the sun and the moon," Dee proclaims triumphantly. "But I would give you the stars!" He adjusts the sphere and lays a piece of curved glass over one of the many holes. Instantly, one of the stars glows bright blue against the ceiling of the Presence Chamber. "This is the North Star, my Queen, and this pattern of stars is what we observed on that most illustrious of days, your coronation. The very firmament of the heavens showered its blessings upon you, for long life, safety, and endless abundance."

There is a rustle of skirts beside me, then Beatrice speaks as the courtiers break out in applause. "I should say our presence here is no longer needed," she says waspishly. "If Her Royal Magnificence is so protected by the stars as that."

Still, Beatrice stays beside me as courtiers and ladies jostle and stare at Dee's wonder. He whisks away the glass and rotates the cage a quarter turn. It appears to rest upon the spindle in such a way that as soon as one series of stars slides out of view, another series slides into position. "And this," he announces, "is the placement of the stars on Your Grace's first birthday celebration as Queen. The stars quite wisely aligned to give you great joy and success the whole year long."

A cheer sounds loudly, giving me an opportunity to step up onto my toes to reach Beatrice's ears alone.

"Beatrice," I say, my voice low, "shouldn't you be at the Queen's side?"

"You would think," Beatrice whispers back, her derision plain. "However, she all but pushed me to the floor in her haste to see more clearly. I won't be missed. But you . . ." She eyes me strangely in the half gloom. "Are you well? You looked positively stricken through most of dinner. You must guard your appearance more carefully than that, Sophia. What distracted you so?"

"And then!" Dee proclaims, recalling our attention. "I ranged forth to find the most glorious years in the future for our Queen, to delight your eyes and warm your spirits." He spins the ball, and the pricked-out holes catch the light as they shoot past, swirling with dizzying speed. I close my eyes against the odd sensation that sweeps over me, and Beatrice shakes my shoulder.

"Look sharp, Sophia!" she says. I struggle to focus on her. She has been given strict instruction from the Queen to help me appear as normal as possible to the court, and it is a doomed attempt at the best of times. But at this moment she has no hope of keeping me grounded to this plane. I am dropping, dropping . . .

Beatrice speaks firmly over Dee's excited babble about the Queen's success decades in the future. Her words catch at my thoughts like rocks jutting out into a waterfall. "Sophia, tell me! What on earth is wrong with you?"

What on earth. I remember saying those words, or something like them. I remember thinking them but a short while ago, in fact—seconds, really—*What on earth! What on earth!*

"Marcus Quinn," I murmur dreamily, the words pulled from me.

"What? Who?"

Dee sets the globe in motion again, the whirl of stars compelling my gaze. "But the stars speak not *only* of far-off futures," he insists, his voice booming at the center of the room. "But of a very curious pattern that is coming together even now."

I suddenly feel that I am on the precipice of the angelic realm, rushing into shadow, into the world beyond as the trance threatens to engulf me like a crashing tide. Before these past few months, the mere idea of dropping into the spirit world in the center of a crowd would have driven me into a panic. And still I tense, blinking rapidly, trying to re-center myself, trying to—

"Sophia?" Beatrice's tone is stern. "Are you well?" She reaches out and grasps my wrist, her tight grip grounding me. "Who is this Marcus Quinn?"

But the manufactured stars across the ceiling of the Presence Chamber choose that moment to shift and shudder, and I shake my head, trying to focus. "Marcus . . . ," I whisper. I *did* see him, once. In my mind's eye, slipping through the shadows, staring through the gloom.

Dee whirls the ball round and round, and I sense myself coming unmoored. "And here we are at last!" he cries. "Here, for one and all. A puzzle and a possibility for you!"

"What is this you say?" It is the Queen who speaks, her

voice as excited as a young girl's. "What night sky do you paint for us, Master Dee?"

"One but a few short days hence," Dee responds gleefully. "At the festival of Samhain. See what the stars suggest!"

I stare as Dee drops scraps of cloth over various pinpricks of light—a blue, a red, a shadowy grey. The colors spill and tumble over me, and my eyelids grow heavy, the trance sucking me into its endless sea. I hear the whispers of angels, their urgent cries, their hissing portents, clawing-catching-grabbing at me, that I may hear! That I may know!

"Sophia!" Beatrice reaches for me, but I pat her hand as if she were a child. Distracted, I mumble the first words that come into my mind, seeing them form and slip away from me into the whirl of colors with which Dee is decorating the artificial sky.

"*He has granted you protection, hidden yet from your detection. Look to find the scrap of Fae to mark the vow that love has made.*"

"What?" Beatrice draws back for just a moment, then grasps my wrists again. "God's eyes, you're seeing visions. Do you mean Alasdair and that infernal Fairy Flag of his?" She curses. "This is *not* the time, Sophia."

I swing away from Beatrice's pinched frown, and it is Anna whose face I see next. Anna, looking up into the enchanted ceiling of false stars, her face alight with interest. Darkness clamps down on me, my voice going spindle-thin.

"*Death descends not once, not twice, blood and lies and blackened knife, three then four then more to come, not till seven is it done.*"

"Sophia, much as I adore you, I'm not going to remember this. Where is *Meg*?"

I am suddenly surrounded by spectral beings. Spirits and

angels, more than I have ever seen before. Some I recognize, most I don't. And they all are talking at once, seeking to fill my ears with words I cannot fully understand, so quickly are they clamoring, their voices blending together into an otherworldly storm.

I pull away from Beatrice, whirling around to see more clearly. The courtiers and ladies are all as ghosts, while the angels are as bright as day. They press in more closely, gasping with delight at the spectacle Dee has created, and I turn, and turn again, not knowing what I'm looking for, until—

There he is. The lone mortal visible among the spirits, standing far to the opposite side of the chamber, his sculpted face almost hauntingly beautiful, his eyes silver-bright: Marcus Quinn. He is lit up like one of the spectral beings, as bright and full as if he walked their dreaming plane like I do. But unlike the angels, who are all looking skyward, Marcus Quinn is staring right at me. Something shifts inside me, and I fall back—

Beatrice pulls me round, and I see Meg moving toward us. Her face does not give me the comfort it usually does, and I blurt the words that clamor in my brain. *"Loyalty shall serve her false, deceit at every turn—"*

"Stop!" Beatrice commands, and her emotion is so intense that I come back to myself. It is like halting a horse by running it into the side of a castle wall. I am left reeling, struggling to breathe. Just then, however, the room visibly darkens. Dee has overlaid the frame of pricked holes so heavily with coverings that the firelight is slowly dying inside, giving the Presence Chamber the illusion of a fading spell.

"And so the stars all must finally slumber," he says ponderously. "Except for our own Gloriana."

With that announcement, Dee tosses a small package at the Queen's feet. The guards surrounding the Queen step forward, bristling, but they are nowhere near quick enough. The package bursts into sudden flame, illuminating the Queen in a brilliant yellow-white light.

Just that quickly, the flame is extinguished.

Complete darkness falls over the room.

Complete darkness . . . and silence.

For one long, heavily weighted moment.

Then Beatrice bursts into wild applause. "Bravo!" she shouts. "Bravo!"

Mad clapping breaks out as the courtiers follow her lead, while the Queen demands that the candles be relit and the music commence. I do not miss the glance exchanged between monarch and maid. Beatrice and Elizabeth are avowed enemies, yes. But they are also allies in a court susceptible to the slightest shift of public opinion. The tiniest hint of any royally sanctioned "grand spectacle" falling flat can all too quickly stir up the gale-force winds of whispered doubts. Everything the Queen does must succeed and be grander than all that has come before. Such is the price of currying favor among a fickle court.

I look to Dee, only to find him staring back. He stands in the lee and patronage of his beloved Queen, smug in his success. But his pride is not only a result of his trick of colored stars, I suddenly understand. John Dee's ways are subtle, and his trap was neatly sprung. I glance right, and see the young man who has left the far side of the Presence Chamber to stand beside Dee. The young man I *felt* I'd met before—though it seemed impossible—the young man I saw quite clearly just now, as visible on the plane of angels as if he too could walk within that hallowed realm. The young man who I now realize is working with John Dee.

Marcus Quinn.

He has been watching me.

I think of my last conversation with the dark angel, the person I felt peering at me in the shadows. I thought it was a shade, some poor deceased soul, but it wasn't. It was Marcus Quinn. He somehow followed me onto the dreaming plane, I am certain of it.

Across the gradually lightening room, I can no longer perceive the angels or spirit beings pressing close around me. They have shrunk away from the noise and the clamor of the Presence Chamber, the clearing of tables and the moving of benches, as the gathered throng of mortals prepares for a night of drink and music.

Instead, all I see is Dee, turning to Marcus and his men, gesturing wildly as he appears to explain how to remove his strange machine, so that he might go and be properly honored by the Queen for creating such a marvelous distraction for her.

But even Elizabeth does not understand the full extent of that distraction. The display of lights and stars was also a ploy to draw *me* out, to prove to Dee what I would never have revealed on my own: that I have developed my Sight far more than anyone suspects, including the Queen.

And now he can betray me.

Dee is determined to prove his worth as the Queen's most trusted diviner, and his chance is before him, with the Queen's need to decipher Mother Shipton's prophecy. If he succeeds, his future is set. The Queen will grant him money, titles, and protection. But he is no fool. He knows that I, too, am being put to the test, along with anyone else the Queen sees fit to question. In Dee's mind, I have become a threat who stands between him and everything he has ever wanted.

And the first step to removing a threat is to unmask it.

Across the room, my adversary tips his head toward me . . . and smiles.

CHAPTER EIGHT

More of Dee's entourage arrived overnight, and the court is alive this morning with rumors that the Queen has made a special, secretive summons to draw another scholar into her presence as well, but no one can guess who. Given the size of Dee's company of learned men, I can scarcely imagine that anyone with a brain remains outside of Windsor. Elizabeth has closeted herself away with Cecil and Walsingham, and for the first time in a brace of days, no one has us running all over the castle.

This means that *finally* we maids can make our journey to Windsortown, to investigate the suspected poisoner, Mistress Maude. The boisterous herb mistress has not returned to the castle since the day the Queen received Mother Shipton's premonition of death, and we don't know what to expect when we reach the town. Will she have fled? Does she truly play any role in the current intrigues besetting the castle?

I shuffle along agreeably at the back of our group, glad to be leaving the castle. I was so disquieted by last night's events that once more I did not sleep.

For what will happen when I do? Will I meet Marcus

Quinn in my dreams? Dare I ever close my eyes again? Has he already breached that most private sanctum, as easily as he has entered the realm of angels? How is it he can watch me, in truth? And *why* is he doing so?

And, God's breath . . . how long has this been going on?

If Dee had suspected I was truly on the verge of making my own connection with the angelic realm a year ago, he never would have shared me with the Queen. I am certain of that. And thus the moment he learned of my abilities, I would think he would have come calling. Yet he has not darkened the Queen's door for months.

This means that his knowledge of my abilities must be recent. But how recent?

Did Dee set Marcus Quinn to the task of finding me? Or did Marcus find me all on his own, and then seek out Dee when he discovered our connection? Is Marcus a villain, or does he not understand that Dee means me harm? The way he looked at me at dinner, and then across the Presence Chamber, was so . . .

I scowl, forcing myself to see things as they are, not as I wish them to be. The way Marcus looked at me last night was simply part of his duty, perhaps seeking to draw me out to get additional information for his employer. And yet, no young man has *ever* looked at me the way he did, as if I were some rare and precious treasure . . .

Oh, leave off.

Of course I'm a treasure to Marcus Quinn. Dee doubtlessly is paying him a pile of gold for any information he can cobble together about me.

As we walk, Anna strides to the fore, excitement quickening her step. "The Queen's cooks were adamant. If we find dragon's blood, basil, lemongrass, or rosemary, Mistress Maude is likely only dabbling in the honesty tea trade—and no harm in that. Turmeric, sage, raspberry, nettle, even licorice . . . all of that's for love potions. The pieces we want to watch out for are bryony, mandrake—or anything you can't recognize."

"Well, that should narrow it down," says Jane.

"Cecil and Walsingham shouldn't be sending us to hunt down Maude. They should be sending us to thank her," Beatrice puts in. "Without her potions, I doubt any of us would have paid so much attention in class of late."

"We could use a good, deadly poison, though," Anna says, in all seriousness. "It would be useful to understand what Maude finds the most potent, and in what doses."

"Well, she certainly uses yew." Meg's words are bitter. She wasn't in the Lower Ward when the guards' horses were poisoned, but she shares my horror for Maude's heartless act.

"A decision we would do well to understand better," I say. "Maude risked much to create chaos in the Lower Ward, and for what? To ensure one old woman slipped into the Queen's presence to deliver a prophecy without anyone knowing who sent her? What has Maude to gain by upsetting the Queen?"

"Mother Shipton's prophecy has done nothing to improve the Queen's mood, that's certain," Beatrice says. "And a frightened Queen is a less generous one. The people of Windsortown have all benefited from Elizabeth's largesse."

"The guards have had no luck trying to find out any information about the old woman either," Jane says, scanning the woods beside us as if the trees were intentionally withholding secrets.

"Oh!" Anna exclaims. "And the old woman herself only adds to the mystery. Our examination of that poor goodwife's corpse was the most enthralling experience I've had since coming to Windsor."

"You frighten me, Anna," Beatrice begins, but Anna will not be deterred.

"I'm serious! There was no reason why she should have died in such a sudden manner. There was no poison upon her tongue or obvious wound, no indication of foul humor in her blood or bile. Her heart just . . . stopped."

"Then it is up to us to find out more," I say. "Surely someone in this town can help. That woman cannot just have dropped into Windsor from nowhere. She's probably lived here all her life." And if the town won't give up its secrets, then I have other sources to ask. Though I am nervous to reenter the angelic realm, I am certain Dee will be so distracted with his plans for the Queen that he will not be focused on me. With any luck, neither will Marcus Quinn.

We part ways outside of town. By previous consent, Beatrice and I were given the easier route. We must find Mistress Maude and her gaudy stall, and keep her occupied long enough to allow Meg, Anna, and Jane the opportunity to discover what they might at the woman's home. Then, when we are quite sure enough time has passed, Beatrice and I might even ask Maude a few questions of our own about the old crone if the moment feels right. We cannot put these questions to the herb mistress too quickly, lest she chase us off. But we are determined to get answers.

From Jane's scouting, we know that Maude's small cottage is quite close, though her stall in town is still several minutes away. Beatrice and I travel on. "They'll not be caught, will they?" she asks. "Not that I can imagine the plight of anyone so bold as to lay hands on Jane, but . . ."

I shrug. "I have a sense that they are safe, but I have no basis for that belief, other than wishful thinking." I squint into the bright sunlight. "I could scry?"

Beatrice's laugh is wry. "No. I've had quite enough of you dropping into a trance in public, thank you. We're far too exposed here." We walk a bit longer in silence, Beatrice drawing the usual attention. She is lovely even in her serviceable skirts and modestly cut neckline. Her clothes are fine, though not luxurious, but her manner shouts out that she is a noblewoman. How do I appear, I wonder? I glance down at my own gown of fine-spun cloth. It's grey, with simple stitching, but there is a light line of elegant embroidery at the waist, hem, and sleeve. It's pretty, I think, though I usually pay no attention to how I look. A new thought unexpectedly strikes me. What did Marcus Quinn see when he looked at me last night? How *do* I appear to a young man?

It's such a strange idea, I at once chatter out the first question to follow on its heels. "Beatrice," I ask, "am I pretty, would you say?"

"Whyever would you ask such a thing?" Her brows lift. "Is this about that young courtier who had you so distracted last night? Marcus Quinn? What did he say to you?"

"Nothing whatsoever," I protest. My lies and half-truths are all twisting together, making it difficult to keep my place. "He is merely a member of Dee's company."

"A member of Dee's company who clearly believes you're pretty," she teases me, her grin wide. Then she relents. "Because of course you are, Sophia. You outshine everyone at court, I tell you plain. Even me, and that's no small feat." Her laughter lightens any sting her words might have. "But be careful not to have your head turned by idle words. They fall too easily from the lips of courtiers."

"Well, then, how do you tell flatterers and fools apart from men of worth?"

"That's easy," Beatrice answers. "They're *all* flatterers and fools, even if they're men of worth."

I consider this. "Because they fall in love so easily?"

Beatrice laughs. "Because they're men, Sophia. They do not think in terms of love, at least not at first. They think in terms of desire. Of possession. This is true from the finest man down to the meanest cur. Men don't fall in love at first sight—they *crave* something at first sight. Something they must have for their own. For most of them, their emotions never plumb any greater depths than that."

"But Alasdair MacLeod loves you," I say, referring to the Scottish lord who even now is embroiled in the Northern Rebellion of the Scots against the French. Though Beatrice was assigned merely to spy upon Alasdair during his recent visit to Windsor Castle, their relationship has become far closer. "He doesn't simply want you like a prized goat."

"Well, he did at first, I wager." Beatrice shrugs. "At first I was a conquest, and then a challenge. It was only later that his desire gave way to something more refined. Though he would not thank me for calling him refined, in any case."

"And you could tell that, when?"

"Immediately," she says, winking at me. "Men are not that complicated, I'm sad to say. Chances are, your young Marcus is looking for kisses and not conversation. If he's after your heart, it will be in his eyes. If he's after your body, well—that proof is yet easier to discern."

"Beatrice!" Blood flares in my cheeks, and she starts giggling madly. I am spared any more of her teasing, however, as we are approaching Windsortown's collection of stalls. The smell of savory pies and sweetmeats fills the air, mingling with the scents of horses and goats and kindling sparking to fire. To my great relief we find Maude working at her stall at the edge of the throng, cackling to her neighbor.

"What 'o!" she cries out when she sees us, recognizing us as past customers to her stall—but thankfully, not seeming to recall me from a week ago in the Lower Ward. Perhaps my covering of dove feathers was an adequate disguise. "Maids from the castle, good day to you. Blessings to you both." She waggles her brows at us. "You've tried my tonic, 'ey? 'As it worked well for you?"

She refers to her love potion, of course, which is all she would give us when we first visited her stall a few weeks ago—claiming she had none of the truth tonic we truly sought. We accepted the love tea as a show of good faith, vowing to return with five shillings, and I sincerely hope Beatrice will not tell her the true fate of that potion—that Jane has dumped the rest of it out in the chicken yard. "It's worked surprisingly well," Beatrice says. "We gifted it to a friend in need, and now she has all the male attention she could hope for."

"So I tol' you it would be! An' yer back, since what Maude says, she means."

"Exactly so." Beatrice surveys Maude's impressive stall. It is filled with bottles and possets, the offerings all wrapped in brightly colored ribbons. "But, oh! You have so many things here! More so even than last time!"

"Look yer fill, ladies! But first, your special mixture." Maude grins, and her shawl shifts as she leans forward, baring a swath of skin. I can see a large mole on her neck, and I try to quell my lurch of fear. Despite my own learned upbringing and my careful studies of the arcane, I still have to resist my completely irrational reaction to Maude's deformity.

To those who are superstitious—which includes nearly all the men and women of England—moles are considered signs of witchcraft or devil-worship. I have seen women slice themselves with a sharp blade, risking terrible injury, to remove a mole from their skin. Most of the time they end up with an unsightly scar, but at least the mole is gone. For some, the truly unlucky, the dark knot of skin returns, almost mocking their efforts, and they must work doubly and triply hard to hide it from the view of idle eyes. Even Anne Boleyn, Queen Elizabeth's own mother, endured cruel court gossip because of the moles on her skin—and such gossip eventually contributed to her downfall. When King Henry grew weary of Queen Anne's inability to give him a son, he used every weapon he could to discredit her. Rumors that she was a witch swirled around her like a dirty fog, in part because of the way she looked.

I, however, should know better. Whether or not Maude is a poisoner, a murderer, or, yes, a witch, has nothing to do with how she appears . . . and everything to do with what she does. And I need more than a mole on her neck or a whisper on the wind to condemn her. We will study the potion she has made for us, and learn what Jane, Meg, and Anna find at the goodwife's cottage. If the evidence reveals her as a poisoner, then she will be judged. But she will not be tried for my fear.

Mistress Maude finishes rooting around in her basket, and emerges with a stubby glass vial with a stoppered top. The whole thing is no larger than a man's thumb, and Beatrice takes it with a frown, holding it up to the light. "Five shillings for this?"

"Use it, an' if you don't think it worth ten I will be shocked. It renders the speaker quite ready to spill his secrets, whether he's asked to do it or no. Just be careful that you're ready to 'ear what 'e 'as to say."

"*His* secrets," Beatrice says. "It will work on any man?"

"Or woman or babe as well," Maude says. "You shall not be disappointed, this I swear."

We both nod, suitably impressed. If Anna can discern what this tonic is made of . . .

Money changes hands, and we turn with noisy delight to the rest of Maude's goods. I carefully scan the crowd as we do so. We attract no attention, which speaks well for

Maude's position in this town. Clearly, no one here suspects her of poor dealings. Instead children run round her stall, and Maude leans over to talk to her neighbor again, keeping one cautious eye on the ladies poking through her sachets.

"How much longer do the others need, do you think?" Beatrice asks beneath her breath. She holds up a pretty fabric-covered pillow that smells like dried lavender.

"They've not been there long, but their work should be quick. When we parted, we had farther to go than they did." I glance back to Maude. "Should we ask her about the old woman who spoke with the Queen?"

"Perhaps not," Beatrice says. "I would rather keep in Maude's good graces, if this truth tonic proves to be useful. The Queen may well send us back for more." She gestures to a neighboring stall owner. "Poke around for a few minutes. Then we can be gone," she says. "And try not to get into trouble."

Beatrice thanks Maude prettily, then flounces off as if to do more shopping elsewhere, and I move to the next stall, making a great business of bending down to inspect its baskets of freshly cut flowers and herbs. One stall leads to another, then another, and I find myself moving farther and farther away from Maude. The air seems to clear with every step, and I realize I am enjoying the pretty fall day. Lavender tendrils in large bound bunches mixed with sage catch my eye, and I stop at another stall, noting the woman's broad collection of herbs. Sage is for purity and protection, and she has ringed it round her cart. She's also taken the time to scatter a bedding of rushes around the space, so that villagers might be more comfortable while they view her wares. Beneath this layer of straw and herbs, the earth is stamped down, the ruts of the wheels deep.

I squint hard, and then I see it—a thin line of salt beneath the rushes, circling the stall. More purification, more protection. Of what is this stall owner afraid?

"Someone there?" A thin, reedy voice startles me away from the cart, and I turn. A hunched old woman leaning heavily on her staff peers up at me, and my mouth goes dry as I see her eyes.

They are milk white with age. The woman is blind.

"Ma'am?" I say, reaching out to her instinctively. "Is this your stall?"

"My daughter Agnes's." She smiles, and I feel slightly more at ease, but the woman tilts her head to the side, as if catching the tone of my sigh. "You're too young to be so old," she says. "You've seen too much, too soon."

"Mother!" A woman comes round the corner, and we both stop short in recognition. It is the dove seller from a week ago, hardly a young woman herself. I blink from one of them to the other.

"This is your mother?"

"Aye. Her name is Bess." The dove seller smiles indulgently at the older woman, who croons at me, stroking my arm. "Yes, sweetheart," Agnes continues to her mother. "She's a lovely young maid. I told you about her, remember? The one who startled my doves away? Fortunately, they all came back again." She gestures, and I see the cages on the other side of her cart, the doves lightly cooing in the breeze.

"She saw them, didn't she?" the old woman says. "Five scolds with only ravens for friends, and poor Sally Greer caught among them all."

"Excuse me?" I blink in surprise. "Is the old woman who spoke to the Queen, then—this Sally Greer?"

Agnes the dove seller pats her mother on her stooped shoulder and glances at me ruefully. "Don't listen to her. Her mind is not always with us."

"I say, she saw them!" the old woman protests. "Sweet, dumb Sally never did have a thought in her head unless someone else put it there. She was no match for ol' Maude." She spits into the dirt. "That one's carried hate in her heart for so long, I'm surprised she hasn't rotted from it."

"Have a care!" Agnes's voice is harsh, and I step back quickly as she moves between us. "I think it's time for your nap, sweetheart," she says, but the ancient woman is looking directly at me with her odd, milk-white eyes.

"Hated the Queen, she did, and hates the Queen, she does. One is the same as the other to her, don't you e'er forget it." Then the old blind woman stiffens, her face going blank. And when she speaks again, the voice that tumbles from her mouth doesn't sound anything like her own.

It sounds like the unearthly rasp of the dark angel.

"Death plays your Queen in a game without end," she moans, her sightless eyes flaring wide. *"It circles and crosses, then strikes once again."*

I wheel back, horrified. This is the first time I have seen the angels speak through a mortal, and to hear such a terrible, choked sound come out of a woman whose voice I verily know seems the height of wrongness. Surely, this should not be allowed. Surely, I am hearing things I should not be hearing! Everything around me seems to press in, adding to my bone-deep dread. I am still in the courtyard, still in Windsortown, only the stalls seem to be no longer scattered through the space as a happy company, but are ringed around me. I whirl round, but there is no way out. Panic clutches my throat. I try to scream, but my mouth seems full of dust. Darkness races toward me over the ground like spilled ink, curling and eddying across the courtyard.

The scene tilts and shudders, and between the two farthest stalls I see a flash—not of light but of bright yellow fire, surrounding a dark and fathomless hole where a face should be. I stare into the hooded cowl of the hunched spirit who haunts the spectral plane, the one who speaks to me in riddles and rhymes. I hear its mocking laugh.

Death comes to Windsor.

A child's piercing shriek rends the air.

CHAPTER NINE

I come back to myself, wiping sudden, burning tears from my eyes, as children race screeching with laughter through the middle of the courtyard. They barrel into Agnes and myself and nearly knock us over in their mad dash. They run heedlessly, their shouts full of sunshine, and I exhale in sudden and unexpected relief before turning to Agnes and her elderly mother, both of them hunched over and wheezing.

"Are you well?" I ask, and then I realize that while the dove seller is in distress, her mother is *laughing*. Laughing!

"You will see! You will see!" Bess hoots as Agnes recovers enough to encircle her mother's thin shoulders with her sturdy arms. Agnes scowls at me, and I shrug helplessly. I have no idea what the old woman is trying to say to me either. *See what? And why will it be so funny?*

"You've quite upset her," Agnes snaps. "Please, leave us alone!" She sweeps her mother up in a protective clasp, and they duck and hurry around the corner of the stall, out of view.

"I didn't mean— I'm so sorry!" Neither woman is paying me any mind, however, and at that moment I hear my name called. I look up to see Beatrice heading my way. I hasten toward her, smoothing down my hair, and present myself with a smile to my fellow maid, whose sharp eyes miss nothing.

"What happened to you?" she asks as she links her arm with mine. We stroll along easily enough, but her grip does not loosen. "I say, where did you go? I looked over, and you were no longer at Maude's, no longer anywhere in the courtyard that I could see."

I peer back toward the dove keeper's stall. It is lost amidst the other carts. "I don't—"

"Tell me you were not *trancing*, Sophia," Beatrice says, using the word as if it were an abomination. "You have to be more careful, especially here in the open."

I press my lips together mulishly. "I am aware of the danger," I say. "I will not put myself at risk. I will not put anyone at risk."

"Right, exactly like you didn't put anyone at risk last night," Beatrice retorts. "I'm serious, Sophia. We need you with us, not rotting in some moldy cell, condemned of witchcraft." She glowers at me. "Or worse."

I am saved from a reply as her chin lifts in triumph. I can almost see the tension easing in her shoulders, her hands. "They're here. Thank goodness."

The three remaining Maids of Honor are chatting like old friends in the shadow of an inn, Meg making eyes at passersby while Anna and Jane appear to be arguing over whether or not it makes sense to enter the establishment, certainly a risky prospect for innocent maids. It's all part of our plan, and as Beatrice and I join them, we prevail upon them to be sensible. We will venture back to our own homes together.

The excitement in our small knot of women is palpable, but other than a quick nod to indicate that the tour of Maude's holdings has been successful, we keep our chatter idle. We, more than most, understand how easy it is to overhear the schemes and secrets of the unwary.

The day is stretching toward evening. We have nearly cleared the town's limits, when a hearty voice cries out a single word. "Meg!"

We stop, and my heart sinks for no good reason. It is Master James McDonald.

"Master James!" Meg does not share my disquiet about this man, and why would she? She has known Master James for many years. He is the troupe master of the Golden Rose acting troupe, where Meg made her fortune before she came to serve the Queen. She and James are fast friends. While Meg greets James warmly, however, Jane sidles alongside me. Her sense of dismay in Master James's presence is of a decidedly different nature from my own. For his part, the dashing troupe master takes note of Jane's reticence even as he moves from Meg to Beatrice. By the time he reaches me, I have composed myself. I have no reason to distrust him, any more than I have reason to distrust Maude based solely on a mark upon her neck. I of all people should be slowest to judgment, and yet here I am, willing to denounce an herb mistress because of an errant mole, and an amiable troupe master because his manner seems too polished.

Who am I to make such rash decisions based on so little?

"Master James," I say with more meekness than I feel as

though I have shown in an age. He takes it as his due and bows over my hand as I sink into a curtsy. I need not worry about his attentions regarding me, though. As I rise, he is already shifting his focus to Jane, who steps back when he would lean in for a social kiss.

He merely grins. "Miss Morgan," he says, then includes us all with his grand gesture. "But say, what brings all of you lovely women into Windsortown, without so much as a word to me?"

"You seem to have found us as easily without the word," Jane observes, and James's eyes dance at his success in drawing her out.

"True enough!" he says. "But it still does not answer the question. What could a poor village offer all of you that the Queen's own castle cannot?"

"Naught but fresh air," I say. "And there is safety in numbers." I watch him with interest, remembering Beatrice's idle remarks about Master James. She's convinced the troupe master is the by-blow of some great house, and in truth I can see the mark of it upon him. He is straight of carriage and strong of jaw, his bright eyes flashing with intelligence and wit. Only, he looks like no nobleman I've ever seen, exactly. Rather, in his way, he looks like all of them.

"Safety indeed, when you are so well protected," Jane says. She is confident in her ability to defend us, and she wears it like a suit of well-fashioned armor.

"But now that you are here, and we are here, we can make the most of this happy event," Beatrice says. "How fare you with the Queen's play?"

"Ah! *The Play of Secrets*, to be held at the festival of

Samhain. Surely it will be an event to stun even a court as jaded as yours, my ladies." James sketches a bow and leaps lightly back, the better to entertain us. He is ever thus, moving so quickly that it is difficult to track him, and now he lifts his arms in a grand flourish. "First we assemble the cast. Mostly men of my company, but perhaps a half dozen more of your nobles, if they dare."

"Why not any of the ladies?" Meg asks in a huff. "We can act a fat lot better than most men, I tell you plain. And a play with all male characters is boring indeed."

"A great possibility! And one I have considered myself, though I've not had a chance to bend the ear of the Queen to gain her approval of such a scandalous suggestion."

"Indeed, sir," I say, charmed despite myself. "You seek an audience with the Queen?"

"That is not necessary. If one of you might bring her a note, that would be sufficient. I can have it delivered on the morrow, and sent to—who?" His gaze roves over us all, resting the longest on Meg, who rolls her eyes. She knows what he is about. "I should insist upon its most careful protection," he murmurs. Then he snaps his fingers. "Miss Morgan! Of course."

"Oh, spare me your foolishness," Jane says. She crosses her arms over her chest.

"'Tis no trouble at all. I will craft a message to Gloriana, to be placed in her hand by her most stalwart of maids. But that is not all I need you for!" James tosses his cape over his shoulder, and while the gesture is intended to impress us with his grace, I find my eyes drawn to the long rapier at his side. That—seems new. The style of the blade itself is popular of late, but this one is finely crafted, judging by its hilt. Where would a hand-to-mouth troupe master find such a lovely weapon? And why would he have need of it?

"I need you to seek out likely candidates for the play," Master James continues. "They must be nobles who are not so highly placed as to be unable to laugh at themselves, but not so low as to be of no interest to the gathered assemblage."

Beatrice snorts, somehow still managing to make the sound ladylike. "I can assure you, you'll find no one willing to mock himself in Queen Elizabeth's court."

"Oh, come now, surely there are a few?" James snaps his fingers again. "Sir Francis or Sir William?"

Meg laughs outright, and I find my lips curving into a smile. "Lord Cavanaugh?" he suggests, and Beatrice places her hands on her hips. "Ah!" he says, before she can speak. "Lord Robert Dudley. Unless I miss my guess, he would be the perfect choice."

"James, I really think—" It is Meg now, instantly sober.

"You think too much, Meg." The barb is lightly intended, but with just enough censure that twin stripes of color flare in Meg's cheeks. I force myself not to frown. It is only because of Meg's loyalty to her troupe that *she* is now in the Queen's service, and Master James and his lot are not branded as thieves. And yet now, suddenly, she thinks too much?

"Robert Dudley would certainly not miss an opportunity to draw the Queen's eye," I say, and even Beatrice slants me a startled look at my confident speech. But if I do not speak, I will scream, such is the tension building inside me. "Still, I think he has secrets he would prefer not to share."

"Once the players are on the stage, there is no telling what shall be spoken. Who can say what is truth and what is falsehood? It will be up to the court to guess!" James says, merry once more. "I wish to cause a stir!"

Anna sniffs. "You wish to cause a riot, you mean."

"Even still!" James laughs. "It will be a coup, you must agree."

"More likely a rout." Jane's tone is flat, and her blade somehow, inexplicably, is in her hands again, as if she must weigh her words against it and see which side comes up wanting.

"And it will be for naught, if we don't get back to Windsor before nightfall." Meg's glance is to the heavens, her manner once again mild, but I catch a feeling of wrongness despite her easy laughter. Meg has a memory that is already legend. A word, once spoken, will always be recalled by her. But that also means a slight, once endured, might never be forgotten.

This time, James takes his cue gracefully enough. "I am, as always, at your service. You will receive a letter from me—"

"Oh, pish," I say, wanting us to be gone. "We'll simply tell the Queen that you have need to speak with her about *The Play of Secrets*. I suspect she will want to see you. It is her way."

"Then huzzah for her mysterious ways, my lady." James reaches out and draws up my hand, grazing my knuckles with his lips like the finest of nobles.

I drop into a shallow curtsy. "And with your dazzling play, Master James, may all the court's greatest secrets come to light."

James pauses for a breath, then lifts his gaze to mine. His eyes are as vibrantly green as emeralds. And just as hard.

"May they indeed," he says.

CHAPTER TEN

We take our leave shortly after, but silence dogs our heels until we are well away from Windsortown yet still some distance from the castle. As if by common accord, we dismiss Master James from our conversation as easily as a cup of turned wine.

"Well?" Beatrice demands of Meg, Jane, and Anna. "What happened? What did you learn?"

Meg opens her mouth to tell the tale, but Anna rushes in. "It was extraordinary!" she breathes. "Beatrice, you've never seen the like. Mistress Maude has the makings of a scientific workshop right within her own cottage. Vials and bottles of every description, a cook fire ringed with shelves, and hooks to hang various potions and elixirs to heat. It was every bit of it marvelous."

"And every bit unknown to her neighbors and to the local constable, I should say," Jane puts in wryly. At our looks, she grins. "Place was filled to bursting with her sacks and bottles, containing God only knows what."

"Her neighbors could tell us very little about her, though

they do seem to like her, in the main." Meg takes up the tale. "I knocked on some doors, begging for work to earn a few shillings to go to the local doctor to heal my child, down with a terrible cough. To a one, the women listened and expressed dismay, then got a furtive look in their eye and told me to hasten back to Willow Lane and find Maude. They told me that she may not say as much in the town square, but she has exactly the thing to keep my baby healthy, mark their words.

"No one was watching the cottage, or paying us any mind either. We walked right up. There were no dogs or men to be found."

"Or anything, in truth," Anna observes. "There are no animals or birds within reach of the house. It was almost uncanny."

"A real witch in our midst," Beatrice says. "Now, that would be something."

I eye her with amusement but say nothing. They've not found a way to describe me as yet . . . though the term "witch" appears to be out of favor, and for that I am glad.

"Witch, perhaps, or fledgling scientist," Anna says, her words staunch. "We've no proof that Maude's tinctures or potions are anything more than an old herb mistress trying new recipes. There was no intent specified in her work room, no list of women to poison or animals to kill, and not a trace of yew."

"And yet no evidence of a family either," Jane says. "She told Beatrice and Sophia the first time they visited her stall that she took care of her husband and her husband's mother in that house of hers. So she's at minimum a liar."

"Or simply a woman who does not wish to have her actions judged too quickly," I offer. They shift their attention to me, as if surprised I spoke, and I don't blame them. I'm the one who labeled Maude a murderess and poisoner, after all. I am the one who insisted she brought yew into the castle. And one old blind woman's mutterings have made me doubt Maude further. I haven't changed my opinion of the herb mistress, but I still have nothing more to justify such a dire accusation than my own grim thoughts and my still-fallible Sight. I have condemned the woman based on nothing but hearsay and hunches.

Still, Bess the blind woman did offer me information we can use, and I hasten on. "Setting Maude's potions aside, I believe I've learned the name of the old woman who spoke to the Queen—Sally Greer."

Beatrice gapes at me. "Who told you such a thing?" she asks. "And when?"

"The mother of the dove seller whose cart I so disrupted in the Lower Ward." I am reminded of the dark angel's words, *Follow the doves.* "I met the mother today, and she mentioned the name Sally Greer—that Maude had given Sally the message to take to the Queen. At that, the daughter became quite distraught. I couldn't ask more questions, but I didn't need to." I grimace. "Whether or not Maude's a poisoner, she definitely has some hand in this Mother Shipton business, for good or ill. Somehow."

"She put the old woman up to frightening the Queen?" Anna asks. "Seems a dangerous game, to lie about a death in the castle."

"Oh, I have no doubt that the prediction is quite real." I shake my head, recalling the dark angel's chilling words. "Perhaps Maude received it in a dream, perhaps she heard it from a wandering bard, or perhaps she conjured it up in a flaming cauldron, if she really is a witch. Who knows? But there are many ways of delivering a message that would not have made the Queen so fearful. Maude chose to make a dark message several times more frightening."

Meg scoffs. "There could be no sense in that."

"Who's to say what's sensible to a witch?" says Jane, who has slipped her knife out of her skirts and is admiring it in the waning sunlight.

Beatrice eyes me knowingly. "Sophia, did you . . . see anything else? When you were away from Maude's stall?"

"No, I did not, truly. I just heard . . . that rhyme again, the one about the circling and crossing." I feel suddenly ill at ease, reliving the dark angel's rasping voice once more. "And then everything became distorted. The carts were all ringed round me, pressing in too close. It felt like I couldn't escape, no matter how I tried."

"Much like one of the Queen's feasts," Jane observes, but I cannot smile. A sudden wash of dizziness is upon me again as I recall the old woman turning to me, speaking the dark angel's words. I reach out, and Anna catches up my hand.

"Good heavens, girl, you've dried blood on your fingers!" she exclaims. "Where did this come from?" She fishes out a handkerchief and rubs the stain away. There is not much, but my fingers are not gashed. Where *did* the blood come from?

We finally breach the walls of Windsor Castle and enter

the Lower Ward by way of the King's Gate. There are plenty of people milling about, both castle residents and villagers who came up to the castle for the day and are now departing.

But I feel something has changed here. This enormous castle now seems too small, too tight. As if it can no longer contain the energies swirling within it.

"Something is amiss," Jane says, and I nod. I move slightly ahead, knowing that I alone can truly see what is happening at Windsor. I step behind her and Anna, and tilt my head . . .

Chaos reigns around me.

With the perspective of my Sight, I see Windsor Castle overtaken by a sudden tempest. Howling winds shoot through the space, racing along the walls as if they are trapped, exactly like the doves were. My fellow spies are replaced by four pillars of fire whose flames leap high and strong despite the storm. The advantage of the gushing wind is that the Lower Ward has been swept clean. There are no more pockets of thick, ugly darkness, there is no line of evil coiling across the grounds. The people, whom I can barely see in the windy torrent, are like mere ghosts, as if their spirits do not shine brightly enough to be discerned.

I feel eyes upon me, and I look up, my Sight sweeping along the walls of Saint George's Chapel and the opening to the Cloisters, where nobles and their families live in small, tidy homes. I skim along the outer walls of Windsor, over the Round Tower and—and somehow *through* it, so that its interior chambers are laid bare to me. My gaze pierces through walls and earth. This has never happened before—and it is not solely *my* doing. I can see so well and so far only because something wants me to see . . . and because that same something wants to see me.

The dark angel? But, no. The strength of this vision does not have an otherworldly feel. I cannot sense my dark angel or any angel within the walls of Windsor. It is as if they had all taken flight.

I squint harder and begin moving again. The four pillars of flame circle around me like a slowly spinning wheel as I advance through the Lower Ward, up toward the Round Tower. And with each step I can see more deeply into the thick walls of the Queen's great castle, piercing the shadows cast by the sconce light. I do not worry with corridors or doorways—nay, I can see through solid rock. Until finally I observe a great gathering of curious souls, as weightless as feathers in the breeze that still blows stiffly around them, never mind that they are far inside the castle walls.

And it is here that I finally understand what lies at the center of this gale that has beset Windsor Castle.

It is not the Queen. It is not her advisors. Even glorious Elizabeth and stalwart Cecil pale beside this man. Even crafty Walsingham is naught but a timid shade.

And it is not John Dee.

For Dee is standing off to the side, and indeed he does outshine the other nobles and their ladies, the Queen and her court. Were he standing in the center of the Presence Chamber alone, he would quite dominate the room. Instead, he is barely a defiant star whose light is drowned out by a much brighter sun. Dee glints and sparks in protest while all the raiment of the universe adorns the man at the center of the room.

A man I have never seen before. A man who turns now, his long grey beard flowing down into two careful points. His deep-set, intelligent grey eyes scan the room until he spies me. He is dressed in heavy, clerical robes, a simple brown stole over his shoulders, and a thick black beret atop his head. He wears no proper ruff of an Englishman but merely a folded white collar, curling over onto his black robes. He looks like a priest perhaps, or a doctor or teacher, in every way but one.

His eyes.

Those ancient grey orbs search across the space, though the walls of Windsor, and onto the storm-swept lawn where I still stand. They fix on me, and I am held in the thrall of a power both great and arcane. A power that has quite broken the mind in which it has sought rest.

I stare as well, as the old man inclines his head to me, his haunting regard never wavering. We are two foreigners in a country—in a world—that is not our own, who yet recognize a strange and terrible kinship with each other.

For through walls and wind and earth, he can see me.

And, astoundingly, I can see him.

Nostradamus, mighty prophet-seer of France, has come to Windsor Castle.

CHAPTER ELEVEN

By the time we five Maids of Honor breach the Presence Chamber, we're not running. Nor are we buffeted by a raging storm. With my Sight dimmed once more, my fellow spies are no longer pillars of flame but quite ordinary girls, dressed for walking and shopping. With all appropriate decorum we step into the crowd of eager courtiers and ladies, each of them straining for a look at the famous mystic of the Continent. And now he is here at the request of the Queen!

We pay close attention to everyone's excited murmurings as to why Nostradamus might be here, but Walsingham and his spies have been quite effective at hiding the truth. The man standing at the center of the Presence Chamber has not been summoned to the castle to solve some terrible crisis for the Queen. No! He has been brought to Windsor merely for her entertainment, along with all the other learned men who have recently graced the castle. The women think the French doctor should be younger. The men think he should be taller. But without question, Michel de Nostredame is the consummate diversion for this perpetually jaded court, and for that, he is a wonder.

Ducking into the rustling crowd, we make our way to the front of the room, and stop well short of the space where the Queen and Nostradamus stand. Since I saw him from my distant location in the Lower Ward, I have tried to avoid looking at the man directly, but he appears not to notice me any longer. Instead, he watches the Queen.

And she watches her people.

Elizabeth appears to have been speaking at length, and she is well into the summary of her pronouncements. While I know nothing of what she has promised the crowd, the thrumming intensity of their interest has not wavered. Of course, with the Queen clearly so entranced by the French seer, it is entirely possible that the clutch of courtiers in front of her is simply smart enough to appear engaged. To seek the favor of the Queen, you must understand her shifting temperament, and adore that which she adores. It is a simple game, to play the part of courtier. But it is a game nonetheless.

"And thus we bid great welcome to our esteemed guest, traveling all this way from France to grace our court with his presence!" Elizabeth cries. A smattering of cheers breaks out. She smiles at the Frenchman, and he inclines his head, looking somewhat mystified, though I suspect that is his usual look. "Would that we could convince him to stay longer, but his travels will take him beyond our sphere all too soon. As he takes his ease tonight, I bid you all to show him the very best of English manners. Tomorrow eve the general court will be free to make merry, while we entertain the doctor in a quiet gathering of music, discussion, and dance."

The entire court hums with expectation, talking in hushed tones. Who will be asked to dine with the Queen? What will be seen and said?

Meanwhile, we maids exchange grim looks. The great prophet Nostradamus will be here only a short while, which means I am almost out of time. I can no longer wait for the angels to come to me with the name of the person doomed to die at Windsor. I must go to them and demand answers. And it must happen tonight.

At that moment I feel a strange pressure, and I look up to see that the quiet grey eyes of Nostradamus have found me once more. He watches me with the odd, unfocused air of a man no longer of this world, and I wonder what he sees in me. A fellow seer, or a pretender to the title? Has he, too, heard the whispers of angels all his life? Have his dreams been beset with terrible visions? I have read *Les Propheties*, of course—Elizabeth's library contains every almanac Nostradamus has published since 1555. But in many ways, Nostradamus's printed prophecies are more confusing than the messages I receive from the angels. Anna maintains that the French doctor has deliberately obscured his prophecies to avoid censure, but I am not so sure. Has he developed some arcane magical rite that forces the angels to be clear, only to muddy the meaning of their words on his own? Or is his connection with the angels even weaker than mine?

The Queen, apparently finished with her announcements, strides into the center of the nobles. Her cheeks are flushed, her eyes bright, her manner brimming over with confidence.

She has done what she intended to do: she has brought together her champions upon her own private battlefield, to tilt for her favor.

Death plays your Queen in a game without end . . .

"I invite you all to tonight's feast!" she exclaims. Now the cheers are in earnest, and the crowd lunges for the long lines of serving tables. The Queen, for her part, processes forward to the high table, but her head swivels around, searching the crowd. At length she finds me.

"Sophia!" she demands. "Attend me."

It circles and crosses, then strikes once again.

With a last resigned glance to my fellow spies, I turn toward the Queen. With each step, I realize that this is what my future shall be. Forever walking into a murky unknown, forever put to the test. Still, I walk with my chin high and my brow untroubled, while both lords and ladies step respectfully out of my way. To be summoned thusly by the Queen is a great honor, but I am not the only one who has been accorded this attention. I see that Dee has already positioned himself to the Queen's left, while Nostradamus has been granted the higher seat at her right. I am grateful for my seat a few rungs below these august personages, as it will allow me to see them all easily, without—

The last courtier stands aside, and my view is obstructed by a face that is already too familiar to me. A face I cannot put from my mind, no matter how much it has already betrayed me. My heart gives a traitorously happy leap, even as fear and mistrust grip my stomach. I am a woman at war with myself.

Marcus Quinn proffers me his arm.

"You shall dine with us?" I ask, but he has no time to answer before Dee waves us forward.

"Sit, my niece, sit," he says, as if he is naught but a kindly uncle. "Good that you have met young Quinn." He bows to the Queen. "Marcus Quinn, Your Grace. A young man of letters and science whom I met when I was last in London. I consider him a colleague and entrust him with my confidence, and pray that you do the same."

"Indeed." Elizabeth's tone is polite while promising nothing, but her eyes are shrewd. She sees Marcus standing close to me—too close, perhaps. Marcus may be Dee's entrusted friend, but he also appears to favor me. That can be for one of two reasons: either he has been beguiled by my great beauty, or he's working for my uncle to gain additional information about me. Neither the Queen nor I believe it's the former. And as Elizabeth's cool gaze slides to me, I sense her orders forming in my mind as if she were speaking them aloud.

I am to let young Marcus Quinn get as close to me as he desires, yet reveal nothing to him. In turn, I am to watch him closely, to gather what information I may.

The first seems fairly easy, as Quinn seats himself close enough to me on our shared bench as to trap my skirts beneath his leg. I'm strangely disquieted by his presence, though he is merely another young man to spy upon, as I have been asked to spy upon so many other members of the court. The Queen's sprawling retinue is fairly riddled with men. What's one more?

And yet, I have not been put to this task so often as have Beatrice and Meg, or even Anna. I have been held apart, much like grim-faced Jane, for other tasks that do not place me in the path of men. I have not minded, to be sure. Still, I feel woefully unprepared for the subtle task before me. My mind races ahead to tomorrow's entertainment. Music, discussion, and *dance*, the Queen has decreed.

I loathe dancing. In the past I could always work up a good swoon to avoid the exercise. Now, were Marcus to ask me, I might actually tread upon his feet. I feel the blush crawl up my neck.

"The Queen does not seem to trust me." Marcus's cheerful words at my ear make me stiffen. "What have I done to earn her suspicion?"

"The Queen does not trust anyone she doesn't know well. And those she knows, she trusts even less," I say easily. Marcus chuckles at my attempt at banter, and I feel strangely victorious, though I've said nothing of merit. Is this how it is between men and women? A smile, a nod, a few well-spoken words, and that is all?

I foresee another conversation with Beatrice in my future. Or Meg, who flirted quite scandalously with her dashing Spanish spy this past summer. I certainly cannot consult Anna, whose understanding of men is confined to the endless books she's read, and not Jane, either. She prefers to deal with men only at the tip of her sword.

"And what of you?" Marcus asks. "Whom do you trust more? Those you know, or those you do not?"

"I daresay it depends on the individual," I reply. "But no

matter how long it takes to gain such trust, be assured, it can be lost in a moment."

He lifts his brows, his cool eyes regarding me steadily. "So you *do* trust me, then."

"I trust you to be exactly who you say you are." I give him a politely chilly smile. "And who is that again?"

Marcus grins. "'A man of letters and science' is as good as any answer, I daresay." We are interrupted by the start of the meal, as servants scurry and Elizabeth speaks and giggles at her own joke, whatever it was. We all laugh in merry response, the ripple of amusement flowing down the table like leaves along a stream. Marcus waits just long enough for propriety before leaning close. "You have determined where you have seen me before."

"I have," I say. "And I would thank you to not follow me again."

"Follow you! How do you know I wasn't there first?"

I don't honor this with a response, and Marcus shifts yet closer, his whisper brushing across my ear. "I can answer all your questions, lovely Sophia, but not here, I think. Perhaps we might have the occasion to speak later, somewhere more . . . quiet?"

My face heats at his scandalous suggestion. "Sir, you are quite bold."

"All your questions," he murmurs again. "About me, and about what I have seen in the angelic realm . . . in addition to whatever you might wish to learn about your beloved uncle." He shifts back, but only slightly. "Surely that is worth a few moments of your time?"

I frown at him as the steam from the feast's heated platters curls around his face, as if he were once more in the realm of angels, watching me. Taunting me.

Whatever I hope to say next is lost, however, as I catch the end of Elizabeth's urgent query, seeming to carry with unnatural volume down the long table. "Can you do it?" she asks, and I can think of no question upon her mind but one. I casually glance to the head of the table, and see that Elizabeth is addressing Nostradamus, who looks at her with a face devoid of any emotion. As if she were asking him to solve some mathematics puzzle, and not predict a death within our very walls.

"By tomorrow moonrise," he says, his voice as clear as bells. And he leans forward to eat his stew.

I blink, taking in Elizabeth's wide smile of relief and triumph.

Then I become aware that I am not alone in watching her. John Dee sits like a hawk on the Queen's other side. He and I are resolutely aligned against each other in this race to unmask the doomed soul at Windsor, it is true. And yet, if we are both of us supplanted by an outsider, then our fortunes shall equally suffer. As much as we cannot be outmaneuvered by the other, we even more cannot let Nostradamus rule the day.

My shoulders sag under the weight of what lies before me. I now have not only one great mind to conquer, I have two. And I, by far, have the most to lose.

Nostradamus's reputation will not be damaged if he is bested tomorrow, that much is certain. And if I succeed and my "uncle" does not, Dee will not be sold into servitude, nor will he starve, I think bitterly. With his wiles and education, with his books and astrological charts and the newest rumors of his alchemical successes, he will survive.

I, however, will not be so lucky if Dee bests me in this test. I do not forget the Queen's dismissal of me last night, that I might serve the Crown in "other ways." If I cannot serve her as a seer, I suspect that she'd just as happily marry me off to some dangerous lord who needs the eyes of a court-trained spy upon him. I also know that I would wither and die in such isolation.

As dangerous as it is for me to be too successful at my role of seer, being unsuccessful is far worse. I *must* discern first who is to die at Windsor, and stop it if I can.

"Sophia, what is it?" Marcus's voice makes me jump, and I realize I am clenching my hands. "What ails you?"

"Nothing at all," I say quickly, and turn to give him my full attention. To defeat John Dee, I must learn everything about him. And if that means meeting Marcus in some quiet place, that he might feel comfortable sharing his secrets with me, well . . . what has this past year of training been for, if not for this?

I look into Marcus's eyes, glinting beneath his dark brows. I see those brows lift as if he could sense the shift of my interest, the increasing of my intensity. I watch his full lips curve slightly as suspicion dawns within him as to what I might say next. I feel him grasp my fingers lightly in his own.

"There is a hall within the castle, quite abandoned," I say, and I almost do not recognize the breathy voice that escapes me, as soft and beguiling as anything I have heard from the most alluring ladies of the court. "Saint George's Hall. Can you meet me there?"

"I will find it and meet you there at midnight," Marcus says, his hand curving over mine. His smile stretches a little wider, the glint in his eye betraying unmistakable interest. *But interest in what?* Am I merely the enemy of his employer, or is there something else in Marcus's gaze to justify my fractured breathing and my hammering pulse at the prospect of our secret meeting?

I nod quickly, but I cannot look away from his bright eyes. The moment stretches between us, soft with promise, and I feel myself shifting again. Not with the sickening spill of a trance, but something richer, fuller, that fills me up with such a heady brightness that it almost hurts to think.

A servant bumps between us, a platter descends and lands on the table with a clatter, and the rush and roar of the feast once again assaults my ears. With an embarrassed flush I draw my hand away, returning my attention to the meal in front of me. In truth, I am grateful for the distraction, to rally my wits and reset my purpose.

I will meet Marcus at midnight in Saint George's Hall, to learn all that he might share—about my uncle, about himself, and about his strange knowledge of me.

But I will meet with the angels first.

CHAPTER TWELVE

The dinner ends with Elizabeth's demand for music. Making use of my slight stature and quick feet, I disappear into the throng of courtiers and slip out of the Presence Chamber before I can be seen. I can only hope that Marcus does not follow me. When I am with him, I can't seem to focus on anything but not looking foolish, and clearly I am failing miserably at that, with my racing heart and ragged breath. This is ridiculous. *I am a Maid of Honor! And a seer, for the love of heaven.* Surely I can manage one young man.

Surely.

Squaring my shoulders with renewed confidence, I step into the darkness of the Upper Ward.

Leaving the castle is an impossibility, but there are still places in the darkness that I might hide, and one of my favorites is only a short distance away, through the Norman Gate and into the Middle Ward, where a parklike stand of trees huddles close along the base of the Round Tower. This earthen mound lifts the tower up high, providing a superior view to anyone so lucky as to be barricaded within the fortified castle walls. I, however, have no need of the security of the tower itself . . . merely the trees that surround it so prettily.

I slip into this small woodland with the comfort of long familiarity. In broad daylight it is not so grand a hiding place, though I have used it in times of need. But most nights it is abandoned, and I move deep into its hushed quiet until I am nigh up against the Round Tower.

Blessedly, I am alone, and I pull out my obsidian scrying stone. I can barely see it in the shadows of this wood, yet dark fire seems to glint from its surface as I roll the stone in my fingers, and I feel the pull of the angelic realm upon me. Not for the first time, I wish I could slip into that place and remain there, searching its endless hills and vales for all the knowledge hidden from the mortal plane. But not tonight, unfortunately.

Tonight I need the truth.

I wrap my fingers around the stone and close my eyes, sinking within myself and drawing deep breaths, and give myself over to the dreaming. I feel the wood around me shift, the whisper of a breeze indicating that I'm in a larger space. I am chilled, and I open my eyes to see that I am back in the misty glade of the angelic realm. A host of spirits awaits, eagerly surrounding me. They speak at once, their voices high and fast, melding together in a hurried song. I wonder at their urgency, and then I understand. My grim specter is not here. In his absence the angels are a clamoring rabble, and I am reminded of those first few times when I crossed over into their realm, and I was overwhelmed with all that they would tell me, all that I could see. Only in time did they grow quieter . . . and that was when I first noticed the dark angel among them.

Was my specter the reason for their restraint? Does it hold them in some sort of check? My heart quickens with excitement, for the dark angel clearly is absent now. I can ask anything—everything!

"Can you tell me what I seek?" I ask, and then I form the question in my mind, for I am loath to say the word "death" aloud. I cannot risk frightening the angels away, and worse—I sense that speaking such a dark word will draw the specter back into our midst.

Ask . . . ask, they respond, and their excitement is palpable. I see their faces more clearly than ever before. The blue-white gilding of their raiment streams around them, reflecting their porcelain skin, their vacant eyes, and their slender, graceful features. They look like Greek statues clothed in ghostlike fire, and I should be put off by their eerie, eyeless faces. And yet I am not. Instead, I spread my hands in supplication.

"Who is the soul doomed by Mother Shipton's prophecy? Is it the Queen?"

Just like that, half the angels wink out like guttering candles, and I swirl around, reaching out wildly. "Please, don't leave!" I beg, and I sense danger approaching. The dark specter is even now bearing down on our small group, I know it in my bones.

But why? Why would he keep this information from me?

The angels that remain seem harsher, their faces no longer serene, their fiery wings spreading wide, as if to encage me. I reach out, and to my shock I see them reaching back. I step forward, sensing that our time is perilously short. *Hurry, hurry!* And as I am trapped within the circle of their wings, something sharp explodes against my skull, like a child's toy shattering against a rock. An impossible pressure rakes through my mind, and I feel moisture welling up in my eyes as an image appears in front of me, as plain as day.

I see the same doomed man as before. But instead of lying dead in his bed, he is robustly alive. Grinning and laughing, he walks through the Middle Ward amidst a group of courtiers. I must have seen him before, and yet I still cannot recall him. But unlike the other nobles, this man is once more draped in a purple sash, and he's carrying a scepter of royalty. Who is this man who walks as a king? I strain to see, my eyes blurring with tears. I hear his name called—I think it's his name—Richard? Robert? Some name as this, but I cannot discern it. He turns and laughs with recognition at the man approaching him.

And this man I do know. I have seen him nearly every day since I arrived at Windsor Castle—Sir Francis Walsingham, his too-serious face now alight with good humor, his manner easy, his laughter unforced.

My heart quails within me, and I stand a moment, bereft, as the scene shifts and tumbles, my vision no longer clear. I see Walsingham once more, at the foot of the dead man's bed. The advisor's face is racked with pain as he stares down at the man's still form. Tears stream down Walsingham's hollow cheeks, though his jaw is resolute, his fists clenched. The doomed man is a friend of Walsingham's? Can this be true? I will have to tell the Queen's spymaster this vision, and yet . . . how does one find the words?

I sigh, blinking away my own tears, lifting my hands to clear my eyes—and then stop short. For the sight I see next freezes my blood.

The Queen lies before me, in a grand gown of gold and black, pearls glistening from the rich fabric, her gold-and-pearl-encrusted tiara knocked askew in her red hair. The field around her is snowy white, but she has fallen at the very center of a large black cross painted on the ground. Her eyes are wide, blank . . . and are staring at a night's sky whose dawn will never come.

She is dead.

At that moment, something dark and furious rushes toward me through the sighing angels, their wings of light scattering the image before me into fragments as I feel a staff pushed broadside against my chest. I trip backward over my obsidian bench, shoved out of the angelic realm as quickly as I slipped into it.

I blink awake, scrambling up, shocked to see I have collapsed upon the ground. Turning around once, twice, I assure myself that no one has followed me, no one has seen me fall. Nevertheless, though it is yet full dark outside, I cannot say how long I have tarried in the angelic realm. My eyes still blurry with unshed tears, I stumble quickly out of the wood. I pause at the Norman Gate to catch my breath, and reach up to brush the tears from my eyes.

I frown. Too much moisture pools against my fingers. I pull my hands down, angling them to reflect the light from the sconces . . . and gasp.

It was not tears that I wiped away from my eyes . . . It was blood. Rivulets of blood, I realize, too much for me to ignore. Scrying has done this to me, I am certain. But how? And why?

I scurry back into the shadows, casting about for something to wipe my face clean. In my haste to enter the angelic realm, I fled the castle without a cloak, and I dare not defile my gown with such a foul stain. I retrace my steps toward the wooded section of the Middle Ward, snatching at leaves to clear the worst of the blood away. But I need water, towels. I need—

"Miss Sophia Dee! I have been looking everywhere for you!"

The words are high-pitched and breathless, one of the court pages. I turn quickly in the semidarkness, praying that my face gives nothing away.

"Yes?" I ask, as calmly as possibly. "Does the Queen have—"

The boy cuts me off. "You are to come with me, Miss Dee! On order of the Queen!" He hands out a small strip of parchment, and for a certainty it's affixed with the Queen's seal.

Before I can speak, the page continues. "I was told to bring you at once, and I have taken too long in finding you." Without waiting for my reply, he darts off, leaving me with no choice but to follow him. Instead of heading back toward the Upper Ward, however, he turns smartly toward the Lower, angling straight for the western walls of the castle.

"What is this?" I ask, hastening after him. "Where are we going?"

His words send an unwarranted bolt of fear through me. "The chapel!" he calls over his shoulder, and then he is off into the darkness, knifing his way through the Lower Ward.

The chapel? What on earth could Elizabeth want of me in Saint George's Chapel, and at this hour?

In a few short minutes we arrive, and the page waves me through. Despite my extreme misgivings, I step inside the chapel's doors, the boy right on my heels.

"Chapel" is perhaps not quite a fair assessment of the place. The main church of Windsor Castle is huge and soaring, built to hold all of the castle's residents. At this hour it appears deserted, and yet it cannot be. I have been brought here for some purpose, after all. The page whispers to me to move ahead, clearly awed by the great space, but I pause a precious minute more, dipping my hands into the font at the front doors of the church as if to sanctify myself. I swipe my face with my hands to clear any remaining blood from my cheeks. Then, at the page's urging, I finally step forward into the church's long, central corridor.

I move down the aisle, remembering Beatrice's thwarted wedding, which was held in this grand space less than two short months ago. How much has changed for us all since then! Beatrice is now in love with another man entirely, I have learned to scry, and—

A sound catches my attention, and I jerk to a stop, peering into the gloom. *What's this?*

Six men stand in a long row just inside the right nave of the chapel, their hands clasped, their entire bodies covered in cloaks and hoods. I recognize them instantly. They are Questioners, devout men dedicated to a higher calling: to root out heretics, Satan-worshipers, or those who defy the Church.

We are no Catholic stronghold, mark me plain. These Questioners are not priests, nor do they have the blessing of the pope—far from it! Elizabeth has no patience for the religious order that branded her as illegitimate. Instead, these Questioners serve God with more of a personal passion. Hidden behind their heavy hoods, they hold forth with pious zeal to rid the kingdom of all that is unclean. I do not know if Elizabeth wonders if their motives are entirely pure—or if she cares. But she certainly understands that under those hoods may lurk the richest and most powerful men in her realm. She needs the support of these men, and their money. And so, for now at least, she gives them leave to wield their holy Bibles like weapons, that all might see that she and her kingdom walk firmly in the light of God.

Beatrice has warned me of these men as well. In recent weeks she has been suffered to answer their questions in the Queen's presence, though she was not the subject of their interest.

I was.

I strain to see into the darkness beyond the men. We are not alone, I am sure of it. Others watch from the shadows. Is the Queen among them? She must be. Her ring shines from my right hand, a symbol of the Queen's grace. By Elizabeth's own decree, no one may hold me for questioning—be they priest, magistrate, noble, or guard—without her presence. And she *is* here. I can feel it.

Which means, what, exactly? She has sanctioned this questioning? But why?

My mind rushes to fill in all the empty spaces. The Queen has demanded that Dee, Nostradamus, and I each provide her with an answer to Mother Shipton's prophecy. We are to give her those answers tomorrow evening. Why would she risk me being labeled a heretic, when she actually has true need of me?

Unless, of course, she has no choice. It was not so long ago that Elizabeth's mother was beheaded amidst swirling rumors of witchcraft, after all. With the Queen's fledgling reign only now taking wing, any accusation of heresy would be devastating. At best, such an accusation would delay her policies and incite her foes. At worst . . .

It seems that even Gloriana's power has its limits, after all.

"Miss Sophia Dee?" The tallest man's voice slides out over the space, and I find myself rooted to the spot for a moment. Beatrice mentioned this man specifically. His voice is eerily smooth, like that of a snake's. Perspiration gathers at my brow and the nape of my neck, and I weigh my response carefully.

"My lord," I say, dropping into a curtsy. I'm not sure in truth whether he is a lord, a priest, or a common rogue, but his voice sounds cultured and learned. And when I rise, it is to hear that same man's words wash over me with mocking censure.

"Do you know why you are here this evening?"

"I am here because the Queen summoned me, my lord."

"And do you always do what she demands?"

"I do. To the extent I may serve her and God, I stand at the ready to meet her every request."

My voice sounds overloud in the wide space, an unusual experience for me. I sense more than hear a shift in the darkness, and force myself not to look. *Who is there?* The Queen, I pray—and yet again, if it is, why has she subjected me to endure this questioning?

"You speak of God!" The voice comes from the left, vicious and sharp. I startle, stepping back. Which is, apparently, the exact wrong thing to do. "Do not move!"

And then a second man, bulkier than the first, pushes out of the line of Questioners. He advances on me aggressively, as if he means to strike me. Instead he thrusts something at me, and I take it without thinking. It is a book, a large Bible, in fact. One of the most lovely bound copies I have ever seen.

Growling, he opens the Bible in my hands, stabbing at a passage while holding a torch high. "Do you recognize this book?" he demands.

"Yes, my lord," I say, the awe in my voice completely unfeigned. It is the Geneva New Testament! I had heard of this printing, but I have not yet seen—

"Read!" he commands.

I squint at the book. He has opened to a passage of the Acts of the Apostles, written by Luke. My eyes fix on the top of the page. *"There were in the Congregation that was at Antioche, certayne Prophetes, and teachers, as Barnabas, and Simeon called Niger, and Lucius of Cyrene, and Manahen, which had bene broght vp with Herod the kynge, and Saul."* I continue on, but I have read the Bible before. This is a particularly fine copy of it, and all of it written in English, not Latin.

Finally the thick man seems to tire of my voice. "Look

here!" he shouts, seeming unduly angry with me. I no sooner look up than I feel the cool pressure of a metal cross against my forehead. There is a gasp somewhere, or perhaps I'm the one gasping, but the man just presses more firmly. Almost firmly enough to bruise. He waits, but I do not explode into flames. He seems fairly disappointed about that.

"Take it away," a new voice commands. Not the slithering whisper of the tall man, but a voice that sounds almost rational. He must be the leader of this group. "Take them both away."

The man rips the Bible and the cross away from me, the sharp edges of the cross dragging against my forehead in its upward arc. If I do not scar from this, it truly will be a miracle.

The new man steps forward. "Sophia Dee, please tell us of your relationship with your uncle, John Dee."

I lift my chin, betraying no alarm. "He is a caring protector, my lord. I am grateful for his kindness in raising me."

"And did you study with your uncle?"

I allow myself a smile. "I saw him very rarely, in truth. When I was young, I played near him while he read his books, in the home of his mother. Does that signify?"

"You did not read those books?"

"No, my lord. By the time I grew old enough to read, my visits to him were more restricted, not less so." I say this as if I were only now reflecting on the oddness of the statement, though not only is it true, but I sense it is the right answer to give. Dee, for all his many flaws, has survived an Inquisition of his own. He knew well how to protect me. "I read the Bible, as well as discourses on the management of country homes, but mostly I worked on my needlepoint."

"You never spoke with your uncle about his studies?"

"No, though I confess that I did want to. What child doesn't want to have conversation with the only parent she has ever known? But my uncle refused to speak on any subjects other than my own studies, or birds, or the weather." I prattle on, desperate to hit upon the right combination of words to satisfy these men.

"And do you ever find yourself staring into the fire, or a stone, or a pool of water, Miss Dee, seeing visions that are not really there?"

"What?" I force myself to laugh aloud as if in shocked surprise. Then, like a girl caught acting immaturely, I school my face into an expression of worried concern, casting my eyes down. "Forgive me, my lord. I am merely surprised by your question. But, no, I do not have time for daydreams. I serve the Queen, and she is an exacting mistress. When I have idle hands, I put them to my embroidery. There is nothing more soothing to me than sewing, I confess. And when my mind is idle, I think on my studies or I read from *The Book of Common Prayer*."

The men seem momentarily at a loss. I suspect they rather expected my fingers would go up in smoke at the touch of the Bible, and with that possibility passed, they don't know quite what to do with me. For myself, I allow a moment of smugness. Meg isn't the only Maid of Honor with the gift of acting, it appears! Here are six men of worth and importance, challenging me with questions that they have every right to ask. I do scry with the intent of actively seeking out the spirit world. I do presume to ask the angels for their assistance in predicting the future. Should I wish, I could enter into the angelic realm at this exact moment and demand to know these men's innermost secrets! I wager the spirits would tell me, too. Even the dark angel cannot seem to resist sharing the mysteries of this world, though it seemed quite upset about doing so when I last saw it. The active pursuit of such knowledge is a heinous crime against the Crown, and I am an unrepentant offender.

But not here, not now, I remind myself. Currently I am naught but an innocent young girl. That is the far wiser course.

I press my palms together demurely, the picture of prim innocence.

And then my heart does begin to pound.

For though I clench my hands together, I can see one long, rust-colored mark between the fingers of my left hand, smeared and drying, but proclaiming to any who would look closely enough, that something very wrong recently happened to Miss Sophia Dee.

My hands are stained with blood.

CHAPTER THIRTEEN

It is nearly full dark around our little group, but I can still see the cover of the Geneva New Testament illuminated by torchlight as the hooded man holds it against his robe. Are there streaks marring the cover? Did I actually just despoil a book of God?

I die a thousand deaths standing here, willing the precious tome to go up in flames before anyone can discover my blood staining its cover, but the fat man does me one better. Turning abruptly to thrust his holy icons at his neighbor, he stumbles in an ungainly fashion and staggers into the man, the two of them flailing for the bound holy book. They keep hold of it, but the sharp edges of the cross the fat man also holds do him no favors. I hear his yelp as he slices his own palm, and then he *does* drop the Bible. It hits the rushes for a scant second before his fellow Questioner catches it up again and clutches it against his rough woolen cloak. With any luck, that will do the trick of hiding any marks from my errant fingers.

I try to appear as small and harmless as possible. Women

have been blamed for men's foolishness, their stupidity, and their sins throughout time. And I am, by these men's own suspicion, a witch—a servant of Satan, coconspirator with demons. How difficult a leap would it be for them to decide I had somehow reached out and made this man stumble?

At the moment, though, I appear to be spared any further scrutiny, as the others turn on the man like rats in a cage.

"Sirrah!" one of them hisses. "You would do well to mind your step as well as your manner, and don the robe of a child if yours is too long to manage."

"A simple misstep," the fat man blusters. "Any of you would have done the same."

"Yet this is not your only misstep," another one says dolefully. "Pray it is your last."

The fat man's tight "As you say" is filled with anger and loathing, and I sense him refocusing on me, eager to lay the blame for his misfortune at my feet. I remain silent, however. For I am still being watched by the leader of this group. And he is by far the greater threat.

"You may go, Miss Dee," that one says at last. And he lifts his voice, as if speaking to the back of the chapel. "We will inform the Queen that you have conducted yourself well."

"My lord," I barely manage. I curtsy deeply, then turn and do my best not to race headlong out of the church. I feel too many eyes upon me as I go, but there is a movement in the shadows keeping pace with me, and that is what I focus on. Someone else, it appears, has borne witness to my questioning. As vast as the chapel is, it would be easy enough for someone to slip inside—but who could it be?

It is not one of my fellow maids, I am certain. The figure is too tall, too masculine. And it is neither Cecil nor Walsingham; his footfalls are too quick. I sense it is a young man. Every nerve in my body prickles with awareness. *Marcus!* It has to be him. I don't know whether to laugh or scowl, to shout with outrage or relief.

And why is he here, specifically? Is he worried for me, or simply doing the bidding of John Dee, keeping tabs on the young woman who is about to defeat him in front of the Queen?

The sudden heaviness of my heart shows me where my true beliefs lie. Is Marcus Quinn about to betray me, once again?

Because I cannot run out of the chapel, though I am sorely tempted, I lose steps as my watcher gains them. By the time I clear the church doors, I have enough time only to see a figure slip around the corner and disappear into the shadows outside. He is heading for the bottom of the Lower Ward.

The Sophia Dee of months' past would have flown back to her fellow spies, her mouth tremulous, her knees shaking, seeking only to hide away, and to attempt not to faint.

But I am no longer that girl.

Marcus is fast, but I have not been training as a Maid of Honor all these long months for no purpose. I gain ground as he moves past the opening of the Horseshoe Cloister and along the wall as if he were making his way to the King's Gate. This ordinarily wouldn't be a poor idea, but there are guards at the gate, and fires burning on both sides of the wall. Surely he will be seen.

As if reading my mind, the man does not hasten toward the bright fires but cleaves to the shadows. I lose him briefly as he blends in with the rocky outcropping of the wall, and then to my shock, I hear a telltale scrape against the stone. I tilt my chin upward and see that he is clambering up the walls, as quick as a pine marten and twice as bold. I curse beneath my breath. Once he is over the top edge of the outer walls of Windsor Castle, I will lose him for sure!

I spend a precious few moments tending to my skirts. I loosen the ties of the Spanish farthingale that serves to stretch my gown out far away from my body, and stuff it behind a stand of shrubs. Then I knot the endless yards of material that make up my skirts and tie them high on my hips, only my shift remaining at its full length for modesty.

And then I'm at the wall.

My fellow maids and I have trained to climb all manner of obstacles, and the walls of Windsor are thankfully far from smooth. Fortunately, most souls are fast abed at this hour or at the very least deep in their cups, and are not out staring at strange shadows scurrying up walls, but I cannot draw attention to myself or I will have far worse trouble than Questioners on my hands.

Quietly, then, I haul myself arm over arm up the vertical surface, grabbing at edges and ledges and pits in the stones. My slippers are no boon to me, and I kick them off after I slide the third time. At least now I can move more nimbly, for all my stubbed toes and torn stockings. I am up and over the lip of the wall in another minute more, but I have taken too long. I can hear the footfalls of a man running far up the twisting pathway along the top of the castle wall, but I cannot see him at all.

A sudden compulsion possesses me. *I need to see!* I swallow, not permitting myself time for fear, and tilt my head, letting my eyelids droop, my body still.

Immediately the scene before me shifts. The narrow corridor of stone atop the castle wall, bordered on each side with ledges tall enough to protect the guards from archers' arrows, seems significantly wider than it did before. It is also blanketed in a weird, ethereal light, all of its treacherous twists and jags laid bare to my eyes. I can easily see my quarry ahead. He is well on his way to the Upper Ward, aiming for the Visitors Apartments. The Queen's men, meanwhile, are camped on the far side of the castle walls. The first set of guards appears fascinated by what is happening on the Thames, while the second set is still down near Saint George's Chapel. If I am quick, I will not encounter either pair of the Queen's men. Then again, neither will my quarry.

I dash off and notice something else. Each step I take while Sighted seems to take me farther than it should, as if I were leaping and bounding, not merely running, as if I were moving at unusual speed. Where the pathway is blocked, I clamber up and over the obstructions. Where it is little more than a rooftop, my feet are solid and sure. I cannot fall, I cannot slow. I am protected in a way I have never felt before.

I have no time to consider this strange experience, however. As I fly up the narrow passageway, I can see the young man ahead of me as clear as full day.

It *is* Marcus Quinn.

Even as I recognize him, Marcus stops short and whirls. I sink down into a crouch, holding my breath. Darkness once more blankets me, and I can only hope that Marcus cannot see me. He has followed me into the angelic realm, and when I look at him with the Sight, he appears unnaturally bright, almost as bright as Nostradamus. What if I appear that clearly to him? I pray this is not the case. I wait a moment more and peek out again, but he no longer stares toward me. His attention is back on the path in front of him.

I squint into the darkness, getting my bearings for where we stand atop the castle wall. We are over the Visitors Apartments, and Marcus is moving much more slowly, taking a few steps along the passage that is now more rooftop than walkway. He pauses to peer over the side of the wall before setting off again, seemingly looking for a particular window. I have to reach him before he goes over the edge and out of sight. There are too many questions I must ask him, to let him slip through my fingers.

At exactly that moment, Marcus disappears over the side of the roof. I race after him and lean over. He is clambering down the wall now, as easily as he came up, and I squint hard, noting the window into which he slides. The moment he is out of sight, I am over the roof's edge and down the wall as well. My hands have begun to object to their rough treatment, and I grit my teeth as the stone bites into my palms. I slide down the last few feet to draw level with the window.

What I see inside confirms my suspicions. Marcus is not alone in the room. He is with John Dee.

I hang against the wall for a moment, unsure what to do.

I cannot stay here, in the lee of the building. Any idiot with eyes to see will spot me. I gaze sorrowfully downward. The ground is yet another twenty feet below, and I am not in the mood to break a limb.

I hug the wall and ease myself down a few more feet, swinging over to grip the windowsill. I glance back into the room, and go rigid with shock.

Dee and Marcus are sitting opposite each other over a large makeshift table, its surface etched deeply with arcane symbols and a complex maze of geometric shapes. Marcus looks glassy-eyed and pale, his face almost ashen in hue. But his mouth is open, his lips moving, and as he speaks, I can hear the rush of angelic voices, all of them tumbling together, yet discernible to my ears.

"Window," Marcus is saying in the strange voice of angels, his eyes fixed on the wall beyond Dee. "Window."

Window!

Dee's face registers his understanding even as I breathe out a curse. Before he can fully turn toward the sill where I am hanging, I push myself out from the wall and allow myself to fall.

CHAPTER FOURTEEN

For the record, falling isn't so difficult. Landing, however, *hurts*.

I manage to tuck my legs beneath me and curl into a tight ball as I near the ground, then roll over and lurch upright again. I move to wrench my skirts down from around my waist, but before I can begin working on the first knot, two strong arms yank me up against the wall.

"Stand fast," Jane speaks into my ear. "He's leaning out the window. He cannot see us, but your shift is as white as snow. Don't let it catch the light."

I force myself to keep my eyes down, working the knots with quick hands until my gown descends again around my ankles. "Your slippers and underclothes are in the bag," Jane whispers, and I notice her rucksack as I hear a shutter bang into place above us.

My eyes widen as I realize the truth. "You saw me?"

"Only by chance," Jane says. "You were gone too long, and it was as good an excuse as any to roam the castle looking for you. I'd just chanced out into the Upper Ward when I heard the page call your name. I followed you both, then lingered outside the chapel and watched who left." Her voice goes flat. "One of the watchers was a woman," she said. "Elizabeth, by her walk."

I nod. "I suspected as much."

"By the time she was safely gone, the man you were chasing was up the wall, with you hard on his heels, and I figured I'd never reach you in time to be of any use." She pauses, looking skyward. "He has not returned to the window. Best that you put on your blasted underskirts before anyone sees us out here."

She stands just far enough away from the wall to shelter me, and helps me free the farthingale from her rucksack, where she has ruthlessly stuffed it. Once I have pulled it on and secured it, she reaches down for her sack and folds it into a tight package that she tucks under one arm. Together we move forward, two proper young ladies taking a late-night walk around the Quadrangle. Our heads are together, like any simpering maids, but our conversation is quiet and tense.

"Those were Dee's chambers, where you were hanging," Jane says. "But who was the boy? He looks like one of the scientists, but they all look alike to me."

"Marcus Quinn," I say. "He was with me in the chapel as well. He saw the whole thing."

"Was there anything to see? You held your own, did you not?"

I shrug. "I passed the trials of holy artifacts without anything going up in smoke, and I defended myself most prettily, if I do say. But I don't believe I'm done with these men."

"Mm. So why send this Quinn? What does Dee gain from having him follow you?"

I shake my head. I wonder the same thing—and it's not as if there were no danger involved. Marcus Quinn risked life and limb to get—what? Confirmation that I would not set a holy book on fire? "Dee's own questioning was not so long ago," I muse. "Perhaps that memory weighs upon him?"

"Perhaps," Jane says, though she does not sound convinced. I am not either. By all accounts Dee remains fast friends with his accusers. Whatever method they used to question him four years ago, it could not have been too harsh.

I do not for a moment suspect I will be treated with similar care.

"Whatever he wanted to learn, I've learned something as well." I pause, considering my view into Dee's window. "Dee has a scrying table."

Jane cocks a glance at me. "A what?"

"You know the stone I use to focus my thoughts and hone my visions? Imagine a table carved with symbols and shapes, almost like a map to a distant country. He has that in his chamber. He was using it to . . . to talk to someone, I think."

"Someone." Jane's voice is as cool as the winter sea. "Someone like who?"

"Someone like an angel, I suspect." I draw in an unsteady breath, hoping she will not think me mad, and hasten on. "Whoever it was, it spoke through Marcus, and its words were clear. It warned Dee that there was someone at the window. Dee immediately looked up, and that's when I dropped."

"How do you know it wasn't Marcus who told him you were hanging there?"

I shake my head. "It wasn't Marcus talking. I'm sure of that."

Jane grunts, and we continue on in silence, the sight of Marcus's glassy gaze and slack face shimmering in my mind's eye. Is that what I look like when I affix my eyes upon my scrying stone? No wonder Beatrice and the occasional guard have been so distressed by my trances. My body must look like an emptied sack, a doll without its stuffing.

Fortunately, Jane has never been one for idle conversation, and she gives me the silence I desperately need as we make our way back into the finally quieting castle. Despite the impossible jumble of emotions I have for Marcus Quinn—outrage, curiosity, confusion—he is not my main concern. My visions are. And I cannot deny the truth I feel in the messages the angels have given me this night. Not one death but two. First, a man in his prime who goes from laughing confidence to a dreadful stillness in his bed, attended by none other than Walsingham . . . and then the Queen.

The Queen.

I turn that second, gruesome image over again in my mind. Her dress—it is like nothing I have ever seen on Elizabeth, black and gold and shot through with pearls. The ground on which she has collapsed is bright white except for that curious black cross, but she is not dressed in a fur-lined cloak, which surely she would be if it were wintertide, unless perhaps she came upon that field but suddenly, rushing forth from a castle or carriage. Her body has not been pierced by any blade, and yet the sight of her lying dead on the ground has a violence all its own, as if she somehow were dashing forward and then tripped upon the hard earth. Is her death an accident that can be forestalled? Or a devious murder, already set in motion?

More than ever, I feel that time is running out.

I must speak to both Walsingham and the Queen at first light. Not to assure my success at the convocation of seers (though of course that weighs heavily on my mind) but to give them both due warning. If Walsingham's friend currently resides in Windsor Castle, then his life is in terrible danger. Still, there may yet be time to save him. As for the Queen . . . if death is to come for her this wintertide, the Maids of Honor shall be prepared. And if my dark vision of her is simply one future among many, then I must be careful in how I present it to her. No one wants to learn they are marked for death, after all. Least of all Elizabeth.

By the time Jane and I reach the doors to our chambers, the clock is chiming nine bells, but my day is far from done. In three short hours there are yet more troubling questions to be answered, when I come face-to-face at last with Marcus Quinn, in Saint George's Hall.

CHAPTER FIFTEEN

The corridors of Windsor Castle often seem like miniature rooms, stretching around the Quadrangle of the Upper Ward like three sides of a square. I expect Marcus will reach Saint George's Hall by traveling through the castle from the Visitors Apartments, where all of Dee's men are staying, as well as Nostradamus. I, however, am approaching the hall from a different direction entirely.

Beneath it.

During the summer, when my fellow spies and I were asked to discover who was causing strange disturbances in the court, Meg and Jane stumbled upon a secret held by the old stones of the castle: hidden passages between and beneath many of the most important rooms, passages that extend throughout all of the wards and into the dungeons below. We don't know what purpose these corridors were originally intended to serve, but they have already proven their value to us—getting us through the castle secretly, and allowing us to spy on members of the court as needed.

Now I take one of the main arteries of this underground

labyrinth, the one that ends in a secret panel that opens up into Saint George's Hall. I slip into the hall and move aside the large drape we have dragged over the panel area for additional secrecy, should any of us have the misfortune of popping into the chamber when it is already occupied. One of the first things you learn as a spy—you keep your advantages to yourself. If any of the court realizes that Windsor Castle is riddled with a labyrinth of passageways, we will never get any proper spying done.

The air in the hall is still, musty. No one comes into this place other than the occasional servant intent on storing away some piece of broken furniture or torn tapestry. As I move through the chamber, my eyes already accustomed to the gloom after my walk in the hidden passage, I wonder at the piles of forgotten treasures our Queen has had neither the time nor the interest to review. Any one of these elegantly carved benches or richly embroidered bolts of cloth would fetch enough coin to feed a family for a full year, and yet here they sit.

I purse my lips, wondering if I, too, will join these relics in Saint George's Hall one day. A seer whose visions have lost their bright luster.

"Sophia." The voice is quiet and sure, the word not a question. I turn to regard Marcus as he moves through the cluttered hall. His walk is steady, though the light from the high windows is barely enough for him to pick his way through the shrouded art and the stacked furniture.

I do not approach Marcus, however. I've seen too much this evening to rush blindly forward yet again.

Marcus seems to sense my uneasiness, and he stops a few paces away from me, testing a sturdy chest before leaning his weight upon it. "I did not think I would find you here," he says.

"What might have kept me?" I ask. "The Questioners you watched at the chapel? The fall from the window outside Dee's chamber? Or merely my disappointment that it took you less than a single night to lose my trust completely?"

Though my words are sharp, Marcus chuckles and stands tall again. "I thought that was you following me. The guards in this palace are impressive, but big. You were as quick as an angel."

More than you can possibly understand. I recall my Sight-sharpened speed along the rooftop pathway around Windsor Castle. What other gifts might the angels provide me, if I gained their trust? My eyes sting in remembered pain. *And at what cost?*

"But you deserve, at the very least, an explanation," Marcus says. "I would give that to you, though I would prefer not to shout it across the room."

I thin my lips. "We are quite alone here. Pray speak from where you are."

I can see his smile even in the dim light. "Very well," he says, offering me a brief nod. "First, allow me to introduce myself properly." He steps forward with a flourish and bows down, his hand sweeping out in a grand gesture. "I am Marcus Quinn, professional channel."

"A channel!" Now my voice does ring across the space, and Marcus straightens, bringing a finger to his lips. "Explain yourself," I hiss, no longer caring that he has edged closer to me.

"What is there to explain? I am the eyes and ears for the spirit realm," he says, hooking his thumbs into his belt, as if this were an occupation as basic as a blacksmith's trade. "Within the circle of a wise man's conjuring, I walk out of this world and into the next, to see what may be seen, and hear what may be heard. This information then flows to my patron, who dutifully transcribes all that I report, for later deciphering."

"Deciphering?" I blink at him. "What do you mean?"

He frowns at me. "I have seen you in the angelic realm many times, Sophia. You cannot tell me that you don't understand what I am saying. The spirit beings all blend together, their voices—" He shudders. "Their voices are as a roar of trumpets or the crash of the open sea. They are impossible for me to discern—for you as well, no?"

I frown at him. It did take me some time to make sense of the angels' speech when I first arrived in their realm and they all spoke at once. But each time I returned, my hearing improved. Surely Marcus . . . "How long have you been serving as a channel?"

He shrugs. "I'm told I have done it since I was eight."

"So young!" I'm glad for the gloom, as he cannot see my patent shock.

"I can repeat what I hear—speak it even as it is being said—but it is gibberish to me. To the scryer as well, all too often, which makes for poor payment, trust me." He eyes me more somberly. "It is not always an easy task, this work. Not every spirit welcomes you into their realm, and some . . . some are worse than others." He shakes his head, pushing away whatever dark images are plaguing him. "Though at least your uncle has proven capable of untangling the angelic song to generate actual words. It is a long and torturous process, to be fair. But he has done it, and I have seen his handiwork. It is how I learned the tale of you, in fact."

That does bring me up short. "What sort of tale?"

"The best tale possible, for it served as a sort of key, if you will. I began work with your uncle this summer, upon his return from the Continent. The very first time I sat down with him at his scrying table, I found myself in a realm of mists and shadows and—noise. God's breath, such noise." He shakes his head. "But though my ears were overwhelmed, my eyes were opened wide. Never before had my vision been so clear. Normally I can perceive naught more than the faintest shapes, but such was the power of Dee's incantation that my journey carried me farther into the realm than ever before. I could actually *see* the spirit beings." His words are filled with wonder. "They were more beautiful than anything I could imagine. The angels surrounded me almost the moment I arrived." He shifts his gaze to me. "They sang of you. Did you know that?" I shake my head, and he continues on, almost as if he were talking to himself. "I didn't realize that, of course, because when I speak what the angels say, I have no recollection of their words, just as I know they are beautiful, without ever remembering their faces. But Dee was quite overcome with frenzy by the time I returned to the mortal plane, writing furiously over every open bit of parchment in the chamber, his clothing, the walls, the bedsheets. Apparently, when he heard your name and recognized what the angels' words were about, he endeavored to copy down the mad wailing of their song as closely as possible, for he was well aware of that particular story already, its beginning, its middle, and its end. And by working backward from what he knew to be true, he could then—"

"He used it as a cipher," I say, suddenly understanding. "He could not translate the angels' words. Not at first. But he certainly knew the tale of my own kidnapping, because he was there. He's the one who stole me. So by hearing a story well known to him, told in a foreign tongue, he puzzled out the angels' words. My own abduction account was the tool Dee needed to pierce the angelic realm."

Marcus nods and takes another step toward me. He is now close enough for us to whisper.

"All those years ago, when you were but a small child, a young, learned man with a fascination for alchemy and divination received a powerful vision," he intones, his voice almost melodic as he recounts the tale, as if it were a story about some other girl, some other time. "In that vision he was promised that which he most craved—the ability to speak with angels. To receive this wondrous gift, he was told to find the three-year-old girl who had been marked by the heavens. She would light his way."

I lift my brows. "Marked by the heavens."

"As surely as if there were a map drawn upon her skin," Marcus says. "Upon waking from this extraordinary vision,

Dee took to his charts and ephemerides. He mapped the stars back three years and studied the portents and signs. After an exhaustive search, he found what he was looking for. On one glorious summer's night, the heavens were positioned above Bristol with such extraordinary symmetry that it left him aghast."

"My father's home."

"He set off immediately, sparing no expense. A child born under such stars as these would be a wondrous light, and he was overwhelmed with zeal to seek her out. As the angels guided him every step of his journey, he found her one grim night and stole her away. He brought her to his family home, keeping her safe and close, trusting that one day, as the angels had promised, she would be the key that would open the angelic realm to him." Marcus's smile is sad, and some corner of my mind registers that he is now only bare inches away from me. "And she was," he murmurs. "You are."

I blink in consternation. "So that's it? That's the whole of my purpose here? I am simply the fulfillment of the promise the angels made to Dee so long ago?" Anger flashes through me. "All of my suffering, just to eventually forge me as his key to the angelic realm?"

"You are not only Dee's key; you are his inspiration. You connect at a level with the angels that is far beyond anything he can attempt."

"But I did not need *him* to make that happen," I snap. "I could have as easily developed my connection with the spirit realm in Bristol, among my family. The only value in Dee stealing me was to serve his own twisted ends!" Rage builds inside me, thick and hot. How many years did I live as an orphan, desperately grateful for Dee's care? How many years did he allow me to feel indebted to him, when he should be indebted to me?

Marcus's gaze never falters. "I thought you knew more of your story than this," he says quietly.

"I knew I had been stolen. I knew Dee had been told by the angels to do it, that he could never achieve true connection without me. But I didn't realize that my purpose was simply to be a crudely forged key."

"More than a key," Marcus says again. "Because you walk among the angels, Sophia. You seem to *speak* to them. Though, of course you could not be doing so, not really." He shakes his head. "That way lies only madness."

"What are you talking about?" I have sensed this fear within myself as well—that to race headlong into the angelic world, away from my obsidian bench, would be to lose hold of my sanity. But to hear Marcus state it so boldly makes me impatient.

His eyes darken, and pure torment flashes in their depths. "Trust me, Sophia," he says quietly. "The angelic realm is far more deadly than you can imagine. I once entered it unprotected. Three years ago, in fact. I was barely fourteen and had no idea of the risk. The conjurer I was working with was too weak, too uncertain. And because of his inexperience, the spectral beings we came upon were *not* born of God, I can assure you. They demanded that I remain within the spectral realm, and I tried to flee. Though the conjurer attempted to protect me . . . they had such strength." He hesitates, his memories draining the blood from his face. "Such strength as I would never have believed. The spectral plane is full of deception and danger, Sophia. You must know this. Even some of the spirits that you believe you've known all your life have been with you but a moment. If they have a mind to do it, they can convince you of any trick of time or space."

I stare at him, my own dark specter looming large in my mind. "What happened to you?" My words are a bare whisper, and Marcus's face goes even bleaker.

"I cannot truly say," he says. "According to the conjurer, I fell into a deep sleep, barely breathing, my entire body appearing racked with terrible pain as I twisted and writhed in his home. He could not call a doctor, of course; he had no idea what had happened to me, or if he would be arrested for conjuring. Days later I awoke, as if from a great sickness, with no memory of aught that came before. It took me months to patch back together the life I had lived up to that point, and another two years before I ventured back into the angelic realm. This time"—he smiles grimly—"with a master conjurer."

"Dee," I say.

He nods. "But I cannot complain. My memory is not what it used to be, and yet—I am here. I am alive, able to support myself quite well as a channel, and a wiser one at that. Why dwell in the past, when there is such a future to behold?"

I cannot argue with that. Still, there is something I do not understand. "If you started working with Dee six months ago, and you learned the cipher of the angels' speech on your very first visit to the spirit realm, then why did Dee continue to seek me out? What more value could I offer him?"

"What value?" he asks. "The value of information, Sophia. Dee is a jealous man. Here he had you to himself all those years, and now when you are under the protection of the Queen and locked away from him, *this* is when you come into your abilities. At first he couldn't believe it, and then he was consumed with the idea of speaking with you in the angelic realm." Marcus shifts uncomfortably. "Through me. To use you to expand his understanding of the spirit world."

"But then the summons of the Queen to solve Mother Shipton's prophecy came down, and—"

"And off to Windsor we went." Marcus draws a deep breath. "Dee seeks to explain the prediction the Queen has received from Mother Shipton primarily through the use of astrology. Our chambers are covered with charts and calendars, and his frenzy is only growing. He is close."

I consider that. Astrology is Dee's first true love, and he is extraordinarily skilled at using the stars as a means of answering his deepest questions. It is no surprise that he has turned to them to answer the question of who will die at Windsor. "And what of the angels?" I ask. "Have they provided you with additional information?"

"They have not. In fact, Dee holds you accountable for that. He believes you have somehow set the angels against him in this question, for they remain silent on the soul who is doomed at Windsor. He's quite upset about it."

"Good," I say, perversely pleased. The angels owe me an enormous debt. By making Dee believe that I was some sort of key to their realm, they sacrificed my childhood to his ambition. The least they can do is ensure I survive this convocation.

"You should have a care around him, Sophia," Marcus says. "Based on his astrological reading, Dee fears that you will somehow divine the answer to the Shipton puzzle this very night. He insisted I seek you out to learn the truth of what you knew. Instead . . . well." He shakes his head. "I did not expect to find you at the mercy of the Questioners."

"You did not aid me either," I say, though this is unfair. Marcus is a channel. His profession makes him as suspect as I am to men who serve God. Worse, I cannot trust him, no matter how drawn to him I am.

Marcus's next words make this all the more clear. "I am in Dee's employ, Sophia," he says. "And it is more than that. Dee helped me to regain my strength enough to reenter the angelic realm, which, after two years of wandering only in the world of man, had become such a powerful compulsion that I could not bear it. And once there, I . . . found you." His expression is wintry but resolute. "For that I will be forever in his debt."

"So what will you tell him of this night?" I ask, the words a challenge. "Will you tell him you have met me and spilled all his secrets? Will you carry back new tales of our discussion to satisfy his thirst for knowledge of me?"

"No, Sophia." He is so close to me, and I am too aware of his energy, his heat. It is as if a spell has been woven around us, lit with possibility. Without thinking, I lift my hand and place it upon his chest, and feel his beating heart beneath my palm. Marcus covers my hand with his, the touch sending a jolt through me. His eyes are once more silver-bright, intent upon my own, and I cannot seem to draw a breath deep enough to give me relief. "Tonight our tale is for our ears alone." He leans forward, his lips almost brushing mine. No young man has ever been so close to me, and my gaze falters, dropping to Marcus's mouth. His sculpted lips part, barely an inch away. "I followed you through mists and gloom," he whispers. "I watched you surrounded by the angels, their light blinding me, still terrifying to behold, but I could not look away." Another breath, and he speaks again, his words a caress unlike anything I've ever felt before. "By the saints, I almost recall . . . I believe I once watched you confront a spirit of fire and ash, and you were not afraid. You never seemed afraid."

"I'm afraid now," I whisper. And I am. I do not understand the panic filling me, the building fear that seems to have no cause nor cure. But Marcus only smiles. He shifts forward that final breath and presses his lips to mine—

A sudden shaft of light fills the space. I wheel away and see that the full moon has edged into the high windows, its sudden brilliance seeming to glare down at us in rebuke. Marcus reaches for me, but I stand back, my hands lifting as if to ward him away. Confusion makes my words bitter to my own ears. "Nay, how can I trust you?" I challenge. "I've seen you only once in the spirit realm, and yet you claim you have watched me for months. You've already told Dee about my session with the Questioners, I assume?"

His expression is all the response I need. "I suspected as much. Stop following me, Marcus. Tell Dee whatever you wish, but no longer chase after me through the shadows, in this world or in any other."

"No!" Marcus protests, looking truly stricken. "You don't understand, Sophia. I don't know why, but I can no more stop following you than I can stop breathing. Especially not now, when danger seems to stalk you everywhere you go." He tightens his jaw. "That first moment, when I breached the spirit world after so long, I was distraught, truly unnerved. Even with a patron as strong as John Dee, I was crippled with fear. And then, when my eyes cleared, I saw . . . you. You fairly glowed, Sophia, so bright in all that darkness. You gave me strength to step forward, strength to return to the world that called to me yet terrified me at the same time. You became the only thing I wished to see in the spirit realm. I dreamed of how you might speak, the sound of your laugh." He sighs, as if the words were a struggle for him. "The way you would feel in my arms, should we ever dance. You became a light not only for Dee, Sophia," he says, his words quickening in their urgency. "You became my light as well."

The spell is stirring again between us, drawing us closer. I shake my head, trying to clear it. "Marcus, you cannot expect me to believe anything you say."

"Then don't," he murmurs. "Believe what I do."

Suddenly his arms are around me, strong and fierce. This time, when he bends his face to mine, he does not falter. He brands my lips with his mouth, his grip almost brutal as he seems to pour his very soul into his kiss, scattering my thoughts in a million directions as a fiery heat wells up within me out of nowhere, answering his demand.

This!

Never have I felt so wanted before, so wanted and needed.

I desire nothing more than to dissolve into Marcus's body like sugar into water, the two of us no longer separate but one. *But he is the enemy,* some ragged part of my mind insists. *He will betray you with every breath!* And yet none of that seems to matter as much as the idea that someone—anyone—could seek to hold me with this sort of strength. Marcus knows who I am and what I am, and yet still he is here! Still he remains! Still he wants to be with me with an intensity that I cannot suspect. His words and his actions may be my undoing, but surely, this is real.

"Marcus!" I gasp as he finally grants me breath, his eyes shimmering with fire, his breathing ragged.

He steps back, setting me away from him with rough regret, as if he were a drunkard and I the last of his wine, too precious to be consumed all at once. "It was so much more than I even imagined," he says at last, his eyes filled with an emotion I cannot discern. "So much more. Everything is different now." The wonder in his voice sounds like a benediction. "Tell me you feel it too."

"I feel it," I whisper.

The bells in the high tower chime one o'clock, shattering the moment. "I must return to my chambers, ere I am missed. It's well past time. We have already tarried here too long." I frown at him, sanity returning now that I am no longer in his arms. "So then, Marcus. What will you say to Dee?"

"That I could not find you." Marcus's words are absolute, as strong as any oath of fealty. "That I searched but you were nowhere to be found, I swear to you."

Something has changed in his manner, and I find my

own breath suddenly quailing in my throat, all of the doubts, hopes, and fears of a moment ago surging once more to the fore.

Marcus's gaze, if anything, sharpens. "Sophia—"

"Go!" I no longer trust myself to be sensible. "I cannot leave until I am sure it is safe."

With one last long, searching look, Marcus nods. He turns and strides forcefully out of the room, once more merely a dashing young acolyte of the arcane . . . and not the young man who stared at me so intently that it seemed as if he wished to draw down my very soul.

I am still staring after him, in fact, my mind playing and replaying our too-brief moments together, when I hear a new sound that roots me to the floor. It is not the wail of angels, nor the howl of wind against the castle walls. Nor is it the strike of Marcus's quick steps, signaling that he has come back to confront me once more.

No.

It is a long-suffering sigh.

"That," says Walsingham, "was most unexpected."

CHAPTER SIXTEEN

"Sir Francis!" I whirl, and see the Queen's advisor emerging from behind an enormous tapestry next to the main doors of Saint George's Hall. He dusts himself off as he strolls through the piles of draped furniture and artwork, pointedly not looking at me. I assume this is to give me time to compose myself after my scandalous interlude, but I find that my utter embarrassment is still not enough to quell the sudden and horrible realization of what I must do next:

I have terrible news to share with Walsingham. I cannot afford to dither over a kiss.

Even if it was my very first.

Nevertheless, as Walsingham draws near, I cannot find a way to begin. I must tell him of the vision, of the man whose bedside he will attend, broken and grieving, but I am suddenly awkward, flushed and ill at ease. They seemed to be friends, after all. How do you announce to a man that his laughing, robust friend is about to die?

Walsingham's abrupt words take the opportunity away from me. "Marcus Quinn works for John Dee," he says, weighing the words as if each must take a measure of his attention. "And John Dee has been set against you in this pageant the Queen has devised, to find the next doomed soul at Windsor."

Both of these statements are true, so I can only agree. "Yes, Sir Francis, but—"

"And yet," he continues on as if I had not spoken, "I find you here, amidst the broken-down splendor of the castle's most abandoned hall, with none other than the hired hand of your uncle, who is also now your enemy. Is this some new alliance in the making? Or are you letting your head get turned by the first young man you meet in the wake of your canceled betrothal?"

My cheeks flush, and I lift my chin, hoping he cannot mark my humiliation in the shifting shadows of the hall. Though clearly, he saw well enough what just took place here between Marcus and me, even if he couldn't hear all of it. "My head is not turned, Sir William," I say. "Marcus Quinn had information for me, and he delivered it. The rest is for naught."

"Ah! Information," Walsingham says gravely. "And perhaps you would like to share this 'information' with me? Or have you forgotten that anything you learn, Miss Dee, is the property of the Crown?"

"I have not forgotten that at all," I say. I still feel the burn of Marcus's lips upon mine, but I am not blind to his betrayal. He has been following me in the spirit realm for months, reporting on my activities to John Dee. So while he may harbor an affection for me, which would be a strange and wondrous thing, it holds little weight against the duty that I owe the Queen. For now that duty must be my guiding star. "Marcus was explaining to me his role with my uncle. He is a channel. Are you familiar with the term?"

That stops Walsingham, and he narrows his eyes on me. "Enlighten me."

"There are many ways into the angelic realm, Sir Francis, for those who seek its secrets. My uncle has chosen to employ the services of a man who would be his eyes and ears, who sees and then reports on what he sees, leaving Dee free to record his observations. Marcus Quinn performs this role for him."

Walsingham wrinkles his brow. "But how? Under some sort of trance?"

"Exactly like that." I blow out a long breath, feeling the moment upon me to explain myself to yet another man who has waited long months for me to finally merit his careful training. For I cannot explain the visions I have had, without explaining how I came to have them. "Marcus met me tonight to . . . to apologize, I suppose would be an accurate description. For following me into the angelic realm, and telling Dee of my activities there."

Walsingham's nimble mind immediately grasps my underlying meaning. "So Dee was telling the truth!" he says, his eyes narrowing. "You *have* mastered the Sight and have not—"

"Ha! There is no mastery here, Sir Francis. I have barely any idea of what I'm doing. Always before, my visions would come to me as dreams or sudden flashes of awareness.

Disjointed and impossible to understand until the events they foretold had already happened. But in recent weeks I have learned how to go beyond receiving such passive visions. I have learned how to slip into my own meditative state and breach the angelic realm. And there—" I pause, for this is the crux of it. But there is no going back. "There I can ask questions."

"Questions of whom?" he asks, though he must suspect the answer.

"Of angels." I watch as Walsingham stiffens, his eyes fixed upon me as he considers my words. "Their answers are not always clear, but with effort I am learning to discern them."

"You can ask . . . questions," he repeats, as if I have altered his understanding of what is possible in the world. "And receive answers. *That* is the nature of your gift?"

"It is. I do receive visions as well, both in dreams and waking hours. But as my skills develop, I can better understand those visions and dreams by requesting clarification." My lips twist into a grimace. "When the angels are of a mind to give it."

"And these angels are of God?" Walsingham speaks quietly, but the chill in his words is unmistakable. For all that he is the Queen's spymaster, Walsingham is a man of faith as well. I can almost see him grappling with the question of propriety. If credible information came from the minions of Satan, would he use it?

Probably. Though he would never admit to such heresy.

Nevertheless, I can put him at ease on this issue. "They are of God," I say, keeping my voice steady. "They are adorned in blue-white fire, each of their wings the height of a man. I sense no evil among them."

Not true, of course, but I need Walsingham to heed the angels' messages, not fear them. Especially given what I must say next.

I speak before he can recover. "Sir Francis, in light of the Queen's announcement at dinner that she wishes us to decipher the prophecy by tomorrow night, I hastened to seek out such answers early this evening. I tried—more than ever before—to get clarity and insight from the angels."

"And they provided the answers you sought?" I can tell Walsingham's mind is still stumbling through the knowledge that his youngest spy now has access to an entire new *realm* of information.

"Indeed." When he doesn't respond, I reach out and grasp his arm. I feel the shock of my sudden touch pass through him as he refocuses on me.

"What is it?" he demands. "What did you see?"

"I saw two deaths at Windsor," I say quietly. "Not one."

"Two." He passes a hand over his brow, sighing deeply. "Of course you saw two. Very well, then, Miss Dee. Let's start with the first."

I compel myself to warn Walsingham of the death that seems more immediate. "He is a man I do not know, but I think you do." I rush into the explanation, hoping that the speed of my words will lighten their sting. "You are at his bedside when he dies. And you are distraught, Sir Francis. I believe this man is your friend."

"Who?" The word is like the crack of a musket. "Who is it?"

“I don’t know his last name, but his first is Richard, or perhaps Robert,” I say. “He is a man of middling twenty years. His hair is chestnut going to red and trimmed short, and he boasts no beard. I couldn’t discern the color of his eyes.” The image of the man assaults me again, deadened eyes staring out, mouth slack. “I think they are blue. He is robust and strong, with an easy smile and laughing countenance.”

“Robert Moreland,” Walsingham says, his tone now more disturbed than angry. “That is whom you speak of.” I am not sure what I expected of the spymaster, but it is not this—cold horror, as if I were an oracle of nightmares. “Tell me exactly what you saw.”

I feel the pressure in my head and will myself to stay steady. “I have seen this man now twice, Sir Francis,” I say. “In both visions he is adorned with a purple sash and holds a scepter—”

“Well, that’s not right at all,” Walsingham interrupts me crisply. “It can’t be Robert Moreland then, but some other nobleman. Very well. What else do you see? How does this man die?”

“I don’t know. There are no visible wounds. He is bedridden and appears gaunt. His mouth is open in a grimace, a thin line of blood trailing from his lips. In the first vision a young woman sits by his side.”

“Describe her.”

“She is wearing a dark grey gown, a veil upon her head. Her hair is blond, and she looks very pretty, though she is racked with sorrow. She is—” I hesitate, then push on. “She is quite pregnant.”

"God's teeth," Walsingham mutters. "Mary Moreland. What else?" he barks at me. "What else is in this damnable vision?"

"You are, Sir Francis." My words are barely a whisper. "You are dressed much as you are now—as you always are. But when I see you, you are standing at the foot of . . . the man's bed. His wife is not present. And you are . . . you have been crying. Your face is set, resolute, but your eyes are red and haggard." I draw in a shuddering breath. "That is all."

"Describe this sash." Walsingham's words are bitten off, and I sense the outrage building anew in him. "Purple, you say?"

I nod. "In the first vision, with the young woman, he is also wearing a crown." I wince at the memory. "The blood trickling from his mouth is purple too."

I draw a sharp breath as Walsingham snaps out a curse, and I instinctively lift my hands up to my chest, as if to protect myself from a sudden blow. The spymaster whirls and stalks away from me, only to return with resolute steps a moment later, his face dark with intensity.

"You do not serve your interests well, Miss Dee, to smear the name of a man who is my friend."

"Nay, Sir Francis!" I protest. "I wanted you to know so you could *prevent* this fell tragedy, that is all!

"If what you say is true, and I pray that it is not, then *prevention* is the least of our worries." Walsingham stares at the far wall. "It is easy enough to discern the truth, in any case," he says, though I have no idea what he means. He scowls at me. "When did you have this vision?"

"I had a brief image of it some days ago," I admit. "But this most clear version was earlier this evening. I decided to tell you and the Queen on the morrow."

"No," Walsingham says, his word a command. "Do not under any circumstances tell the Queen. Not until I have time to determine the truth of this."

"Of course, Sir Francis," I say, overwhelmed with the strength of his emotion. My head is pounding, and I force myself to lower my clenched hands to my sides. I have to ask, and yet I fear I already know the answer to my next question. "Pray tell . . . this man is not at Windsor Castle?"

Walsingham lets out a choked laugh. "Of course he is at Windsor Castle," he says. "I invited him here. Him and his young wife, Mary, who is heavy with child." He sighs, then shakes his head. "But we must attend the task at hand. I came looking for you for a reason, when you were not in your own chambers. Nostradamus has retired for the evening, safely within the Visitors Apartments. We have accorded him a gracious room and assigned him servants for whatever his needs may be."

I frown, my mind swimming. Why is he telling me this? "I'm sure you've done your best to make him comfortable," I say.

"Indeed," Walsingham says. "However, we have also done our best to aid our own Maid of Honor in her quest to prove herself as the Queen's preeminent seer."

I lift my brows. "You have?"

"I have left a guard at the door to the Visitors Apartments. This man will take you to a specific alcove and then depart.

Go inside the door there and climb the narrow stair. Be careful not to make a sound. Though the walls are stone, I do not fault the hearing of our esteemed French guest."

My eyes widen as I grasp his meaning. "Are you certain he will seek his answers this night?"

"Why wouldn't he? Dee has been holed up for hours, and you, yourself, sought out your angels. Nostradamus is every bit as keen to impress Elizabeth, for all that she is not his Queen. But look sharp, Sophia. Tell no one what you see, what you hear, until you speak with me."

"Of course," I say, but when he would turn toward the chamber's doors, I raise my hand to stop him. "There was the matter of the second death, Sir Francis."

Almost against his will, he stops himself, fixing me with his tired eyes. "So you said." He shakes his head. "From your manner, I can only assume it is the Queen?"

I nod quickly. "Yes." I rush on to unburden myself. "She falls on a white field, Sir Francis, a black cross at her feet, and—"

Despite my dire and stumbling words, however, Walsingham seems to relax, lifting his hand to stop me. "There's snow on the ground?"

"Well, I don't really—" Impatience flares in his eyes, and I stammer on. "Y-yes, Sir Francis. The field is covered in snow."

"Very well." He gestures for me to precede him out of Saint George's Hall. "Since it is not currently snowing at Windsor, then it appears we have the luxury of focusing only on your first prediction this night, distasteful as it may be. Go, then, to your post at Nostradamus's chamber."

I open my mouth to protest, then shut it at Walsingham's black look. Together we move down the wide corridor that will lead to the main doors of this side of the castle, such that I will have only a short walk across the Quadrangle to reach the Visitors Apartments. At the next intersection of rooms he halts, waving me ahead.

"You have given me much to consider, Sophia, and much work to do this night," he says. "But now you must take your focus away from what you have seen and fix it upon whatever Nostradamus is searching out."

Walsingham's expression is both grim and strangely wry. "If indeed the prophet-seer is conjuring spirits in his chambers, let's make sure he gives them a good Windsor welcome."

CHAPTER SEVENTEEN

I find the guard awaiting me exactly where Walsingham indicated, and only then do I realize that I have no idea how the Queen's spymaster found me, there in the gloom of Saint George's Hall. It's not as though I told the other maids where I was off to. What other spies lurk in the halls of Windsor Castle?

Either way, I do not envy Walsingham the task before him: explaining to his friend that he must leave Windsor at once. My vision showed quite clearly that Robert Moreland will die at Windsor Castle if he remains. This of course makes no sense, since Mother Shipton's prediction talks only of royalty. I recall the chilling words of the prophecy in the old crone's croaking whisper:

A royal house defeated,
disaster unforeseen.
Death comes to Windsor
to court the maiden Queen.

How could Robert Moreland have anything to do with a royal house? Still, it doesn't matter if I do not understand the vision I've received from the angels . . . only that I act upon it. Or, rather, that Walsingham does.

When the guard sees me, he turns without comment, leading me down the long hallway at the base of the Visitors Apartments. When we reach the alcove, he departs just as silently. I hasten to the door that Walsingham mentioned. When I give the panel a gentle push, it swings open without a sound.

I step inside and reseat the door, checking twice that it will open again for me when my work here is through. Satisfied I will not be locked in this secret stair for eternity, I turn round, willing my eyes to get used to the darkness. No sconces here, for certain. If there are holes riddled into the walls, any light would give me away.

As silently as I can, I creep up the circling stair, my hands sliding ahead of me along the wall. At length, there are no more stairs and the space opens wide enough that I can stand on a small landing. Once again I reach out with questing fingers to trace over the walls, touching lightly to mark several grooves in the stone. Each appears to be stoppered with soft, fresh clay packed into a small fabric bag, and I wonder if Walsingham inspected this closet himself before allowing Nostradamus to be housed next to it. I choose a groove at random that is at a comfortable height and, holding my breath, remove its covering from the wall. When the small plug comes easily away, I lean forward, pressing my face to the wall that I might observe what the great Nostradamus is doing in his lair.

The great Nostradamus appears to be . . . sleeping.

Squinting to see more clearly, I note what I can of the

room, given my limited view. The French doctor is slumped forward in his chair, his body slack and loose, his back to me, his head bobbing in uneven rhythm as he snores with a rough wheeze. The chair itself, what I can see of it beneath his coarse-spun grey robes, seems to be more of a stand than a proper chair, a brass tripod that is perched next to a large, shallow bowl on the floor.

Beyond the doctor I can see a broad table where a cluster of golden candles sits, their light sending flickering shadows all through the room. I see books gathered there as well, and a silver globe, along with the dull blade of a ceremonial knife . . . but, intriguingly, no skulls or other instruments of the arcane arts. I wonder at the books Nostradamus has brought with him on his rushed trip to Windsor Castle. Does he have *De Mysteriis Aegyptiorum*—a copy of which Anna has now stolen twice from Dee's library—a tome of ancient magic from Egyptian, Chaldean, Greek, and Assyrian practices? Or perhaps the *Clavicula Salomonis*—the Key of Solomon—which would give him the names of all the demons known to mortal man? Are these the books that provide his pathway to the angelic realm?

An odd scent filters to me through the spy hole, and I pause. It's sharp but not unpleasant. Nutmeg? That is a costly spice, but Nostradamus has been well compensated by both the French court and the countless souls who have bought his almanac for the past several years. I have no doubt he can afford all the spices he might wish to sweeten his nightly meditation.

Something moves deep in the room, and I press my face to the stone, refocusing my attention on Nostradamus.

I stretch up onto the tips of my toes and peer at the floor beneath the good doctor. All of the rushes have been swept away, and there is a thick line drawn around him in heavy chalk, surrounding Nostradamus in a perfect circle. Small, stubby, unlit candles rest around the edge of the circle, and beyond those another shape has been drawn on the floor. That one is a triangle. No candles line its edges, but I can tell that Nostradamus has chalked words and symbols I cannot decipher along each of its three sides.

Instantly I understand what is happening here, and my hands tighten into fearful fists against the wall.

Nostradamus is not stepping into the spirit world, like I do. He is bringing the spirit world to him.

At that moment, the doctor rouses himself abruptly. He stands up from his small chair. His grey robes float around him as he stoops to light the candles around the edge of his chalk circle, and I can barely hear his muttered words, though I discern that he is reciting in Latin.

As he speaks, however, I notice something else. The basin of water at his feet begins to bubble and roil, its water sloshing against the brim, lapping over the sides. I watch in wonder as a sound floats up from the water's surface, a thin, creaking moan. Nostradamus does not appear to be alarmed at this strange noise. Instead, he sets down another candle beside the basin and pauses a moment over the water, peering into its murky depths.

He murmurs more Latin, once again too soft for me to understand all of the words, but I do hear him speak the name of God. His face is beatific in the steam now rising from the basin, though how steam can be produced, I do not understand. There is no flame beneath the shallow bowl.

Still, Nostradamus's grey eyes are alight with wonder and even a simple joy. He is connecting with the spirit realm, whether solely in his own mind or perhaps through some image appearing to him in the water. The visions he sees transport him into a kind of mild trance, his hands moving over the water as if to caress the steam that is now billowing more heavily. It spills over the edge of the basin as he recites lilting invocations to whatever lies within that watery tomb.

Then the smoke dissipates, and the thin moans are back. Only, now it is many voices threaded into one, a building and ebbing wail. The angels have never spoken with such anguish to me, thank heavens. It is as if Nostradamus were tapping into a deep well of pain with whatever question he has put to them. The doctor leans forward, and in his eyes I see something new. A holy fire has been lit within him, his face now almost level with the basin of water, his lips moving quickly but silently, as if these final incantations are meant only for spectral ears.

A sharp, discordant clatter sounds behind Nostradamus, and I jump almost as high as he does. The doctor turns just as the candles spurt around his circle, their flames leaping into the shadows. Then the triangle drawn on his chamber floor begins to shift and shimmer.

Something is scratching at the edges of the chalk, desperate to escape.

I barely forestall a squeak as an image seems to burst up from the floor, the wraith of fire and shadow filling the space constrained by the chalk triangle. I immediately think it is my grim spirit, but this creature is far older and seems far more dangerous. Its back is hunched, its long robes are in tatters, and its arms are buried under thick sleeves of charred wool. It spins around, clearly enraged, and seems to fix its attention on Nostradamus, though in truth, I cannot see its features in the black hole beneath its hood. Like my dark angel, this one's cowl is ringed with fire, but it is a wilder flame, deep red in color, that seems to blaze in fury when the dark spirit spots the man standing in the chalk circle a few feet away from him.

"Venia, venia," Nostradamus says, holding out his hands. The creature hisses in rage and pain, and the doctor titters nervously, the sound of his laughter almost as frightening as the keening wail that soars up from the basin. "I would not ask, but to confirm," he implores.

The dark spirit pauses, seeming momentarily confused. Then it leans its head back, its hood falling slightly away but not enough to bare the face hidden beneath. It speaks, and I hear the roar of a thousand voices, each more pained and wounded than the last. Is this what Marcus heard when he first stepped into the spectral realm? As strident as angelic voices have seemed to me, they have never been so loud as this. At length, I am able to piece out four distinct phrases, all of them combining into an anguished scream.

"Where the muddy river runs white
An eagle shall be born of a wren.
Doomed to fly into the jaws of a wolf,
His blood shall turn to gold."

Nostradamus staggers, overwhelmed by the sound that seems to shake the room, but by the time he has recovered, the creature in the triangle has slipped back into the floor, with only a wisp of black smoke remaining to mark its passage.

The doctor moves quickly to the basin, but it too has gone quiet. Frantically, he pats his heavy robe until he finds a pouch and stylus hidden in its drape. He pulls out a small, bound book, leans over, and begins writing fiercely.

I reel away from the tiny spy hole, blinking in the darkness, the demon's words ringing in my ears. No wonder Nostradamus's prophecies are so confusing! He cannot do what I do. He cannot truly cross over. Instead he must pull his spectral messages out of the very firmament of Heaven—or Hell.

The words of the demon echo around my skull, battering my mind. Verily, if I had to rely solely on such garbled howls as these for my sole source of information from the angels, I *would* surely go mad.

I hear the doctor's strange, high-pitched laughter and immediately press forward, resetting my eye to the spy hole. Nostradamus has broken his circle. He is now pacing the length of his large chamber, the little notebook to his chest, his eyes fever bright. And all the while he laughs. Laughs until he cries, laughs . . . like a man whose mind is broken.

Unbidden, Marcus's words return to me. *That way lies only madness.*

After watching Nostradamus for several minutes, I reach out to make my way back down the turning stair. What Nostradamus has done is heresy. He did not passively receive that vision, as if in a dream. He sought it out, drawing it from a demon he conjured into this world. If he is ever discovered, his life will be forfeit.

But he won't be discovered, I know. His prophecies have grown too powerful, and with power comes safety. And clearly, Nostradamus believes he has completed his task. Tomorrow night at moonrise, he will have his answer for the Queen.

I have my answer too, but unlike the good doctor, I am not wandering about in tight circles, giddy with what I've learned. Has he been shown a different person than I have?

Is my fell prediction the correct one?

Or, yet stranger still, are both of our conclusions the same?

No matter the answer, I know that in barely eighteen hours, my future will be made.

Or lost.

CHAPTER EIGHTEEN

"This is foolishness." The disgust in Jane's voice is palpable, and I am in full accord.

We are gathered in a corner of the mercifully abandoned Presence Chamber, the long tables pushed up against the wall. It is the last place in the world I wish to be. Walsingham has rejected every attempt I've made to speak to him, though he must know I have information about Nostradamus. Is this some sort of test of my patience? Of my will?

If so, I am failing it miserably. I have nearly gone mad, trying to stay quiet. If I cannot seek out Walsingham soon, I fear I will burst.

Still, for the moment at least, I am beset with an entirely different type of misery. A clutch of musicians has assembled near us, tuning and plucking their instruments, graciously providing accompaniment as we practice dancing. All five spies are present this morning, plus Rafe de Martine, who has just arrived from London, to Meg's great joy.

Meg and Beatrice are competent dancers, skilled enough to make the rounds while drawing their partners into conversation. The rest of us, however—Anna, myself, and Jane—lack even a modicum of comfort with the art.

But tonight, perhaps to balance the more dire nature of the Queen's convocation of seers, there will be music. There will be dancing. And, by the Queen's own decree, there will be *men*, without the usual round of women to escort them. The most select group of nobles in Elizabeth's court, in fact, handpicked because they have all earned her favor.

And all uniquely positioned . . . to serve as a test for Maude's truth tonic.

It was Anna who first suggested this plan, but the rest of us agreed quite readily. Put a little of the tincture in their wine, and courtiers one and all should be spilling secrets faster than they can spin us round in a country reel. Even the Queen has approved Anna's suggestion, though with unanticipated results. Elizabeth is now apparently considering whether she should make Maude some sort of official court herb mistress, the better for us to study her craft.

Now, that really is foolishness.

However, our plans are set. Tonight, we shall dance. Which means today, we must practice.

I smooth my skirts down, using the movement to wipe dry my sweating palms. I have barely slept an hour since leaving Nostradamus's chambers, eager to meet again with Walsingham and tell him what I have learned about the French doctor and his conjuring . . . and about the Queen. But Walsingham has been locked in his chambers all morning, and at last I had no recourse but to join the others here for this required lesson.

Rafe is currently paired off with Anna, whose blushes cannot seem to be stemmed. Her ginger coloring does her no service in this regard; her emotions show clearly on her fair skin. Currently her emotion appears to be "mortification."

"I *am* sorry," she blurts, having trod once again on Rafe's toe. "I'm just so nervous."

"Preserve me from this," Jane mutters. She fishes a small bottle out of one of the pouches at her side, and tosses it to Anna, then pushes her aside. Rafe, startled, flourishes the traditional stance of any modern dance, the Honor. Jane executes hers with the precision of a knife thrust.

"What is this?" Anna asks, wrinkling her nose as she uncaps the flask. She gasps. "Jane, this is aqua vitae! Where did you get spirits this strong?"

"Drink a full measure of it," Jane says. "You'll never get through this otherwise, and neither will I."

The musicians strike up a soft flow of music, and Jane and Rafe go through the sedate paces of the Pavane, stepping up and down the room as Beatrice surveys them critically. "I will not perform the Volta," Jane says, her voice clipped, though no one has asked it of her. "I will consent to the Trenchmore, and the Galliard and Almain. I'll kill someone before I get drawn into a Gavotte, however, I'll tell you plain."

"How do you know any of these?" Beatrice demands. "I have never seen you once upon the dance floor. Ever."

Jane shrugs as she shifts toward Rafe. "Your Scotsman convinced me to learn."

"Alasdair?" Beatrice fairly squeaks the word. "When did you have a conversation with him about dancing, of all things?"

"Here at Windsor, when you were sparring with the Queen and he was being driven to distraction by your absence." Beatrice's brows go up, but Jane turns in a tight arc, not graceful so much as precise. Fluid. The musicians are as shocked as we are, however, unable to take their eyes off her sinuous form. She is long and lean and deceptively strong, but she is still not at home on the dance floor. I suspect she agrees with this assessment, else she would not suffer to practice in our company. "We discussed dance as warfare. He said you gave him the idea."

"Well. I did no such thing." Beatrice sniffs.

"He has a point," Anna supplies helpfully. She has capped the bottle of Jane's flask, and does look the better for having taken a drink. "I've certainly wounded more than my share of dancing partners, never having drawn a blade."

"And you have learned your craft excellently, Miss Morgan." Humor laces Rafe's voice as he holds Jane's hand aloft. "'Tis a question of subtlety, naught more. An easing to your manner. Perhaps, as a suggestion, I would urge you to think of the effort more as a game than an attack?"

"Mmph."

I laugh, even as a short knock sounds at the door nearest our company. Rafe and Jane split away from each other and instantly balance on their toes, which I marvel at—they are both so primed for action, so ready for battle at the slightest provocation. What would it be like to have violence as your guiding star?

So entranced am I with this idea that I do not turn to see who enters our small group, and thus the young man's words strike me unawares. I am glad that only Anna can see my face blanch in dismay.

"Good day, my ladies, sir. I beg your pardon for the interruption."

"Master Quinn," I say, masking my nerves by turning quickly to him and holding out my hands. The effect of seeing him again is stronger than I expected, and my face heats despite my determined smile. Was it really less than twelve hours ago that we spoke? That we kissed? It seems like a century has passed, and my fingers tingle with anticipation, my heart lurching into an ungainly gallop. "What a surprise to see you."

"Pray, are we not yet so acquainted that you might call me Marcus?" He eyes me with keen interest as he walks the short distance to me and takes one of my hands in his. His kiss across my knuckles is the soul of propriety, but it still sends a skittering thrill through me. "I was walking with your uncle when I was blessed to cross paths with Her Majesty and her advisors. We spoke at some length; then she dispatched me here."

I frown at him. "She did?"

"In truth, it was Walsingham's suggestion," he says, and I have the fortitude not to flinch. Marcus bows to me. "I understand you are in need of a dancing instructor?"

"*You* are a dancing instructor?" Beatrice's words are patently disbelieving, but Marcus strikes an Honor to her, his elegant body perfectly posed in a flourish to rival even Rafe's splendid form. "There is no mastery in dancing with me," Beatrice says. "If you can instruct, then instruct.

Gentlemen?" She gestures to the clutch of the Queen's musicians. "A Galliard, if you would."

Jane instantly turns to Rafe, giving him a wink. "Stand up with Meg," she says. "I have no need to practice this."

She doesn't have to ask Rafe twice. He steps gallantly forward and gathers Meg to him in a brief embrace, before standing back as the dictates of the Galliard demand. For myself, however, I am immediately distracted as Marcus approaches me. He is devastatingly handsome this cool morning, his doublet of black velvet the work of a master, his breeches and hose spun of ebony thread. The jaunty hat on his brow is black as well, save for a single milk-white stone—an opal perhaps? It seems too bright for moonstone. He makes a great show of removing his gloves and straightening his white, ruffled cuffs, another shock of brightness against all that black. All thoughts of his attire are chased away, however, as he performs the flourish of the Honor, and I am forced to curtsy. Then I place my hand in his—and all is lost.

His touch shoots through me like a lightning strike, creating an awareness so big within me, so full that it threatens to swallow me whole. The surprise of that contact lasts only a moment, but I am left shaky, trembling, as if I have suddenly been transported to the angelic realm by naught more than the brush of his fingertips. Worse, he clearly knows it. He watches me intently, pulling me into his sway. It's as if he sought to ensorcell me . . .

And, heavens save me, he just may achieve his goal.

We move in the semicircle that the dance requires, the

light, skipping steps quickening my pulse. I'm sure the steps are the reason for my increased heart rate, and not Marcus's soft words, loud enough for me to hear over the sprightly strains of music wafting from the musicians' corner. He tells me to turn, to skip and nod my head, to hold my chin and hand this way and so, to glance from the side and steady my breathing. We part, and I watch him dance with an elegance that Robert Dudley, the Queen's favorite courtier, could scarcely better, and then he gestures to me to begin my part. My eyes are on his mouth, my ears attuned only to his words, and I hop and flutter and smile as if I were born to the music.

Then his hand is again on mine, and we spin around once more, the room practically shimmering around us. We are laughing and dancing, the music slipping from one song to another, and then to a third. I am performing well enough, and Rafe changes partners, allowing Anna to stand up with him and practice her steps. But for me there is only Marcus. I relax in his arms, the movement coming naturally now, as easily as breathing. I turn, and turn again, and once more my vision shifts.

The Presence Chamber seems suddenly filled with a curious trick of light, as if the sun were streaming through mists that swirl upon the floor. I am *not* in a trance, and yet, encircled in Marcus's loose embrace, everything seems magical. I sense eyes upon me and peer up at Marcus, but though he is looking at me and laughing, his is not the gaze I feel.

As I glance to the side, something moves in the shadows of the Presence Chamber, something just outside our circle of maids and musicians. Something that seems to cleave the shadows in two, the darkness falling away, only to rush back in to fill the gap.

It is the hooded spirit.

It watches me with a fierceness I feel across the small space, and I cannot think what has brought it here. I remember all too well its furious attack on me just last night in the angelic realm. My grim specter shoved me out of its plane quite effectively, as if I should be banished, never to return. That rude action was the closest I have ever come to touching the angelic beings, and I certainly won't be inviting the experience again anytime soon.

But now the dark angel is standing here, on the other side of the veil, and once more it seems angry or . . . Perhaps "anger" is not the correct word. "Protective," maybe. Intent upon our company, whirling across the floor. But why?

I look sharply around me. Following the dictates of the dance, we circle, my feet finding their way as I follow Marcus's careful instruction. No one seems to notice my split attention. But still, every time I turn, I see the dark angel there, waiting and watching.

How much do I know about this hooded specter? I believe I have felt it on the edge of my consciousness since I was very young. Still, it made its presence known only recently, whispering everything dark and dire. Has it truly haunted me all my life, or barely for a moment? Has it deceived me, as Marcus said it might, giving me memories that never happened? I cannot understand how that is possible. And yet . . . I want to understand.

The wisp of fire seems to burn a little more brightly at the edges of my dark sentinel's hood, as if it wanted to give me the answers that I seek. But for all the revelations I have received from my specter, there has been no true clarity in its messages. The other angels—those who remained when I asked them to reveal the doomed soul at Windsor—*they* had no problem telling me what I sought. Of course, they left me with blood spilling out of my eyes as well. How much more damaged would I be if the dark angel had not returned to push me from the spirit realm?

Was it, somehow, protecting me?

I sense another shift in the room then, as my heart takes up a strange, thumping beat, and I focus on the dance to ground myself once more in the world of men.

Jane is talking to the musicians as they play, Anna and Rafe are laughing and dancing, Beatrice is looking on with satisfaction, and Meg is using the opportunity to stare at Rafe without censure. The love in her face for her Spanish spy is impossible to miss, and I feel my own heart swell with the emotion. The strength of such happiness fills me to the tips of my fingers. I am so delighted for Meg, for the simple pleasures she takes in life, for her courage in going after the one thing that she would not give over to Queen and country.

I laugh for the sheer joy of it, and then swing my gaze again out across the Presence Chamber, to where my dark angel stands. I frown, then stumble badly, causing Marcus to shout an alarm and the music to stop in a discordant, startled clash.

It is gone.

CHAPTER NINETEEN

It is another hour before the maids and I can gather again in our chamber. After our dancing lesson Marcus tried to speak with me, but I fended him off. I am too raw, too out of step to talk with him. Further, I have reached the limits of my tolerance for Walsingham's disappearance. Once more, I sought out the Queen's advisor, traversing the entire length of the castle. Once more, I was denied. The man may be the Queen's spymaster, but he is also being insufferable, to make me wait so long. To make all of us wait, indeed.

If Nostradamus's strange words do in fact hold the key to deciphering Mother Shipton's prophecy about a death at Windsor castle, well, why shouldn't the Maids of Honor use that information to either verify or dispute my own angelic vision? Whether I am right, or Nostradamus is right, or we *both* are right, I will go into the convocation of seers well prepared.

"Well, go on, Sophia," Beatrice speaks up now. "You look like you have just eaten a bird. What is it you learned last night?"

Meg leans forward, and Anna clasps her hands together,

her eyes mirror bright. Jane shifts onto the balls of her feet, as if she were preparing to do physical harm to any words I might speak that would put us in danger. Even Beatrice's face is pinched with worry.

Walsingham ordered my silence, but it is not Walsingham who will fight alongside me, should the battle lines be drawn.

I release a long breath, then begin the tale that already has been etched into my bones.

"I scried last night," I say. "The angels' message was clear. There is not one, but two threats we must beware of at Windsor Castle. The first is an immediate one, a member of Windsor's household doomed to die in his bed. The second seems further off but is far more terrible: the death of the Queen upon a field of white."

Something subtle shifts in everyone's demeanor then, bright and firm. The Maids of Honor recognizing a threat to our monarch. Unlike all too many young women our age, however, we do not flutter or gasp, or cry out in fear or worry at this terrible news. For Walsingham and Cecil have trained us well. We are spies for the Queen, yes, but we are also warriors. And warriors do not lament the terrible things that stand before them. They go about knocking those things down.

"White?" Jane speaks first, her words measured. "So, wintertide. We have some time to prepare, at least."

"And a field means she is in the open country," Anna says. "We'll be in London ere long, and we're not likely to find any open spaces there by the time the snow begins to fall. So perhaps not until late winter, or early spring."

I nod, unable to dispel the strain I feel, despite their quite reasonable assessment. Just as with Walsingham, the maids have quickly driven to the heart of the matter. The Queen is under no immediate threat, not if she is to fall upon some snowy field. But still, something nags at me . . . something I cannot quite dispel.

"But what of this first death?" Meg asks. "That seems as though it will be the focus of the convocation of seers. How did the Queen phrase it?" She snaps her fingers, then assumes a rigid posture, her chin high, her hands curved into fists upon her hips. If her hair were red instead of dark brown, and her skin paler, she could pass as Elizabeth herself. "Who will die next at Windsor?" she demands, her voice flawlessly mimicking the Queen's. "And when, and how?"

"I'm going to have nightmares," Beatrice mutters.

I feel my tension loosening, as it always does when I am with my fellow spies. I sit on my pallet and lean forward, my elbows on my knees as I share information so secret, not even the Queen has heard it yet. "I don't know the man, though Walsingham does. I told him my vision last night, and he recognized the person I was describing right away. He said it was Robert Moreland."

"Moreland!" Beatrice speaks now, clearly surprised. "Whyever would he be at risk? He's no more royal than Meg."

"I can be *extraordinarily* royal if the situation demands it," Meg protests. "And I know the man as well. Tall, broad-shouldered? Red hair."

"That's who I saw in my vision, yes."

Jane shifts on her pallet. "It doesn't matter who he is,"

she says. "If the Queen thinks he's from some sort of royal house, and therefore a potential claimant to her throne, then the death that's been predicted will likely come from her own hands. She doesn't suffer competitors lightly."

I frown, considering this. *Thank goodness Moreland is Walsingham's fast friend, or he might be in danger indeed.* "It could mean something else entirely, but on his deathbed there was a scepter and crown, and he was draped in a mantle of purple."

Meg's laugh is rueful. "Definitely sounds like royalty."

"But it's not possible." Beatrice is up on her feet, pacing. "Moreland cannot be in line to the throne. He's a merchant from Gravesend, if I'm remembering the gossip correctly, and his very-pregnant wife is also the daughter of a merchant. His business is . . . wool, I think."

"Perhaps the royalty connection is indirect, then?" Anna asks. "A brush with greatness once, naught more." She frowns. "I canna imagine the Queen would wish him ill in that case, especially if he's a friend of Walsingham's."

"Oh, I'm sure not," Beatrice says drily. "I confess, I know nothing more about him, though. Where are his rooms?"

"Horseshoe Cloister," Meg says. "Cecil assigned the Cloisters to me after Shipton's prediction upset the Queen. Your Robert Moreland was belting out a fairly bawdy tune the other day when I passed by him, and it was one I recognized from the western coastal villages. I asked him how he came to have heard such a song, and he confessed it was his mother's favorite. He seemed to care for the woman quite dearly, though I got the impression she's passed away. I liked him for that."

I grimace. "Well, good son or no, that brings us no closer to understanding how Moreland could figure into a prediction about a royal house."

"'A royal house defeated,'" Anna says, quoting the Shipton prophecy. "It does seem quite clear."

"Unless the defeat is simply that the Queen could not keep this man safe?" Jane puts in, but I raise a hand to stop their conjectures.

"I have more to share, though it's no easier to understand," I say. "Last night Walsingham bade me to go spy upon Nostradamus in his chambers." I feel my cheeks color, even as I disobey the Queen's advisor by sharing yet more without his permission. "I was to tell no one what I saw."

"Oh, excellent. Then exactly no one could help you," Jane says, irritation clear in her voice.

"Did Nostradamus scry?" Beatrice's words are sharp with curiosity. "Surely he suspected we'd be watching him."

"If he was concerned, he gave no sign of it. I entered a small corridor—"

"With a winding stair?" Jane asks.

"Spy holes stoppered up with clay?" Meg chimes in. The two spies grin at each other in triumph, pleased to be familiar with yet another cubbyhole cut into the castle walls.

"The very same," I say, laughing. "And once I was in place at the top of the stair, I did watch Nostradamus scry." I smoothly skip over the whole "dark spirit trapped in a triangle" part. Even my friends might not be comfortable with the ideas of demons visiting Windsor Castle. "And he received a prophecy."

"No!" Anna fairly bounces with excitement. "Do you recall it exactly?"

As if I will ever forget it. "I do. It makes no sense, of course, but perhaps you might be able to help me puzzle it out. Here are the words:

> *"Where the muddy river runs white*
> *An eagle shall be born of a wren.*
> *Doomed to fly into the jaws of a wolf,*
> *His blood shall turn to gold."*

Instantly the Maids of Honor are alive with movement, walking and talking, staring and mumbling. "Muddy river turns white," Anna muses as she strides over to a pile of books she's arranged on a side table, the precious tomes stolen from Dee's library. "That has to be the Thames. Frozen over? Or perhaps merely the Thames at wintertide, hmmm." She hums a little, poking through the stack. "It seems to me there's a journal of seasons here . . ."

"An eagle is clearly a sign of royalty," Beatrice puts in. "Blood to gold, as well, though that reference is more obscure."

"The wren is the key, though," Meg says, triumph in her voice. "What do we know about wrens?"

"Small, brown menaces," Jane says. "Don't try to stay abed once their clamor starts up."

"They're songbirds," I say, my heart doing a little flip. "Like Moreland's mother."

Beatrice's laugh is sharp and derisive. "And Moreland

looks to be about twenty-five, yes? Clothed in purple, with a scepter in his hands and a crown upon his head?" She rolls her eyes. "I bet I have the right of it. You don't grow up at court and miss those kinds of hints. In 1534, King Henry would have been still hale and hearty, and certainly not one to ignore a pretty distraction."

"He took up with Moreland's mother." Anna nods, frowning.

"Not even that, I wager," Beatrice says. "Merely a night's dalliance, I suspect, while he was married to . . ." Her smile sharpens. "Well, well. The Queen's own mother, Anne Boleyn. That certainly would be a 'disaster unforeseen,' if what Nostradamus *and* your angels say is true. If Henry bedded Moreland's mother, young Robert could potentially claim the throne. The way would be murky, but pretenders have waged campaigns with lesser cause."

"Robert Moreland is the *least* likely pretender to the throne I've ever seen," Meg says firmly. "He told me his father died when he was very young, that he cannot remember him. His mother remarried thereafter, and he's lived a very happy life. He's a wool merchant, not some lost prince pining after his crown."

"His opinion wouldn't matter," Beatrice says. "If it's merely suspected—and it will be, ere long, if both you and Nostradamus share what you've seen—then Moreland's life is in danger."

"But my visions aren't always accurate," I protest. "And Nostradamus receives prophecies so jumbled that they can be read sixteen different ways. Surely that is not enough to kill an innocent man over."

"Here it is!" Anna's voice draws us all over to her side of the chamber, where she stands with an open book. "The Thames doesn't freeze over every year, of course, and not everywhere along its course when it does. But in 1534, right around the time when Moreland would have been born at Gravesend? It absolutely did. Or so it was recorded in this history. That year boasted one of the coldest winters ever."

I turn back to Beatrice, and her face is grim. "This does not bode well for Moreland," she says. "Or for his wife and child."

A chill settles over me, but I try to push it back. "Again, all of these are but portents and possibilities," I say. "We're drawing connections to support a vision that I may not be understanding correctly."

"Yes, but first you, and then Nostradamus?" Anna holds her history book against her chest, almost like a shield. "Walsingham was closeted away this morning, but it's nearly high noon. Where would he be now?"

Jane's voice is hard and certain. "My money is on the Horseshoe Cloister." She stands up briskly, shaking out her skirts. "What say we all have a look?"

But we are wrong. The five of us all but run to the Lower Ward, but once we reach there, we can do nothing but mill around like confused ducklings. The Cloister is as lively as it ever is, but the small apartment where the Morelands are quartered looks quiet, as if the family were out for an early afternoon stroll.

"Perhaps Walsingham has already warned them?" I suggest, but something still seems off to me. Uncertain.

"Perhaps." Beatrice sighs. "But if he hasn't, then Robert Moreland remains in desperate danger, at least until we can clear this matter up. For even if Walsingham gets to him in time to spare his life, his troubles are not over. Not unless he can convince the Queen he's no threat to her crown, anyway."

"Surely that's a simple enough task," Meg says, and Beatrice nods.

"Yes, but one we'll have to handle delicately. If we can't speak to Walsingham before the convocation, it's up to us to draw his attention away during the event itself. Ideally *before* you and Nostradamus are set up to tilt at each other, Sophia. Until then, we wait."

The others agree to the right of this, but as we leave the Horseshoe Cloister, I cannot return to the castle with my fellow spies. I am too disquieted by the day's events, nervous about what the night may bring. And unlike the other Maids of Honor, I do *not* have to tolerate the waiting. Meg may be a master thief and Beatrice a master manipulator. Jane may have her knives, and Anna, her books. But I am a *seer*, for the love of heaven. *Whatever I seek, surely I can find.*

And after all, tonight's revelations cannot center only on one poor man and his questionable birth. The Queen is also threatened. For all that her demise is linked to her collapse on a snow-dusted field, and we are still enjoying a robust autumn, it is no small thing that she is at risk.

Death plays your Queen in a game without end. It circles and crosses, then strikes once again.

I think of the dark angel, watching me silently from its shadowy realm as I danced with Marcus. Did my grim specter appear this morning because it wished to speak with me? If so, I am willing to listen.

Once my mind is set, I am eager to be away. The need to run burns within me, but I force myself to stroll toward the King's Gate. As I move through the Lower Ward, I fold my arms tightly against myself, as if I were cold. No one much notices me, and the space is more than half full for market day. Yes, I am a female walking without escort, but I am also a maid, constantly directed hither and yon by the Queen. Not even the guard Will Seton notices me, though Ladysweet lifts her head and nickers, forcing me to quicken my pace to hasten through the gate. Still, the sight of the mare once again healthy lightens my spirits somewhat. No matter if my Sight is not always trustworthy, at least it helped me to save her.

My thoughts darken as they return to Maude and her deadly yew. I cannot be mistaken in thinking she deliberately set in motion the events of that day: pressing the poor old woman, Sally Greer, into service as her messenger, and getting her in front of the Queen to deliver Mother Shipton's prediction of death. To hear Bess tell the tale, Mistress Maude hates the Queen for some fell reason of her own. But I still can't puzzle that out. This is the Queen's first year on the throne! In the past several months she's worked hard to earn the love of all her loyal subjects. Whatever could she have done to enrage a village herb mistress?

Once I have left the castle walls, I feel safer somehow as I angle toward Windsor Forest. It will take me another half hour to find my hallowed glade, but my heart no longer has that strange, clamped-down feeling it did within the castle's embrace. I can breathe again.

I walk beneath the heavy cover of trees, loosening my shawl. Even in the full light of day, it seems the forest is close and quiet, sheltering me. I finally reach the glade and glance about, immediately locating the small stone bench that I found the first time I chanced upon this clearing. I have no idea how the bench was brought here, but I entertain myself with thinking that I am not the first wandering soul to seek refuge in this glade. Certainly neither the deer nor the birds ever do. It is always empty, a balm to the soul.

I seat myself on the bench and will myself into a state of calmness. If the dark angel awaits me on the other side, then I must be ready for it with all my questions. About Maude, the Queen, and especially poor Robert Moreland, whom I pray Walsingham has spirited out of the castle, to ensure that neither Nostradamus's prophecy nor my terrible vision has a chance to come true.

Once I am ready, I pull out the obsidian stone on its long chain and hold it up in front of me, wrapping my fingers around its smooth surface.

I feel the door within my mind ease open, and I step across—

Only, everything is different.

Or, rather, I am different.

Every time I visit the angels, I arrive as I am dressed on the mortal plane. This time, however, I am completely changed. My gown is white, richly adorned, my hair heavy with a net of pearls that hangs down over my shoulders. I have rings on my fingers and bracelets of gold and silver on my wrists. I look like a bride on her way to a wedding, or a Queen before her own court. How did this happen?

Around me there are easily a dozen angels, murmuring among themselves—but not my grim specter. I resolve to ask my questions of the angels instead, but they do not move toward me. They appear to be waiting and watching, eager for some scene to unfold. After several moments of this, I hold out my hands and step away from the obsidian bench, welcoming any of them to approach me and speak.

A rustle of movement sounds to my right, and, smiling, I turn . . . then freeze.

It is the dark angel.

And for the first time ever, I realize my grim specter is a *he*.

The heavy hood still hangs over his face, all flames banked for the moment, but the dark angel's cloak is flung back to reveal a powerfully built masculine body. He is nearly as robust as Beatrice's Alasdair, and his clothing is as fine as any courtier's in Elizabeth's circle, all in jet black: doublet, breeches and fine black hose, leather boots. I don't recognize that I'm staring at those boots until the spirit's feet shift, and I realize he is performing the Honor, the first step in any proper dance.

Startled, I lift my head to search his face—and meet only shadows.

I do not trust myself to speak. Never before has an angel tried to approach me in this way. I sense it is forbidden, an unwritten rule of the realm. I am mortal, they are spirit. Never the twain shall meet, else . . .

Madness.

Ignoring my mute objection, the dark angel moves around me, mimicking the dance he observed naught but a few hours ago. He watches me from the darkness of his hooded cowl, and I find myself curtsying to him in turn, then rising up. He positions his hands as the dance requires, and I place mine next to his—close, but not touching him.

The dark specter sought me out in my own realm, after all. Clearly it—he—wants to speak to me. If he wishes to dance with me as well, I can be accommodating.

"What can you tell me?" I ask. My voice is breathless, though we are circling each other most sedately. Still, I feel tired, as if my energy were draining away.

Life, it is this dancing, stepping forward, hastening back.

The dark angel's words recall me to his face—or, rather, to the darkness that passes for his face beneath the cowl. I smile tentatively, not sure how to respond.

"Yes," I say. "Life *can* be a dance, good sir."

His head comes up then, anger riffling between us. I have said something wrong. I bite my lip and try to give him a better answer. "We seek to come together, yet all too often find ourselves pulling quickly apart. We cannot stay but that we seek to leave; we do not leave but that we wish we could stay."

He nods, and I breathe a tiny sigh of relief. Still, no sooner have I relaxed than his words sound again. This time, however, they are solely in my head.

See this gathering of spirits.
Look but quickly, then away.

They would seek to draw your breath,
To dance your dance, to ever stay.

I frown, but I do as he instructs, glancing over at the collected assembly of spirits. The dark angel is correct, I suppose. There is an intensity in the way the other spirits watch me, but no more so than I felt in the dark angel himself as he watched me dance with Marcus.

The laughter that skates across my senses is low, dangerous. Can the dark angel read my thoughts? If so, I dare not wait any longer to ask my questions.

"Please," I say, though there is no supplication in my tone, only bold demand. "You and the angels showed me the Queen's own death last night. You must tell me how to stop that from happening."

But my grim specter remains silent, watching me from his cowl's hooded depths as we engage in this caricature of a dance. "I cannot fail in this," I try again. "I beg of you."

Do not rush into this madness.
Do not fall, ever to stay.
Do not heed the call of sirens.
Flee this place, away, away.

"Enough!" I cry in frustration, pulling out of his mock embrace. "If you cannot tell me, then please withdraw and allow another to speak!"

He moves so quickly then that I can only gasp. His gaunt-leted hand reaches out and cups my chin, lifting my face up to his. *How is he touching me? This is not allowed!* And yet, at the moment when I feel the dark angel's forbidden touch, my mind is filled to bursting with sounds, images, and words.

I see the young, chestnut-haired man in his bed once more, dead.

I see Walsingham at his side.

I push these images away. "What of the Queen?" I ask. "I saw the Queen die! How can that be stopped?"

The dark angel shifts his hold on me, loosing my chin but crowding close. My sight dims further, until I am wholly blind. I feel the lightest pressure along my cheek, as if the angel has drawn his finger down my face. With that touch my vision brightens once more, in sharp and vivid clarity:

I see five women, my fellow maids and myself, in the midst of some great revel—as if we were part of it but with our own unique roles, a play within a play.

Positioned like the tips of a five-pointed star, each of us holds a sword high in the air between our clasped hands, our eyes glowing bright. We are possessed of an eternal inner fire, able to see in utter darkness.

At our center is the Queen, and we all stand upon a circular snow-white field, bisected with a black cross.

I remember this place, of course. It's where the Queen will die! I am smote with an impossible urgency, and suddenly I understand. When the Queen takes to this white field, I will be close enough to save her. If I move quickly, she will vanquish death. I simply need to reach her. *I must reach the Queen!*

The dark angel seems to shudder, and I sense that both his hands are pressed to either side of my face as he stares intently at me, my mind filling with bright, discordant images. Now I am back in the Lower Ward, rushing through the collection of carts and animals and people. I seem to be searching for someone, desperate to find her, when the carts suddenly give way and I dash into the open space.

Before me an old woman in heavy shawls whirls around to gape at me, her hands flying up in a violent frenzy as if to warn me away.

Her eyes are as white as milk.

Pain explodes in the back of my neck.

I scream in agony, reeling away from the dark angel as a bolt of fire lashes through me. I am nauseous with a heavy, roiling wrongness.

At that moment a roar besets the glade, wind racing into the sacred space. I stumble to the side, half-collapsing onto the obsidian bench. I feel a cloying wetness on my cheeks and brush it away, but when I pull my hand back, my horror surges anew to see my fingers red with blood. My eyes are once again bleeding! The raging storm grows, and I realize that the dark angel has stepped away from me and is lost in the gale. "No!" I scream into the wind. I squint across the open space, but I cannot see the dark spirit anymore.

"Don't leave me!" I am dizzy with physical pain, but the sudden wrench of the dark angel's disappearance hurts me worse, as if, having transgressed so far as to touch me, he may be taken from me forever, never to return. Never to show me his face. "Who *are* you?" I demand, grasping at something—anything—that will keep us connected across the planes. For I cannot lose him. Not now, when he has given me a way to see visions with such a startling clarity. Not now, when I am so close! "Come back to me!"

But I can already sense the angelic realm slipping away, even as I feel the brush of something against my cheek, as light as a feather though it seems to scorch me to the bone. *Arc,* speaks a voice in my head, more pictures and thundering music than words, a word full of fire and desolation and loss. *My name is Arc.*

My eyes pop open. I am in the quiet glade of Windsor Forest, staggering around like a woman gone mad. But my head is clear, and my neck no longer feels as though it has been set on fire, despite the fact that my eyes are streaming with what should be tears. With what instead, I suspect, are thin rivers of blood.

I rub my hands against my face, gently wiping away the worst of it. *What just happened?* Never before have I been touched by any of the spirits. Never before have I danced. Never before has the dark angel held my face in his hands as he poured out images too intense for my mind to accept.

Arc, he said, and I wonder at the word, turning it round in my mind. So that is his name? Can I now summon my grim specter, like Nostradamus called up the fire spirit? Dare I even try?

A branch cracks in the distance, and I look up in sudden concern, at once aware of how far I am from the castle. How far, and how alone.

No, no. I urge myself to calm. *There is no one in the glade. I am alone. I am safe.*

Half-right, anyway.

CHAPTER TWENTY

I make my way back to the castle slowly, dread gathering around me like a heavy cloak. Though I must find Walsingham the moment I breach the walls of Windsor, my feet have become leaden, and it is almost more than I can bear to put one of them in front of the other. Surely all the cares of Windsor Castle will still be waiting for me, no matter when I arrive.

There seem to be yet more carts heading into the Lower Ward for market day than there were when I passed this way earlier. They choke the narrow opening of the King's Gate. I fall in step with villagers seeking entrance to the castle, grateful for this moment's rest to walk normally among normal people, all of whom seem blessedly *normal*. They look over at me with only a passing interest, taking in my simple dress. To them I am as any villager walking to the castle, with no concerns but what provisions I might buy for my family.

I'm jostled into the center of the group as we wend our way forward, and then it seems we must wait again as the guards engage in some discussion at the gate. I stretch my neck, trying to relax, and a movement up ahead catches my eye. There's something immediately familiar about the woman's hunched shoulders, the wild hair peeking out of her cape, the colorful shawls wrapped round her frail body.

It's Bess, the old blind woman from Windsortown. I squint hard to see who she is talking to. Sure enough, her companion is her daughter, Agnes, the dove seller. Even as I watch, Bess grips her daughter's arm with easy familiarity, using her as both support and guidepost.

The memory of my vision in the angelic realm floods through me—the chase in the Lower Ward, the clearing of the carts. Bess turning back to me, urgently warning me away. I marvel at the blossoming ache of remembered pain in my neck. *What was that vision about?*

There is only one way to be sure. I push through the crowd, taking advantage of the stalled carts to slip in and out of the villagers. A command is shouted from the gate, and we all lurch forward once more as the next wave of people is let inside the castle walls. The delay has served its purpose for me, however. I move up alongside the dove seller and her mother.

"Agnes?" I begin, and the woman glances to me, instantly recognizing me. To my great relief, she doesn't scowl but grimaces at me ruefully.

"Aye," she says. "With a mother who would not rest but that she had to come to Windsor this day."

"Windsor Castle, bright and fair," the old woman croons, and the look Agnes sends her is so filled with sadness that I feel sudden tears prick at my own eyes.

"Is she well?" I ask quietly, but the old woman's cackle is immediate—and sharp.

"I'm blind, not deaf," she announces, and that earns us chuckles from our neighbors. Her daughter gives me another wry smile.

"She's as well as she can be, for a woman whose mind is *touched*," she says quite audibly, and her mother laughs again. Agnes glances at me with the tired eyes of a daughter who understands which battles she cannot fight. "I would make her time as easy as possible." She shrugs. "She has been good to me."

"And you to me, sweet Agnes, you to me." Bess pats her daughter's hands.

I nod, sensing the underlying message in these words. I fear this might be the last trip to Windsor Castle for the old blind woman, her days now dwindling down. Looking at Bess, I cannot see how she could become so distraught as she seemed in my vision. I consider warning Agnes, but how do I put into words what I have seen?

I can't, I decide. I can only make sure that whatever danger is to befall Bess, it will not be this day. "It looks as though all of Windsortown has come up to the castle," I remark instead, and Agnes snorts in agreement. She glances at me, and I mouth the word "Maude?"

Agnes's eyes reflect her understanding as she shakes her head firmly. No wonder she felt safe in bringing her mother here. I am relieved too. If Mistress Maude is not at market day, Bess will be safe. "That woman Mother mentioned before," Agnes says, keeping her voice low, though I can tell from the tension in her mother that the old woman can hear every word. "It's best that you forget her name. The guards have been all over the town asking after her, but no one will talk. I'm only grateful they didn't stumble upon my mother, since she can't shut up."

Bess laughs once more, but I stay focused on Agnes. "That woman could be important, Agnes," I urge. "What do you know about her?" After all, if I don't fully understand the truth behind Maude's actions, the Queen may pay with her life.

"Sally was a widow with no more living children," Agnes says at last, though I can tell she doesn't want to talk of this at all. "Daughter died last year in a fall. The cart vendors had been taking care of her, none more so than Mistress Maude, in all truth. Sally felt she owed her, and she did. Owed her enough to take a message to the Queen, certainly."

"Owed her enough to die while she gave that message?" It's only a guess, but it hits home. Agnes flinches. "What did Maude use?" I ask.

"I cannot be certain." Agnes's words are tight and low. "But if I had to guess, it'd be monkshood. Maude grows enough of it behind her cottage to fell a bear, and let me tell you, she's not using it to treat headaches."

"Monkshood." I try to recall what I know about the deadly poison. "But there was no sign of Sally's lungs failing."

"She didn't need much to push her to death. If she didn't strangle, then the damage to her heart alone was enough." Agnes shakes her head. "Her time was short."

"Still." I wince, thinking of the sight of poor Sally Greer, crumpled on the floor of the Presence Chamber. "Why did she have to die at all?

"It has you talking, doesn't it?" Agnes's mother interrupts us with a croaking laugh. "If ol' Sally had marched up to the Queen and told her piece with a wink and a smile, what would have happened? She'd have been questioned by the guards, is what, her head cuffed for her troubles, and then ignored. The Queen wouldn't spend a minute worrying, and how would that serve ol' Maude? Maude hates the Queen, always has. A wound that deep is not easily staunched. She'd sooner spit at the woman's feet than kneel at them, and that's for certain."

"Mother!" Agnes draws her mother to her more firmly, as if she's a child to be scolded. But Bess just laughs.

"She plays a long game, mark my words," Bess says. "A long game indeed."

"But what issue could she have with the Queen?" I ask the question that is likely to drive me mad. "Elizabeth has ruled for less than a year."

Agnes shakes her head firmly. "Pay my mother no mind," she says. "Maude's a troublemaker to be sure, but she's no fool. She wanted to cause a fuss, for her own sick purposes, but she'd never make the Queen her enemy outright." She grimaces. "You didn't see her walking up to the Queen to tell her Mother Shipton's prophecy, did you?"

I sigh. "True enough. But how did she get that prophecy in the first place?"

"Miss Dee!" Before Agnes can respond, I hear my name called. I glance up to the King's Gate, which we are almost through. The guards there gesture to me with an urgency that cannot be denied, and I'm forced to leave Agnes and her mother behind. I make my quick good-byes and hasten forward. When I reach the King's Gate, it's Will Seton who grins down at me.

"There you are," he says, but though his eyes are warm, he wastes no time with idle chatter. "A page was sent for you more than an hour ago. The Queen has need of you."

Dread lances through me once again, and I squint up at the sun. I have not been gone that long. "Have you any idea why?"

Will Seton laughs. "Who can guess what stirs the mind of a monarch? But I'd be on my way, were I you."

I thank him and edge away. Still, the gratitude that shines in his eyes warms me. I am glad I saved his horse from Maude's poison. Though my skills are meant to be bent to the Queen's service, where I can help others, I will.

Scant minutes later I rush into the Queen's Privy Chamber almost breathless, my overheated skin instantly becoming clammy in the cool confines of Elizabeth's inner sanctum. "Your Grace," I say, sinking into a curtsy.

"Get up, get up," the Queen snaps. She appears agitated, but there is no one else in the room save Cecil and Walsingham, and they are removed to a corner, conferring on some matter of their own. Still, the sight of Walsingham makes my heart leap. *At last I can speak to him!*

"Where have you been?" Elizabeth demands as I rise. I force myself to not touch my hair, my face, to not call attention to my state of dishevelment. I open my mouth to speak some falsehood, but the Queen's eyes are too sharp.

"Approach me, girl," she says, her voice overloud. What has disturbed her so?

Still, I do as she bids. Behind me there is some commotion, and I realize that both Walsingham and Cecil have moved to engage someone outside the doors of the chamber. Under cover of their conversation, I draw closer until I am a bare three feet away from the Queen. Elizabeth leans forward in her throne, as if she can sense where I have been from my appearance. She tilts her head, her gaze holding mine. "You had another vision?" she asks. "Dee told me you did, just now. Said he saw it in his own angelic session."

"Dee!" I exclaim, while in my own mind fury erupts. Marcus Quinn was spying on me again! Not three hours after I left him with his pretty words and meaningful looks on the dancing floor. "I cannot imagine how he thinks he can see such a thing, Your Grace."

"And yet he has said as much to me. So who is telling me the truth, I wonder?"

And this is it. Elizabeth's first real demand that I reveal my abilities. She is my Queen, my ruler. I owe her my life and my fealty. But the images in my head are all jumbled, and I cannot shake my most recent vision of the five Maids of Honor, with glowing swords and eyes, ready to protect the Queen upon a field of snow. We cannot fail her then, and I cannot fail her now. For until I know the truth, I dare not reveal too much.

"I did *try* to reach the angelic realm, Your Grace," I lie. "I set out to do just that, but it was for naught. The angels remain silent, though I feel they will speak soon, truly."

"Mmph." Elizabeth sits back in annoyance, eyeing me. "See that they do," she says curtly. "I have no wish to be made the fool."

I frown. "Your Grace?"

"Your uncle has been quite convincing about your abilities, Sophia," she says. "And I tell you plain, I am inclined to believe him." Her jaw tightens. "It would be best that you don't fail me this night."

We stare at each other for a long, frozen moment. Then I curtsy as demurely as possible, my mind racing with her not-so-subtle threat. "I understand," I say.

I'm still looking at the floor when she blows out a frustrated breath. "Walk with me, Sophia," she says. She stands and sweeps down the short stair that extends from her throne, and holds out her arm imperiously. Confused but not stupid enough to deny her anything, I slip my hand into the crook of the Queen's elbow. We pace the length of the Privy Chamber and then move farther out, to where the servants are busily preparing the Presence Chamber for the evening meal and entertainment.

"Sophia," she says, and her voice is quiet. "You need to start trusting me if this is ever going to work."

I stiffen in her grasp, utterly surprised. "Ma'am?"

"Don't play the fool with me," she says. "I have eyes. Every time I enter a room, you watch me warily, as if I'm going to hang you from your toes at any moment. But that is not my intention, Sophia. That has never been my intention. I have only ever wanted to keep you safe."

Immediately my mind skips to my memories of the

questioning in the chapel. The Queen was there in the shadows, watching the Questioners try to brand my skin with holy objects. That was her idea of keeping me *safe*? Still, I hold my tongue. And the Queen does not need a response to continue talking, of course. It's one of her many graces.

"But I need *you* to keep *me* safe as well," she says, and this time I do glance at her, only to find that her profile remains serene . . . and deadly serious. "I plucked you from your uncle's care because the kind of service I need cannot be relegated to this plane alone. I value Dee's astrological prowess highly, and still more his alchemical research."

She pauses, and I sense that I should make some comment here, though I no more believe that Dee can change lead into gold than that he can fly. "Of course, Your Grace," I reply.

"Do not 'of course' me. It's no small matter," she says, and I barely avoid a wince. Once more I have said the wrong thing. "I inherited not only a kingdom from my dear, departed half sister; I inherited its debt as well. With gold in our coffers procured from the Philosopher's Stone, we can go a great distance toward satisfying the demands of the people while holding off the encroachment of our enemies." She tightens her hold on my arm as we walk. "And with foreknowledge of events that may affect my court, I can rule with an assuredness that will silence my detractors and confound those who would seek to overthrow me. Yes"—she nods with grim satisfaction as we turn at the far wall, heading back toward the Privy Chamber—"to strengthen my throne I would reinforce my defenses on all sides, including within the realm of angels. And for that, Sophia, I need you."

I feel a hard kernel of dismay form in my stomach, like a knot of twine. Part of me wants to share with the Queen the vision I had of her, and yet I sense this is not the right time. Not now, when she is speaking to me so earnestly, and with such clear hope about the future. And I cannot deny my relief and gratitude that she is treating me with favor. The servants all notice it, and the ladies who pass by us—curtsying to the Queen and then taking in our positions, as if we were bosom friends. The Queen's support opens all positive doors and closes all negative ones, and I would do well to remember that.

For despite the wonder and beauty of the angelic realm, I do not live there. I live here.

And in the mortal world, there is no power so great as the Queen's.

"Your Grace, Miss Dee." Before we have barely breached the Privy Chamber's doors, Walsingham is before us. He looks haggard to my eyes, but then, he is Walsingham. He always looks haggard. And with his arrival, my mind crashes back to all that I must tell him. "We must begin our preparations for tonight's convocation," he says. "Please, allow me a moment with Miss Dee."

CHAPTER TWENTY-ONE

The Queen grants Walsingham permission to draw me away easily enough. But Walsingham does not stop at the doorway to the Presence Chamber. "Walk with me, Sophia," he says, and strides toward the corridor, forcing me to nearly run to keep up with him. The cool hallways of the castle seem too dark and oppressive, and when we step out into the still-warm afternoon, I lift my face to the sky, wishing we were still in midsummer and not on the doorstep of winter. I shall miss the sun once the darkness of the frigid season is upon us.

Walsingham's brisk pace takes us into the Upper Ward, and we set out across the Quadrangle. "Your vision, Miss Dee, about Moreland. It was most unfortunate, but I thank you for it nevertheless. I discussed the matter with him at some length. In the end, I think he understood."

Relief rushes through me. Walsingham has sent Robert and his young wife away, ensuring that the prophecy shall not be fulfilled! "I'm glad, Sir Francis," I say quietly. "It pained me to share what I saw with you."

"No," he says. "You did right by telling me. You should

always tell me such things. For the good of England, and for the Queen." His voice nearly breaks on the last words, but he rallies, stiffening his back. How difficult it must have been for him to chase away his friend! No doubt Moreland felt deeply betrayed to be dismissed, but what else was Walsingham to do?

Still, at least with the resolution of this terrible prophecy, we can leave off tonight's folly of a convocation. "So what will happen now?" I ask. "Have you told the Queen that we need no longer go forward with the convocation tonight?"

"What do you mean?" Walsingham asks sharply, and I blink at his sudden anger.

"But . . . my vision," I say, stumbling over my words. "The prophecy is resolved. You've spoken to Moreland already."

A tremor ripples across Walsingham's face, making him seem centuries old. "Mother Shipton's prophecy may be read in many ways, as all prophecies might," Walsingham says, shaking his head. "We have addressed your interpretation of it, but that does not put an end to matters, I'm afraid. No. The convocation of seers shall proceed, and the Queen alone will decide who provides the answer she most prefers."

I prepared myself to assure him that I already knew Nostradamus's interpretation, but his final words stop me in my tracks. "The answer she most prefers? What does that mean?"

"It means the answer she most prefers, Miss Dee. If the Queen agrees with our assertions, then all well and good. If she doesn't, then we must simply remain content that we knew what was right and true. That we performed our work for her as quickly and completely as we knew how. That is our role, as her servants and protectors. That is our charge."

I nod, taking in his words. It is overwhelming, and it should be gratifying, to have Walsingham's confidence in me. But still, he looks so shaken that I cannot feel smug. And my own fears still twist and roil within me, refusing to be silenced.

"And what of my prediction about the Queen, Sir Francis?" I ask. "I saw a white field, marked with a black cross, and the Queen fallen upon it without a mark on her. Surely we should explore that vision further as well?"

"Surely we should *not*," he says severely. "We will defend the Queen in the time and manner that is best for her, and for England, as we ever do. Accordingly, we will shore up our protection for the Queen the moment the first snow falls, and not before. There is no need to frighten her. No monarch can rule ably when gripped with fear."

In the face of my budding protest, he speaks first. "Say not another word about this, Sophia. Not to me, not to anyone. Your work is done on this score."

I purse my lips, but in truth what can I say? Other than, "Of course, Sir Francis."

We arrive at a set of stone benches, the afternoon suddenly seeming far too cool to me. Walsingham bids me to take my rest, then stands there, looming over me. "I confess, there is another question that weighs heavily upon me, in light of all that has passed today. Something I would ask of you, if you are able to grant it." He doesn't wait for me to respond. "The vision you shared with me this past night led me down paths I did not willingly tread, to realizations I had not fully considered until I found myself in the small hours of the morning, thinking . . . unthinkable thoughts," he says. His voice is almost despondent, for all that it is strong. "Such thoughts as I had never wished to be mine own."

"Forgive me, Sir Francis, for causing you this pain," I reply, for I feel I must say something. "At least you were able to do what you could."

He continues as if he didn't hear my words. "My service to the Queen is paramount. It goes far deeper than my work in Parliament, or my role as her counselor. I have tied my fortune and the fortunes of my family to Elizabeth. I do it willingly, and with the knowledge that she is the best hope for our country to achieve its goals and reach a level of greatness unmatched across the Continent. I am willing to sacrifice much for that—more than I ever would have imagined."

"She is blessed to have you," I say, and he grimaces.

"'Blessed,'" he says. "It is one way of looking at it, I suppose." He turns to me more fully then and plunges on, his question at once concise and wide-ranging: "Can you tell me what *my* future holds, Sophia?"

I draw back, startled. "Your future?" I should be offended, as if this were some sort of test, some trick for the court fool to entertain the gathered throng.

"Yes," he says. "I wish to understand what lies ahead of me, given what my service has wrought thus far."

Something in his voice gives me pause, and I resolve to assist him. I slip the obsidian scrying stone off my neck, grasping it in my fingers. I have never sought to ask a question that was more than a clarification of a vision already received in some part from the angels. But today, on this cool bench in the shadowed protection of Windsor Castle, it seems the right time to begin. And this is for Walsingham, I remind myself. Walsingham, who is the Queen's trusted advisor, yes, but also the man to whom I gave an incomprehensible vision of his friend's death, and who didn't laugh in my face. He took my information for what it was—a guide, a warning. An important thread to consider in the whole embroidered cloth. And he acted upon it.

I can do this for Walsingham.

I gaze down at the obsidian stone, and slip into the angelic realm just that quickly. I do not wait for the angels to form before me this time. Instead, I ask my question into the mists, to any angel who might be listening, my words no more than a sigh. *"What lies ahead for Sir Francis?"*

Something shifts in the darkness before me, and I feel the eyes of a spirit seek me out through the gloom. Quite without my intention, my sigh lengthens, the exhalation becoming at first a gasp and then a sort of strangled moan. Then, suddenly, the outdoor space I am occupying with Walsingham becomes an enormous chamber. It is filled with light and music and—people. So many people! Everyone is dressed in the silks and velvets of a formal dance. It is a masked revel, the women's hairstyles, plunging necklines, and easy manner bespeaking a world far less circumspect than Elizabeth's court. I hear chatter and am drawn forward. It is lyrical and bold—*French!* They are speaking French.

The dancers move and create an opening, and I see Walsingham, only not the Walsingham I have come to know. He is haggard and worn, and there is something not quite right about his skin. It looks stretched too thinly over his bones, a trick of the light that seems to vary as I watch him. First he is healthy, then he is sick. First he is robust, then he is wan. I track him through several steps of the dance, and always he is different. Time seems to pass with the rush of music, building to a crescendo, then crashing to the earth. Over and around again, over and around. At length the Walsingham in my vision seems to feel me watching him. He looks at me across the space, and I shrink back, the full weight of his desolation catching me up, tears filling my eyes. *No!*

"Sophia!"

I feel arms around my shoulders and a cloth at my face. My vision clears, and I realize that, back on the mortal plane, Walsingham is holding me, as a man might hold his dying grandfather or wounded son. I have toppled off the stone bench, my skirts are tangled on the grass, and Walsingham crouches over me. There is no intimacy in the embrace, for all that he holds my body close as he half-kneels upon the lawn, propping me up.

"Did I fall?" I ask.

"You damn well didn't stay sitting. Here." He dabs my face a final time, then helps me back up to the bench and offers me his handkerchief. I take it, not missing the bloodstains that darken the rich fabric. I do not need to ask Sir Francis whose blood it is.

Instead, staring at the marred white cloth, I begin talking. And I do not stint in my account.

"The vision I saw would place you years from now, Sir Francis," I say, still not looking at him. "Perhaps another two or three decades. I cannot be certain. You are penniless, though you have the air of a nobleman. You are in France."

He flinches back, astounded. "I am no longer serving Elizabeth?"

"Yes, you are," I say, and now I do look up. "You are under the Queen's protection. But, Sir Francis, I believe she has bankrupted you. You are forced to be in this place, a diplomatic envoy to convey her every whim, and she has not settled enough coin on you. You are angry and dismayed, for all that you are the perfect courtier. You remain her spymaster, but you—you—"

"After all of this, I am still undone," Walsingham whispers. "My wife, my family . . ."

I feel my own heart wither at his bleak tone. "They are the reason for your weariness, Sir Francis. They remain in good health, but you had not expected it would come to this." I clutch his handkerchief in my grasp. I know without asking that he believes me, which perhaps says something more about the Queen than the clarity of my vision. The idea of her bankrupting him is not a surprise. Diplomats sent off to foreign lands do so on their own coin, monarch's blessing or direction aside. If Walsingham is required to remain in France for any length of time, he will find his coffers drained.

"Twenty years hence?"

I favor him with a small smile. "You're older, Sir Francis, by a fair margin."

"Not so fair as that, from what you say." His answering grimace is pained. Then he straightens on the bench beside me, staring at the flurry of activity as market day continues in the Lower Ward.

At length he speaks. "We are the two of us caught in a

world that would break us, Miss Dee, if we give it the chance."

I nod, straightening the handkerchief on my skirts, folding it over to hide the telltale blood.

"And yet," he continues, "we also find ourselves in the unique position of possessing some control over our lives. Perhaps not our futures—only God can truly alter any man's course—but our present, to be sure. That, we can affect with shrewd and careful work."

I hesitate. "I do not understand your meaning, sir."

"I mean we must look to ourselves and those we love," Walsingham says quietly. "And prepare for futures we cannot imagine." He stands, and it is like he is a different man. A man with a new course set in his mind. With every court grace, he holds out his hand to me. "Just as we never imagined the events of this day, I warrant."

"Assuredly not." My dry laugh feels as worn as he looks, and I allow Walsingham to pull me to my feet. We move toward the Lower Ward and the market day festivities, and I think of all that this long day has already held:

The quicksilver Marcus Quinn in Saint George's Hall—and my very first kiss.

Nostradamus in his darkened chambers, conjuring spirits.

Two different dancing floors, in two different realms, with me swirling in the embraces of two very different partners.

And finally, this—a vision, a conversation . . . and an unexpected connection with the Queen's grim spymaster.

None of these things I could have predicted, and the day is not yet done.

The convocation of seers still awaits.

CHAPTER TWENTY-TWO

The Lower Ward is bursting with activity, and Walsingham and I walk into the throng with the air of two people desperate for distraction. We are granted it. The scents alone would be enough to turn anyone's head—the savory aroma of meat pies, the rich smell of cinnamon, even the sharp tang of mulled wines fill the air, as the villagers resign themselves to the season drawing to an end. With winter seeming to come on earlier and earlier every year, the blessings of the harvest have become more important; and the celebrations of food and ale to stave off the long winter's privation, more merry.

It certainly is an auspicious omen for Elizabeth's reign, I think, as I meander through the brightly colored stalls. I should be glad to see her people filled with joy and hope as she closes in on the end of her first year as Queen. This time last year she was naught but a princess kept under close watch, her relationship with her own half sister, Queen Mary, fraught with tension. She did not know what her future held, or when her station would change for good or ill.

What a difference a year has made in her life.

What a difference in my own as well.

Walsingham takes his leave of me, and I suspect he is as happy for us to part ways as I am. It is one thing to know you can ask the angels any question. It is another to live with the answers they provide.

"So pensive, Miss Sophia, and on such a pretty day?"

I turn to see Marcus Quinn by my side, his eyes guileless as he regards me with open interest.

"Indeed, sir." The scowl I give him seems to have no effect, so I draw myself up stiffly. "Have you decided to simply follow me in open sunlight instead of muttering over a scrying table to track my path into the spirit realm?"

His smile grows broader. "Why do you believe I followed you there at all?"

"Because Dee told the Queen I had a vision," I say coolly. "And how could he have known that, but that you told him?"

"Did he say such a thing?" Marcus shrugs the matter away. "Well, it was *all* I could tell him, really. Yes, he bade me look for you, and yes, I saw you enter the angelic realm. But then the entire place was overtaken by infernal winds. I could not see you through it, and the sound was like to kill me. Not even Dee could decipher my ramblings." He crooks a brow at me. "Were you on the other side of that gale, or in the thick of it?"

I lift a haughty brow, remembering my dance with the dark angel. "I was in its very arms."

Marcus grins at me. "Then the storm was quite lucky, I know from fond experience. But say, Dee is all caught up in the evening's convocation. I would be a poor retainer if I did not ask you: Have you solved the Queen's riddle?"

"What? You jest!" I blink at him, amazed. "You cannot expect me to give up my position so easily."

"You *have*, then!" His eyes are alight with merriment. "Dee is quite satisfied as well. I can't imagine how the Queen plans to choose a winner, if all three of her champions put forth the same information."

This does make me frown. "Dee knows?" I ask, thinking of Walsingham's gaunt face. "He has seen who was—is—to be killed?"

"I do not think he's put so fine a point on it as that." Marcus shakes his head. "Be fair. He's had only a few days to assemble all his charts and measures. He has studied the astrological markers, however, and is quite sure of what he does know: the timing of the death, and the nature of the victim. He seems quite beside himself with pride, I will say that." His face softens as he looks at me. "If you have the answer as well, then so much the better."

"Seems a poor attitude for an eager retainer to take," I say.

"'Tis mine all the same. Here. You look like you haven't eaten in weeks." Marcus stops at a market stall selling pies, the small fire at the cart's side tended by two children with open grins. The pastry is too hot for my hands, and he gives me a fine handkerchief to wrap it, appearing not to care that the buttery pastry will ruin the cloth.

"And how is it you have such coin that you can spend it on pastries on market day?" I ask. "Dee pays you so well as that?"

“Dee is a miser who would spend his money on naught more than books if he could.” Marcus laughs. “But he realizes that I am his only link to you, and for that he must make an exception.”

“How sad you will be when this day’s work is done, then, and you’ve no reason to track me down in this world or any other.”

I recognize the words for what they are—clear flirtation. Still, I cannot stop them.

Marcus looks at me intently, the smile on his lips reaching his eyes. “Who says that I have any wish to stop?”

The force of his gaze burns into me. I try to smile, but I cannot quite make my mouth curve, and my words, when I do form them, seem foreign to my ears. “You cannot stay with Dee forever, Marcus,” I say. “Eventually he will tire of sending you after me.”

Marcus’s words are equally soft. “I would not need to track you in the angelic realm at all, Sophia, if you would allow me to court you in this one.”

“Court me?” My words are overloud, my shock serving to make me coarse and unrestrained. I straighten and proceed again more civilly, though my heart has begun thudding once more. To have Marcus look at me as Rafe looks at Meg, as Alasdair regards Beatrice . . . But still, neither of those relationships have the Queen’s blessing. And given her need of me, I cannot believe she will countenance this distraction either. “You cannot court me, Marcus.”

“Whyever not? You are unmarried, I am unmarried. I cannot see the objection.” His eyes light with amusement. “I can't stay forever with Dee, as you say, and you can't remain in service to the Queen the whole of your life."

I think again on the Queen's words, the tightness of her grasp as she held me to her side. "I wouldn't be so sure of that."

"Nonsense," Marcus says. "And I am sure your uncle would approve the match."

"I can only imagine." My words are less certain, and I struggle to match his easy banter. "Though you might find he would expect you to work afterward for free."

"A price I'd gladly pay. Here, give me that, since you aren't eating it anyway." Marcus plucks the meat pie out of my hands and tosses it to a passing child. He turns back to me and entwines his fingers in mine, bringing them to his lips. "Give me the word, Sophia, and—"

"Marcus, no." I draw my hands away from him, glancing around. Surely, in this crush, there are no guards watching us. And yet I cannot allow any whispers of impropriety to begin. I have enough of every *other* sort of whisper following me already. The line of them stretches halfway around the castle! "I serve the Queen. You know that. My time is not my own, my hand is not my own. They are both given over to Her Grace, to do with what she wills."

"But what of your heart?" Marcus insists. "Surely she cannot lay claim to that as well."

"And yet you would?" I laugh at his boldness. "You would lay claim to such a thing, having met me only a few short days ago? I question your sincerity, good sir."

"Never that." He shakes his head. "Doubt my honesty

about my work with Dee if you must, but never doubt that my affection for you is sincere, Sophia. Would that I could prove it to you—"

"Pardon!" Marcus's words are cut off as a woman jostles us. It is Agnes the dove seller, her face a mask of fear. "Forgive me, miss, but have you seen my mother? I stepped away for only a second, and now she's wandered off. I cannot find her anywhere!"

"Bess?" I scan the space. With all these people packed into such a tight space, how in the world could we find one small woman? "Have you asked the stall-keepers where you were standing?"

"They remembered her, of course. How can you forget a blind woman?" Agnes shakes her head. "But they didn't see her when she slipped away. She does that more and more, it seems, never mind that she can't see! She says her feet have eyes of their own and guide her way." She wrings her hands. "She could fall and no one would notice, in such a throng as this."

"We will search." I look to Marcus, and he reaches out to squeeze my arm.

"Seems logical she might head for home, if her feet have eyes," he says, and I do smile at him now, grateful for his aid. "I'll head to the King's Gate and ask the guards if they've seen anything awry."

"Thank you!" Agnes says as Marcus strides away. "I'm worried for her, I tell you plain. I would swear I saw Maude in the crowd."

I stiffen. "I thought you said she wasn't here today."

"I thought she wasn't. Maybe she still isn't." Agnes twists her hands in her skirts, as if she's decades younger. "I thought I saw her just for a moment, but a moment was all it took to strike me through with fear. I went to collect Mother, and of course that was when she decided to disappear." Worry tightens her lips. "I suspect she does it simply to unnerve me. I'm going to retrace my steps to where I lost her."

I nod. She is aiming left, so I will aim right. "Then I'll search this way."

Agnes dashes off, and I turn resolutely forward, then consider something else. The dove seller's mother is no ordinary woman. Her mind is touched, and she is near death. And I saw clearly how easily the angels slipped within her, speaking to me their words of prophecy from her own mouth.

I can find a woman like that, for I have the eyes to See her.

And with any luck, Marcus won't be looking this way, to witness me shining, fire bright with the Sight. Although, if he did, would I mind so much? I cannot deny drawing some pleasure from the fact that *someone* understands the paths I walk. That someone else has seen what I've seen, heard what I've heard. That someone knows my gifts, as well as my challenges.

Enough of that, I think grimly. *For now, your challenge is to find Bess.*

I blink, accustoming my eyes to the Sight once more. Around me, thankfully, there is nothing to suggest that evil has returned to Windsor Castle. The market day bustle remains robust and cheerful, and there is no sense of darkness here.

I refocus on the crowd and immediately sense the old

woman, deep in the thick of the carts and vendors. I plunge forward, threading my way into the throng, and catch sight of her. I am immediately taken aback.

She is running. Or running as fast as a blind old woman might, her body taut, her hair streaming behind her. She reaches out with wild hands, touching this person and that, so lightly that they cannot notice her as she speeds through the crowd. What is she running from?

I scan the carts behind her, but they seem too closed in, too dark all of a sudden. I am reminded of another market day, when Maude drew all the carts together, hemming in the doves, the people . . . even me. But I do not see Maude here, and I cannot worry about her.

I give chase. My legs are stronger by far than the old woman's, but it's still a trick to catch up with her, as thick as the crowd is. At one point she turns, glancing over her shoulder, and I catch her wave of fear. Someone is definitely chasing her. Someone means her harm!

Confusion washes through me. Who could possibly seek to harm an old blind woman, soft in the head? But as I dash forward, I am convinced she is trying to evade me as well. I get close enough to shout, and the word comes out almost harshly, my own fear welling up. "Bess!" I cry.

The old woman halts with a jerky clumsiness as a space opens up between us at the edge of the carts. Then she wheels around. Her milk-white eyes are wild, her manner frantic. "No!" she gasps, and I sense her looking past me, as if even in her blindness she could see some horror racing up behind us. "No!"

I try to turn, but it is already too late. A body crashes into me, round and soft, and I feel a narrow blade sink deep into the skin at the base of my neck. A dagger! Fiery pain explodes downward, and I can almost feel the slick surface of the knife plunging through my entire body, whatever liquid smeared on its blade surging through me like a sickness.

The death you don't seek is the one you should fear. It aims for the blind, but catches the seer.

"No!" I struggle, but the pressure lifts immediately, and I am shoved away. Arms windmilling, I regain my balance and whirl, only to see Maude grinning, her fists now on her round hips, her manner both surprised and delighted.

"Well, then!" she exclaims. "That was unexpected, but bless me if it doesn't make me 'appy just the same." She leers at me. "Gave ol' Maude a fright, you did. I wasn't looking where I was going and bumped right into you! Silly fool, I am! Are you well, girl?"

I lift my hand to my neck and draw it away. I felt a pinch there; clearly I was cut. But still, there is so little blood!

"What have you done?" I growl, and Maude wags her finger at me.

"Whatever could you mean, pet?" Her face goes a little harder. "I wasn't following *you*, after all, but that nattering chatterclack from Windsortown. But you got in my way and she was right there, so yer pain serves as a warning to 'er just the same. Mark my words, none will trace your mishap to poor ol' Maude. So you just be glad of your strength. It will save you, I warrant."

"You poisoned me!" I try to shout the words, but fear

clamps down hard on my throat, rendering my accusation little more than a squeak. Maude merely clucks at me, waving it off.

"Poison?" she says. "Never say such a thing. I sell paints for pretty women, and droplets for their eyes, no more. And besides all of that, you could never prove 'twas me that caused you 'arm." She takes another step toward me, leaning close. "I didna see your death this day, poppet, and I would 'ave. But that doesn't mean you won't suffer. And just as well. Next time you'll stay out of my way, eh?"

Marcus's voice rings out to my right, and I stagger away from Maude as he rushes up to me.

"Marcus!" I cry, gratified to find that my voice has returned to me. "Find a guard. I need to report that this woman—"

But as I turn back, I see naught more of Maude, not even with my Sight.

"What woman?" Marcus asks, looking at me with concern. "Are you all right?"

"I think so," I say, taking a step. Instantly, my legs wobble beneath me, and it's only with Marcus's aid that I'm able to stay standing.

"What is it, Sophia?" he asks, worry sharpening his voice. "What happened to you? You look as pale as a ghost. And your eyes . . ." He stares at me, his expression darkening. "What's wrong with your eyes? The irises have gone completely black!"

"Anna!" I say, my mouth slipping and stumbling over the word. "Please, we have to find Anna!"

CHAPTER TWENTY-THREE

I don't know how we reach the maids' chamber. Marcus's grip is tight around me, and I sense he is half-carrying me, but we somehow have managed some measure of propriety to have reached thus far unaccosted. At one point he spoke to someone else, explaining my weakness, dizziness, and whatever he has seen in my eyes. The voice that responded sounded male, and familiar, but my mind is awash with a buzzing I cannot quell, far worse than the cry of a thousand angelic voices.

I feel those angels too, pressing close. They watch, ever eager, and that gives me the greatest pause of all. Am I so close to death as that? But Maude said . . . *What did Maude say?*

"There you are. No, don't lay her down. I need to see her eyes."

This voice I definitely recognize. I feel a finger beneath my chin, and Anna lifts my face up, Though she is right in front of me, I cannot see her clearly. "There you are, Sophia. We have you now."

She waves her arm, and someone new appears, carrying a tray with what might be a half dozen bottles. Meg? "Rafe told us only what Marcus said, Sophia. Can you talk?" When I only blink at Anna, the words clamoring in my mind but impossible to be spoken, she continues. "And what he said to me was clear enough. You've been poisoned. You understand this?" I nod, the movement barely a bobble of my head. "And by quite a strong dose, from your manner. Dizziness, loss of vision." She peers at me. "Thirsty, yes?" My involuntary shudder must be answer enough. "Only a few poisons act so quickly, and as it happens, we have no yellow frogs at Windsor—at least, not that I am aware of. Though, if you see any, tell me immediately." She blows out a sharp breath.

My vision swims, but I think I see her move certain bottles to the back of Meg's tray. "Given the state of her eyes, we can eliminate this, this, this," she says. "Which leaves belladonna. Ordinarily I'd prescribe a purgative, but she didn't drink the stuff."

I feel my hair brushed back from my neck, cool fingers touching a point that sends a bolt of fire through me once more. Someone else speaks. "Barely a knife at all, almost more of a sewing needle sharpened to pierce leather, though thrust with a jagged plunge." Jane's words are detached, but a fine edge of anger rides them. "It isn't the cut that is harmful, but the poison."

"Distilled down. . . . Has to be, to cause such an effect with so little of it," Anna says. She is pouring small bottles of fluid into a cup, and I watch her with an odd detachment. At that moment there's a commotion at the door, and I swing my head around slowly to see Beatrice burst forth, her hands clutching a tankard. I think it's Beatrice, anyway.

"You have it." Anna's relief is palpable.

"The only good thing to come of my mother's addiction, yes. I have become a master at identifying the right mixture of opium and wine for stupor, and that for death. Not that I would wish either upon even my worst enemy." Beatrice strides forward and thrusts the tankard at Anna. "What now?"

"This first." Anna quickly pours some dark red liquid into a cup and brings the cup to my lips. "Drink it all, Sophia. As fast as you can."

I stare at her, still numb, but I do not resist as she pushes my head back and pours the liquid into my mouth. I splutter as I feel the burn of it hit my throat.

"She'll choke!" Suddenly Marcus is at my side, holding me still, but Anna doesn't cease the gentle pour.

"She drinks it or she dies," she says. Her voice is as cold as frost, and I wonder at it, blinking to try to see her more clearly. Never before have I experienced Anna being so sure, so certain. Surrounded by her science like a fine raiment of light.

"There you go." Marcus's arms tighten, but it is Anna who speaks, Anna who sets a quarter hourglass on its head. "In short order, once the opiates have a chance to enter her bloodstream, we'll give her the steeped herbal brew. She'll want it, too. Belladonna poisoning is noted for its parching effect. Then more of the laudanum, and brandy besides."

"How long?" Beatrice asks.

"An hour," Anna says, rocking back on her heels. I watch her, but it's as if she has moved a fair distance away from me, impossible to track. My sight seems to shimmer a bit, and a curious warmth spreads through me. I sag, but with Marcus encaging me, I've nowhere to go but to lean more heavily against him. He takes my weight without comment, and I feel the stroke of his hand down my back, his whispered words against my hair.

I slip in and out of consciousness, but there are three constants every time I awaken that steady me. The first is someone pouring liquids down my throat; some that burn, some that soothe. The second is Marcus holding me so firmly, it seems he is made of stone. And the third is the presence of the Maids of Honor, all of them ranging round me in unwavering guard. With their presence I hold more firmly to my grasp on reality.

When I am not with my fellow spies, however, I am by no means alone. The spirits press and howl in the angelic realm, their presence all around me like a crashing storm. But the dark angel is absent, nowhere to be found in the gale. I remember his warning, which I heeded too late. I remember his gloved hand upon my cheek, allowing me to see so much more than I ever have, to see and to believe what I saw. He tried to warn me as best as he was able. And I did not listen. I dared not listen. For if *all* my visions are now correct, what does that mean for poor Robert Moreland, whom I saw dead upon his bed just last night? Shouldn't I have a new vision of him now, riding over the countryside, hastening away from Windsor's walls? And yet, nothing comes.

Something like sleep claims me once more, until I am jostled awake for what seems like the fiftieth time. Anna is in front of me, and I flinch away from the bright flame she thrusts toward my face. "Leave off!" I say sharply, and my own words startle me. They are as crisp and sharp as a flint strike.

Anna's smile is the stuff of magic. If I did not already feel my fog lifting, the healing strength of her beatific grin would burn it all away. "Recovering," she says, sitting back.

I straighten, and realize that Marcus is still beside me. I offer him a smile, suddenly shy, but then draw in a startled breath as he leans forward, planting a chaste kiss upon my forehead. His entire body is shaking, and he stands up abruptly, almost pushing me off my pallet in his haste. "I must away," he says, and his voice sounds strange, his words too rough, too thick. He bows to Anna, the other girls, but does not look again at me. "Ladies, my thanks evermore. Sophia." He still does not turn to me but away, and strides hastily out the door.

I blink in confusion, wondering if I am still lost to my dreams, but Beatrice gives a soft laugh.

"He's lost that battle, and lost it hard," she says.

Meg snorts a laugh. "Completely conquered."

"He's the one who'll have need of recovery, not Sophia," Jane agrees, a rare grin lighting her face. "Though he'll never find it, I wager."

I gape at them until Anna gathers my hands in her own, her candle set aside, her face still wreathed in smiles. "Pay them no mind, Sophia. They're only teasing you," she says, and I finally understand the others' words. I feel the blush climb up my cheeks, and Anna squeezes my hands more tightly. "That doesn't change the fact that they're right, however," she says tartly. "Marcus Quinn is quite obviously in love with you."

Other than having to endure my fellow spies' continued laughter and ribald comments, the next two hours are easy enough, with multiple trips to the garderobe (I must have drunk my body weight in laudanum and herbal tea!) and yet more stiff medicinal concoctions to chase away the intoxication of all that wine. But by the time we enter the Privy Chamber for the convocation of seers, I am more or less upright, more or less steady—and more or less prepared to meet my fate.

The gathering is a small one. In addition to the select group of courtiers the Queen has invited, Cecil and Walsingham are present, as are John Dee and Nostradamus. Marcus is here as well, watching me across the small space, but I dare not look at him. I blame the aftereffects of the poison and the wine . . . but having him here both unnerves and supports me, like I am a woman walking a narrow plank, held steady by both her hopes and fears.

The Queen drifts easily from courtier to courtier, smiling and laughing, confident in her power. There will be dining and dancing, and then she'll excuse the great majority of these men and meet with her champions in secret.

Then this farce will be done.

We dine in easy companionship, and I feel better with each passing minute. I allow myself a measure of relief. I have shared all that I have seen, and in so doing I have saved Robert Moreland—and saved myself, too, if you count the death presaged against the seer.

As the meal draws to a close, a loud burst of laughter at the door to the Privy Chamber breaks across the space, and we all look up, startled. Even Jane straightens in surprise at who is there, brushing off the royal guards as if they were naught more than a nuisance to him.

Troupe Master James McDonald bows before our company, his grin as bold as his manner. The Queen stands, then strides forth from our table to confront him. There is no need for her to do so, but her impulsive actions have ensured that all eyes are upon her, which is her preferred state of being. "What is the meaning of this?" she demands.

"Your Grace." James does not bow to her. He kneels, one knee sinking to the floor like he is some medieval knight to whom she is about to give her favor to carry into battle. It's a master stroke of flattery, and the Queen's countenance instantly changes, her face alight with interest.

A nervous guard speaks up. "Your Grace, he said you had commanded him to speak to you before he departs the castle, without fail."

"Did he say that?" Elizabeth's tone is arch, but she is smiling, flirtatiously coy. "I do not recall giving you such an order, Master James. Might you be mistaken?"

"I cannot be," he says. He does not rise, but he has the audacity to lift his face and stare at her with hot eyes. "If your lips did not grant me entry, Your Majesty surely did, to ensure that the grand spectacle I have planned for the Samhain celebration these few days hence meets with your royal favor."

I frown, and even Elizabeth seems surprised. Is Samhain

and Master James's *Play of Secrets* so soon? Seers and prophecies have distracted us all.

But she inclines her head gracefully. "Then, Master James, as you have stated your case so prettily, I bid you to rise. What manner of entertainment do you have prepared for us?"

"An event to delight the senses, my Queen," James says easily as he stands again. "I bid you set the stage as I direct, to ensure your lords and ladies have a tale to share back in Londontown, ere you make your way to that city for the Christmas celebration."

"You presume much to think we'll leave so quickly."

Master James laughs. "I presume nothing at all. Where better to showcase your magnificence than on a stage so grand as London? With all your people flooding into the city, waiting for a glimpse of their beautiful Queen in her first holiday spectacle. I'm sure you already have festivities planned to delight your subjects there, yes?"

I can almost hear the Queen's brain churning. I suspect she has nothing planned for London, given how filled her mind has been with Windsor's dire portents of death. But now she can see such revels on the horizon, and the thought clearly pleases her.

"Indeed, Master James. But you run ahead of yourself. It is the festival of Samhain that concerns us at this moment."

"And what a festival it shall be," James declares. "Dinner first, something light, with plenty of wine to loosen tongues and spirits."

The Queen sniffs in derision. "We've had our fill of loose spirits of late, I fear."

"Say it isn't so," James says with mock horror. "Then this night will be one to make all forget the troubles of these recent weeks. Sweet confections too should be in evidence, soul cakes and warm bread, all frosted with sugar, so that your tables look like they have been graced with stardust itself, a tracing of fairy silver spread over all. In the candlelight the effect will be stunning."

"Mmm." There is little Elizabeth likes more in this world than sugary pastries and candies. "This is something we could arrange."

"There will be laughter and music throughout the dinner, setting the mood for a night of gentle phantasms and moonlit fantasy," James continues. I marvel at him as he beguiles the Queen. He is truly a handsome man, and his charisma is breathtaking, even in the company of a figure as striking as Elizabeth's. "And then, when all are well and truly sated, we will adjourn to the Upper Ward for the spectacle itself."

"An outdoor spectacle?" Elizabeth asks. "Surely that is begging for a storm."

"Not on a night blessed by Your Grace," James says. "Besides, only the Quadrangle is large enough to allow a platform to be built in its center as a makeshift stage." James raises a finger. "And such a stage as this will be, you cannot imagine."

Elizabeth's brows lift. "And what will my courtiers see upon this stage?" she asks.

"A play of great wonderment, I assure you, featuring your very own court! Upon this stage, before their fellows, they will talk of secrets—and of love."

"Love?" The Queen's laugh is wry, and her chosen attendants laugh along with her, pleased to be hearing such remarkable plans firsthand. "You'll find not many of my courtiers comfortable with talking of secret love."

"Ah, but on this most special of nights, my goal is for you to see who truly loves you. Whose hearts you fill with happiness and adoration, who will follow you not only as their Queen, but as their joy and solace."

"And how do you propose doing all of this?" Elizabeth asks.

James spreads his hands. "You have only to watch, my Queen, and be amazed."

"You promise much, for a court you have rarely seen."

"I promise nothing more than what you deserve, my Queen, and quite a fair amount less, in fact. Would that I could show your glory to the whole of your kingdom in every city." He lifts his hand to Elizabeth, as if he is waving to an unseen, adoring crowd.

The Queen nods. "Very well," she says. "Then not only my court should see it here. We'll allow the villagers to come into the Upper Ward as well, any and all."

"As you will!" James agrees. If he is dismayed by her pronouncement, he does not show it—yet another shrewd decision on his part.

Not the last by far.

The Queen bids Master James to tarry awhile as the music begins, the second portion of this evening's trials officially underway. Each of the maids has an assigned duty, including myself. We carry trays of fine wine the Queen has sanctioned for this night, poured into lovely cups of gold. And into each of those grand cups we've also placed a few precious drops of Maude's truth tonic.

Despite my own thwarted poisoning, which of course no one knows about but the Maids of Honor, Marcus, and Rafe, Maude's skill as an herb mistress still needs to be confirmed. Accordingly, in the brief time since we took the vial away from Maude's stall, Anna has tested the tonic on subjects, both with their permission and without it, and is convinced the potion works. The Queen, ever one to kill multiple birds with a single stone, eagerly agreed that this evening is the opportune time to test the brew. Neither Nostradamus nor Dee will be fed the tainted wine, of course. Those two worthies sit by the Queen, still engaged in lively conversation with her.

But any other courtier is fair game.

As is Marcus Quinn, I think, my cheeks stinging anew as I recall the laughter of my fellow spies. Perhaps it is time for him to betray his secrets as well.

Cecil and Walsingham remain in the shadows of the chamber, their expressions unreadable as they watch us perform our roles.

To Beatrice and Meg they have given the most challenging assignments, two of the court's richest lords. To Jane and Anna fall the next tier down, a young marquess for Jane to cow into submission, and a puffed-up patron of science whom Anna is to coddle into revealing the nature of his latest experiments.

And as for me, my task is equally simple, and equally profound—to draw out one Marcus Quinn about what else

John Dee is working on, when he is not bent to the Queen's command.

If I happen to ask *other* questions while I'm at that task, well . . . who could blame me?

We gather at the edge of the makeshift dancing floor, ready to go after our quarry.

"Ah!" A sudden exclamation startles us. "My favorite ladies of the court."

"Master James!" Meg recovers first and curtsies to her former troupe master. Beside me Jane draws up to her fullest height, one hand twitching upward before she schools it to remain clasped in the other at her waist, as the proper maiden she pretends to be. I do not need the Sight to understand her intention. Some weeks past, Jane received a quite unusual gift—a slender necklace of gold, as fine and lovely as it was unexpected. Her benefactor? None other than James McDonald, the troupe master seeming determined to engage her affections. Jane is wearing the necklace tonight. Had she suspected James would remain in the Privy Chamber, close enough to her to matter, she would have already removed it. As it is, she cannot do so now without him noticing.

"So, you are staying for the music, then?" I ask, drawing his attention to me.

"Your lovely Queen suggested that I meet some of her most favored courtiers, that I might better fashion an entertainment for them. I think she rather likes me."

"Someone ought," Meg jibes, and Jane coughs beside me, earning a censorious look from Master James. His gaze drops to her neckline, spying the strip of gold. His smile is immediate and triumphant, fading not one bit in the face of Jane's scowl.

"Begin!" The Queen's voice rings out over us, and music flows through the chamber. James turns smartly to Jane and steps into the Honor, bowing to her with a flourish. She has no choice but to respond with a curtsy of her own, though there is murder in her eyes. She offers him a cup of wine with a hard smile, but James merely sets it aside.

"The music calls," he says, holding out his hand.

Jane pulls back. "I do not dance."

He reaches for her fingers and draws her close. "Then there is no better time to begin." The two of them step into the line of dancers as the music strikes the first measures of an Almain.

"I could not speak the line better." I jump and am immediately trapped by Marcus's hand upon mine. I shiver at the touch of his light fingers. "Shall we practice the steps we have learned, Miss Sophia?"

"Of course," I say. "But first, a toast to you?" I proffer him the cup of wine, and he takes it readily enough, tipping it to his lips under my careful scrutiny. Then he, too, sets the cup aside and draws me onto the floor. The Almain is a simple dance, but there is nothing simple about the way I feel with Marcus so close. He dances with a sense of assurance and grace, as if he were born to the world of noble finery, yet I sense this is not the case. Rather, he is a bit of a chameleon, able to take on the sense of a place, and of its people, in order to fit into his surroundings more easily. In that regard he is well matched to Master James, the ultimate actor. But whereas James's actions were born in the world of theatre, I cannot guess what drives Marcus.

"You are thinking very hard for a young woman entranced by her first official dance with a handsome young man. Are you quite recovered from your trying day?" Marcus's words are deliberately provocative, and I flush.

"I am," I say. "And how do you know that I am not thinking about you?"

"My favorite subject, to be sure. So what are your thoughts telling you? That you should be very careful around me? That I am danger itself?"

"Never that." We are walking in sedate circles, fast enough to give the illusion of movement but slowly enough to grant plenty of time for a meaningful look, a practiced glance. I suddenly understand why Beatrice considers the dancing floor more fraught with danger than the battlefield. Every time I come close to Marcus, I experience a strange tremor along my skin. As if I lost my sense of self and flowed into him, then back. As if we not merely touched . . . but blended. It is a heady experience, and I feel the blood rising in my cheeks, the thudding of my heart.

"I have met many people in my travels, Sophia," Marcus says. "But you are the first to capture my attention so completely. How do you do it?"

I flash him a look at his bold words. Is this the wine at work?

"Is it with your eyes? They are so blue as to seem violet, the color of spring flowers newly opened. Your soft lips, your fair skin? Is that how you weave your enchantment?"

I shake my head, suddenly unnerved by his candor.

"They feel it too," he murmurs, and I glance around. No one is paying attention to us, all of the court whirling and twirling, the music drifting around us in a grand clamor of sound.

"Look more deeply, Sophia." His words slide over me strangely, and he holds my hand aloft in the arching twirl of the dance. Our fingers touch, and the scene before me shifts and slides.

I do see them, then. Like one painting over another, too many people for too small a space. I know those figures, silent and watching, and know their yearning, so intense that it is discernible even across the veil. The angels have gathered to watch the living dance, but they are not focused on the riot of colors and sound; they are focused on Marcus and me. As if they were aware of something profound between us.

What is it that they know?

"So you *can* see them, without Dee's conjuring spells," I say, and his smile is almost sad, though he says nothing. The movement of the dance takes us away from each other, and brings us back moments later. Then he gives his answer.

"I can see them because I am touching you, Sophia, and only because of that. I do not have the gift of Sight without a seer." He shrugs. "I cannot remember much of my life before my accident, though, when the conjurer sent me into the angelic realm unprotected." He regards me with an air of melancholy. "What is it like, Sophia? What is it you see on the other side of the veil?"

I think of the grim specter. "Only the angels," I say. "Just as you have seen."

"Well, they shall never have you completely," he declares. "You belong in the mortal realm."

His words strike an odd, discordant note with me, as if I were drawn to disagree. I direct our conversation to more important topics—important to the Crown at least. "Your work with Dee, does it stray only to the angelical realm?" I ask, trying to sound guileless. "Or do you help him in all manner of projects?"

"All manner," Marcus answers.

"Indeed," I say as he turns me in the dance. "Even his alchemical pursuits? I have heard those can be exhausting."

"'Exhausting' is a good word for it!" Marcus says. "Day and night he works to find the correct equation for the transmutation of elements. It is the most frequent question he bids me to seek out in the angelic realm." He chuckles. "When he is not searching for you, of course."

"And has he received an answer?" I ask, trying to keep my manner light.

"Not even a murmur." Marcus's candor surprises me, and I make a note to confirm to Anna that Maude's truth potion does indeed seem to work. I ply him quite unashamedly as much as I dare, and the evening spins on, the familiarity of music drawing us ever closer in its soft embrace.

Eventually, of course, the dancing must end. Marcus bows to me as I sink down into a curtsy. As I rise, however, I feel another familiar presence in the room, dark and fierce. The Queen announces that the evening has drawn to a close, and dismisses the musicians and her courtiers, and Master James as well. Marcus steps off to the side of the room, then returns to hand Dee a large armful of documents and some device I cannot see. Then Marcus bows to me, quietly bidding me good night, and he is gone.

Finally, it is time. My fellow Maids of Honor withdraw to stand by Cecil and Walsingham, able to watch the convocation of seers but not to intervene. I stand in a row with Dee and Nostradamus, the least of our number in every measure that could possibly matter.

Still, I will not be alone, I realize, as I make my stand before the Queen.

Across the Privy Chamber, my grim specter looms once more. I feel safe, almost secure, and I allow my face to ease into a smile, my heart to swell—

Then he raises his hand.

And darkness swallows me whole.

CHAPTER TWENTY-FOUR

The black veil rips asunder, but I am no longer in the Queen's Privy Chamber, nor in the company of my peers. Instead, I am in what must be Robert Moreland's sitting room, in his apartment in the Horseshoe Cloister. There are comfortable chairs and tables neatly stacked with books and papers, and the two men occupying the room are smiling at each other, cups of wine in their hands. I watch, and Robert drinks fully and deeply of his cup. I watch, and Sir Francis lifts his own cup to his lips, not taking the slightest sip.

Horror quakes through me. The scene rushes forward then, galloping on the devil's hooves, and I see Sir Francis reach for Robert Moreland as the man falls forward and slumps into Walsingham's grasp. He carries his dazed and failing friend to the bedroom even as Moreland weakly tries to fight him off.

I shake my head, desperately trying to clear it, but the vision will not abate. At last the tableau is struck that I have now seen already too many times: Robert Moreland in his bed, surrounded by the fading symbols of scepter and crown.

Walsingham at his feet, tears coursing down his face, mouth clenched hard in a rictus of agony.

And then I see something more. A grey-haired woman, round and foul, standing at the edge of Moreland's room, watching the scene before her like I am, her laughter harsh and full-throated. And lying at her feet is a young woman in a gorgeous gown, her crown knocked from her head, beautiful red hair streaming over her shoulders.

The Queen, dead by Maude's hands, because no one is watching over her. No one is protecting her.

Suddenly I am awash in the screams of a thousand angels, and my head pounds as I stumble back, drawing startled humphs from Dee and Nostradamus.

My Sight winks out, and I am no longer in Moreland's sickroom, no longer seeing the horrible image of my fallen Queen. Instead, I am back in the Privy Chamber, my hands gripped at my sides, my entire body shaking. No one seems to notice, or if they do, they must surely ascribe my tremors to my fear of presenting before Elizabeth.

Well, I cannot say my reactions have gone entirely unnoticed. Across the rush-strewn floor of the Privy Chamber, Walsingham is staring at me. *What has he done?* His face is gaunt but resolute, exactly as it looked earlier this day in the Upper Ward, when he pulled me aside to speak in confidence.

Had he just come from murdering his friend? All based on my vision? *What have* I *done?*

Oblivious to my mounting horror, the Queen retires to her throne, and her gaze sweeps over the room. Then her words root me in place, her voice sounding overloud in the quiet chamber.

"You are well versed in the question," she says, leaning forward. "The prophecy given me by Mother Shipton, through a villager who traveled to this very castle to tell the tale.

"A royal house defeated,
disaster unforeseen.
Death comes to Windsor
to court the maiden Queen."

She curls her lip, as if the act of repeating the fell pronouncement offended her anew. "I am confident that you can tell me the truth of this prophecy," she says. "Who shall suffer this death at Windsor? How it is to strike? And when?"

I cannot bear this charade any longer.

"Your Grace!" I stand forward. It is already done, the death occurred, the riddle tragically solved. "Allow me to—"

"Silence!" The Queen's command brooks no opposition. "You will get your chance, Sophia. I choose John Dee to begin."

I'm too distraught to argue as Dee steps forward. The astrologer, to his credit, looks every inch the scholar as he strides with arms laden to stand in front of the Queen. At his direction, Cecil and Jane carry a table to him and set it by his side. Upon the table Dee places his sheaf of papers, weighting them down with the device, which I recognize as an astrolabe. Then he bows to the Queen.

"The question you have set before us has many angles to pursue, Your Majesty," he says, his words ponderous and forceful, a teacher talking to willful students. "I have addressed each of those angles in succession, by careful study of the stars above us."

The Queen tilts her head. "The stars can tell us who will die at Windsor?" she asks. "Then surely this information should have been provided to me long before now, should it not?"

Dee doesn't flinch at her rebuke. "In a manner of speaking, yes. If you suspect that death will come to Windsor, say, in the fall of 1559, then you can look to the stars to see if they bear out this prophecy, because we have a specific place in time. And in fact, I can say categorically that Mother Shipton's prophecy is *true*." Dee's words are simple, but they still have a powerful effect on the room, and my own dull shock is momentarily pierced. Given her soft gasp, the Queen apparently had not been fully convinced of Mother Shipton's prophecy. From the look on Cecil's face, he hadn't been either. The Maids of Honor appear unfazed by Dee's pronouncement, but then, they know the truth, and do not merely have to believe the words of some hump-shouldered witch in the north of England.

Yet even they do not know the fullness of Mother Shipton's horrible prophecy-come-true.

Dee continues, more pompously. "The stars are most inauspicious for this exact moment in time for Windsor Castle. When I presented the grand spectacle for you, Your Grace, be advised, I was looking for *positive* angles and harmonious conjunctions, not the opposite. But looking through a darker filter, I see quite clearly: death shall come to Windsor."

"When?" The Queen's question is sharp, but Dee raises a hand, as if to hold off her impatience.

"This very week, Your Grace," he says. "I cannot be more exact, I fear. But as to how," he rushes on, seeing the Queen stiffen in disapproval. "How, I can tell you with certainty. As the good doctor here can well attest, there are many ways to die in times as difficult as ours. But a death that would come by plague, for example—"

"Plague!" The Queen has taken his bait quite neatly, and she slides to the edge of her seat. "Say that some soul has not visited plague upon this castle!"

"Not at all," Dee says smoothly. "But you'll agree, it was an important consideration in my calculations, to discern what was likely and what was not. There are also the possibilities of death by strangulation or blade. Death by poison or a physical battle. Death by musketfire or death by natural causes."

"Or death by boredom, good doctor," the Queen says, her elbows on her throne's armrests, her fingers gripping the carved gold edges. "What, precisely, did you find?"

"The death to be enacted at Windsor Castle is definitely a murder."

Once again this is not an unexpected statement, and yet the chill that rolls through me is not about what may be, but what is already done. Across the Privy Chamber, Walsingham's face is a mask of resolve, his eyes never leaving mine. "With the moon in Scorpio, and the bitter sadness of Chiron in opposition to watery Neptune, all signs as to the manner of this death point in only one direction.

That of poison. Death comes to Windsor on the tip of a poisoned tongue."

I glance at Anna, only to find her staring at me. We are up to our ears in poisons this day.

"And finally, we come to the nature of the doomed soul." Dee's words drag me back to this Privy Chamber of horrors. "Without a full accounting of every birth date of the castle's current residents, of course, it was impossible to identify him exactly. However—"

"Impossible?" The Queen cuts Dee off, her manner subtly charged. Here, at last, she has an opportunity to put her former tutor in his place. "I set for you a simple task, Dee. To determine *who* would die at Windsor, and *when*, and *how*. You have quite ably completed the last two aspects of this challenge, and yet you would tell me that you fall short on the first and most important? That you cannot name the doomed soul among us? Surely, that is a poor showing indeed."

"If you do not accept my findings, Your Grace, I can retire without saying anything further. I presume, however, that you would be interested in learning what else I have to share." Dee's reply is arctic, and I am inclined to agree with him. It is no easy feat, to pluck a single person out with nothing but the stars. Then again, Dee did find *me* all those years ago.

"You presume wrong." The Queen's voice has taken on an additional edge. I wonder at the balance of power between these two. Dee was one of the Queen's most trusted and beloved instructors throughout her childhood. Yet here she is suddenly treating him as an insolent courtier. Is she punishing him for some perceived slight in his tone tonight? Or does she merely want to assert her authority over her onetime instructor?

It doesn't matter, in any event. Dee turns to his table, and the Queen lashes out once more. "You may remain, John Dee," she commands. "We are not yet finished with you. But I call to make his pronouncements the good Dr. Michel de Nostredame, that he might succeed where you have failed."

Dee stiffens, but he remains in his place. I find I cannot speak either. It is as if I were watching the events of this chamber from outside myself, unable to predict their outcome, unable to even predict my own actions. After a moment, the French doctor steps out from beside me and moves to stand before the Queen. He nods to her, and she graciously inclines her head, the soul of civility once more.

"Good doctor, you have kindly taken your time and expended great effort and energy to join us in our hour of need," the Queen says. "We are most grateful for your visit to Windsor Castle. You grace us with your presence."

Nostradamus watches the Queen throughout this short speech, merely nodding again to her as she finishes. "I am honored that you choose me to address such a prophecy of great and powerful vision," he says. His voice is soft but strong, and I find myself wondering how he was greeted throughout France and Italy in the towns where he ministered to his patients, particularly those towns beset with the Black Death. His first fame came as a plague doctor of extraordinary success, and I suspect his healing powers likely extend not only to the cures that he directed the town's apothecaries to concoct, but to the solemnity of his voice, pitched to calm the most frantic of patients.

He is certainly calming Elizabeth now.

Me, alas, not as much.

"Your court is truly a wonder to behold," Nostradamus continues, and the Queen accepts his flattery. "Long have I traveled, throughout many countries, and rarely do I find a Queen so beloved. You will be remembered throughout time for your grace and dedication to your country. Your reign shall live in glory long after you."

These words have the ring of a prophecy in and of themselves, and I am not the only one who thinks so. The Queen has returned to a full and delighted smile, that she tries unsuccessfully to hide with her next grave words. "I thank you for your kind speech, good sir, but our need today is grim indeed. Have you any guidance to give us in the question of the doomed soul of Windsor? Who is next to breathe his last within these walls, and how, and when?"

Nostradamus bows with due humility. "I too have learned, as the great scholar Master Dee has, that the timing and manner of death is as he states. This murder does happen, and it does happen through the use of poison."

Despite myself I glance to Dee, seeing that he, too, has noticed Nostradamus's neat evasion. How easy it is to simply confirm the two items that another man has already discerned in this challenge! For then you may stride forth with the third element, content that no one may gainsay you. I think back to what I heard in Nostradamus's chamber—the mournful dirge of the water, the hiss of the fire spirit. I recall precisely what he was told, and the means and timing of Moreland's death were not at all included in that prophecy. But there is no way for me to prove his lie.

Nostradamus continues. "To illuminate the man who shall meet his death here, however, I can go yet further. The information I have been given on this question is thus for the ears of this company alone."

He draws a deep breath, and everyone in the room strains forward, so as not to miss a word of the great prophet . . . though half of us have already heard this message:

"Where the muddy river runs white
An eagle shall be born of a wren.
Doomed to fly into the jaws of a wolf,
His blood shall turn to gold."

Silence follows hard upon his pronouncement as we all take it in. Across the chamber, I see my dark specter shift back further into the gloom.

Walsingham straightens, his gaze hard on Nostradamus. I can see in his face what he is thinking. He knows the symbols of royalty as much as any man in this room. Based on my visions of a purple mantle, scepter, and gold crown adorning Robert Moreland, he decided his friend was a threat to the crown, and killed him because of it. And now his actions have been validated. Nostradamus is saying quite clearly that the doomed man is an "eagle," yet another royal symbol.

These are the words that justify murder!

Nostradamus, for his part, stands at his ease in the center of the room, comfortable in his prediction.

As well he should, I think peevishly. For without what I have seen, who could make any sense of what he's saying?

Except Dee now faces Nostradamus, his face transfixed not with outrage, as one would expect, but with excitement. "An eagle, yes!" He cries. "Of course, that is exactly right!"

"What is this?" Elizabeth's question is like a shot across the chamber, stilling both men.

Dee turns to her. "The part of my response that you have not yet heard, Your Grace," he says. "I could not countenance it, because it was disturbing to me, as you might imagine. But I, too, saw this in the skies as they arch over Windsor Castle in these dark days. The doomed soul is born of royalty. It is an eagle who will die."

Once again, I am smote with the image of Maude laughing over the body of the Queen. While they are so focused on Walsingham's murder of a potential pretender to the crown, they are failing to see the real threat!

"What are you saying?" Elizabeth's words are cold, her brows raised and her face like marble. "You dare to predict my own death to my face, and with the zeal of excitement lining your words?"

"What? No!" Dee says hastily, and even Nostradamus looks startled. "Your Grace, no," Dee continues. "That is not at all what we are—"

"And you, Sophia?" Elizabeth turns to me. "What do you have to say to the statements of these men, who so willingly put forth the idea of my own demise as if it were a topic of scholarly debate? Have you, too, seen my death by poison, here in the halls of Windsor?" Her words are steady, but there is no denying the weight that looms beyond them. I have the feeling that I am standing at the edge of a great precipice, and the faintest breeze will knock me over into the abyss. But I can't fight the rising tide of my own fear any longer. Fury catches me up and hurtles me over the edge as the Queen's tone grows sharper. "Answer me!"

"It is already done!" I retort, my words so loud, they seem to reverberate off the walls. "And all of you have been deceived!"

"Stop, Sophia!" Walsingham's voice strikes out like a gunshot, but I can no longer stop myself. I can no longer stop any of this.

"You have been deceived!" I say again. They must understand the truth: that Mistress Maude's plan all along was to *distract* the Queen with this prophecy—so Maude could execute a far darker plan. A plan that would change the course of history. "Yes, the vision of Nostradamus and the calculations of John Dee are true, but they speak not of you but of a man. This man exists—existed—within the halls of Windsor, but he breathes no more. Still, I beg of you to listen. You have other, more terrible problems to consider, Your Grace. Your own life is in danger!"

"No!" Walsingham bursts forth from where he stands and strides into the center of the room. "You are overwrought, Sophia. I demand you to be silent. I have removed any threat to the Queen. It is done!"

"It is *not* done!" I counter. "And how would you know

if it were? You condemned a man based upon my visions alone. You did not have the extra testimony of Nostradamus to guide your hand. You did not have John Dee's calculations to ensure you were correct."

"There was no time!" Walsingham roars back. "Moreland said enough to sway me. *You* said enough to sway me."

"Who is this Moreland?" Elizabeth asks.

"Forget Moreland. He is not the threat that you should truly fear!" I try again. I whirl round to the Queen, who is staring at me with abject horror. I can only imagine what I must look like, my hair wild, my manner crazed. "All of this is only a distraction! You are going to die, Your Majesty!"

"Enough!" Cecil strides forward, and with a jerk of his arm, he summons forward two guards who must have ventured into the Privy Chamber at the commotion. They march forward like sentinels of doom and grab hold of my arms, fairly lifting me off my feet. It's a testament to the Queen's alarm that she makes no protest regarding my rough treatment. In fact, she seems almost relieved. "Walsingham is correct. You are distraught, Miss Dee. You shall not say another word."

"But—"

"Silence!" Cecil waves to the guards. "Take her to the holding cell. Await my instructions there." He scowls again at me, his face implacable. "If she continues to speak, gag her."

But there is no need. I fall mute, suddenly shaking free of the terrible thrall that has held me. I see everything as if in frozen miniature: the dismay of the Maids of Honor, the Queen's patently shocked face, Walsingham's and Cecil's outrage. *What have I done?*

Silently the guards half-carry me from the room. When we pass through the doors, however, they pause for a moment. One of them speaks, and the voice is so well known to me, I almost slump in renewed mortification.

"Stand, Miss Sophia," Will Seton says quietly. "So that all might not suspect what has happened."

It takes me only a moment to understand. Most of the court is in the Presence Chamber, laughing and talking, and we are but a breath away from that room. If I am seen being hauled off unceremoniously, gossip will fill all of Windsor so quickly that the very ceilings will burst from the strain. I force my feet to move, my back to stay rigid, as the guards and I process through the long corridors, as if I were merely being escorted somewhere with their protection.

We are completely unnoticed.

It is only when we reach the deeper corridors of the castle that I begin to falter. We move away from the softer rooms of Windsor and into the rough-cut hallways, down stairs lit only by the occasional torch. The "holding cell," as Cecil calls it, is a rude chamber with a bench and table bolted to the floor, a chamber pot that mercifully looks unused, and no light whatsoever. Will Seton pushes me inside, his touch as gentle as possible.

"Wait in here," he says. "If you need aught, you've but to ask."

The door shuts behind me, and darkness falls like a stone cloak. After a moment, I hear the scrape of something at the door. Seton has set aside the covering for the grate, which normally would be opened only if a guard needed to check the status of a prisoner. Instead, he has given me the only gift he can. A precious square of light on the stone floor, shimmering with the torchlight from the corridor beyond. With that tiny grace, I breathe more easily.

But not for long.

CHAPTER TWENTY-FIVE

The creak of the door wakens me, and I jerk to a sitting position. At some point in the evening, I must have curled myself onto the bench, for I am stiff with pain. I feel strung out, lost, the events of the convocation nothing more than a jumble in my mind. If I dreamed this dark night, I can't recall, which I take as a slight mercy.

A man steps into the room, and despite myself I cringe back. It is Cecil, his face still looking like an executioner's. A guard follows behind, carrying a tray bearing two carafes. Another guard affixes a torch to a sconce by the door. Flickering light floods the room, and I wince away at the sudden brightness.

"I brought you ale and water, some bread," Cecil says gruffly. The guard sets the tray down on the table and stands away from it, but I make no move toward it, though in truth I am so parched, my tongue cleaves to the roof of my mouth. The guard departs, and Cecil stands in silence for another few moments, then pulls the door shut behind him. I notice the panel has been replaced over the grate.

He leans against the wall, studying me. "Walsingham

spoke with the Queen, after your bit of dramatics," he says. "We ushered out Nostradamus with thanks and gold, and assured Dee of her satisfaction with him. He did not show too much concern for your well-being, and he went peaceably enough. His assistant was a bit more of a problem."

That last statement makes me smile, a fact that I'm sure Cecil doesn't miss.

"You can return to the maids' quarters, Miss Dee," he says. "And to the court, to the grace of the Queen. We have but to come to an understanding."

"Of course, Sir William." Now I do rise and move over to the tray. I pour the water out onto a cloth and rub it over my face. I feel better, and realize that, too, is part of Cecil's ploy. He wants me to feel safe, not too deep in the mire.

But this is also the same Cecil who half-drowned Meg, over and over again, to get her to betray her secrets. Why is he treating me with such care?

The answer hits me squarely: Walsingham. Sir Francis must have told Cecil about my vision of Moreland, and of the Queen. Perhaps my vision of Walsingham's future as well. My lips tighten in derision, and I'm glad Cecil can't see my face.

When I don't turn toward him, however, he speaks to my back. "The Queen has need of a seer with your skills, Miss Dee. You have proven yourself ably and well."

I do turn around then, confronting him. "I have caused a man to die, Sir William. My words, and mine alone, drove Sir Francis to kill Robert Moreland."

"Action that was warranted," Cecil says severely. He forestalls my outburst with a raised hand. "Despite your accusations, Walsingham *did* speak to Moreland. And to ensure he spoke truthfully, we used Maude's truth tonic as well." His smile is grim. "Once that took hold, Robert told Walsingham the tale easily enough. His mother's chance meeting with the King during a historically cold winter, his conception and birth. The man who married his mother in spite of her fatherless child, raising Robert as his own. She never spoke to her son of his father until she fell ill with delirium, shortly before she died but a year ago. He hadn't considered the story since, or so he told Walsingham."

"Then he is a fool," I say derisively.

"The world is full of them." Cecil shrugs. "But his mother *did* tell him this tale. Robert Moreland never intended to pursue the matter, thinking the woman quite out of her mind." He shrugs. "He also said he never told another soul."

"Not even his wife?" I ask. "Or is she now dead as well?"

"Not even his wife," Cecil says. "The Queen appears to believe Walsingham that the wife is blameless in all this. Which is in the young woman's favor."

"Mine as well," I say. "Then again, what's two more lives upon my head, when I've already the one to carry?"

"You were completing your *assignment*, Miss Dee," Cecil retorts. "An assignment given to you by the Queen. An assignment that is still yours to have, if you can restrain yourself from such unseemly outbursts as last night."

"My *outburst*, as you call it, was justified! Walsingham walked into Moreland's chambers already planning to kill him. How else can you explain the poisoned wine? He laid the man down on his own bed and watched him die, Sir

William! His friend! What would he do to you or me, if he'd kill his friend with such coldness?"

But Cecil doesn't seem to be listening to me anymore. Instead, he's gone very still, his eyes huge in his tired face. "How did you know about Walsingham—the manner of his killing blow?"

"What?" I fold my hands over my stomach, but I am already caught out. "It simply came to me," I said. "A vision I did not seek. At the onset of the convocation."

"And you *acted* upon what you saw in that vision, no verification of the facts needed."

"I hardly *acted*, Sir William. It's not as though I lifted a cup of poisoned wine to a man's lips."

"But you believed what you saw," he says, unrelenting. "Just as Walsingham believed what you saw about Robert Moreland. How is that any different?'

"Because Walsingham should not believe everything he hears! He questioned Moreland, yes, but his mind was already set. And why? Because of what I said? Do you trust every scrap of intelligence that comes to you from your spies and their encoded letters? Do you trust every prisoner who gives you a confession? No! It is one thing for me to see something in my head and know it to be true. But to stake a man's life on it!"

"We are staking a kingdom on it, Miss Dee," Cecil replies, his voice razor sharp. "So you'd better get used to the experience. You've demonstrated your skills masterfully. And you shall do so again. And again."

"Or what?" I fume. "You'll kill me?"

Cecil has the temerity to laugh. "Kill you? I think not, Miss Dee. You're worth far more to us alive than dead, as yesterday's events amply illustrated."

I stare at him, understanding his meaning, as blood drains from my face. "You cannot make me talk."

"Oh, but we can," Cecil says, quite recovered, his words almost cheerful. "The only question is, where will you do the talking? For all I care, you can spend the rest of your life in this room, never to see the stars. If you know nothing else about me, know this: I am a very patient man. Eventually you will tell us what we seek, when you have forgotten what a blue sky looks like, or the feel of the sun on your face. Eventually you will share your visions, when you long to hold flowers in your hands, or to hear a friend's laughter. It may take two days, it may take twenty. It won't take *years*, though, mark my words. For if you wait too long, I fear you will be able to predict the deaths of every friend you ever had, the other maids, even your young Marcus Quinn." He does smile then, to see the shock upon my face. "The Queen can forge another assassin, Miss Dee," he says quietly. "Another thief, another scholar. And I assure you, it will give her great good pleasure to have cause to rid herself of Beatrice. Is that what you want to have happen? For your fellow maids to pay for your unwillingness to do your job?"

A long and terrible silence stretches out between us, and in it I see the life I am to live. A prisoner in velvet chains, cozened perhaps, but no less trapped. For Cecil has the right of it, I feel it in my bones. The Queen may tire of Meg's sleight of hand. Jane may lose her touch at death. Beatrice may run out of secrets and Anna out of solutions. But a woman such as Elizabeth will never tire of learning about the future. Especially her own.

"Yes," Cecil says, watching me closely. "It does not take the Sight to puzzle out the truth of this. Eventually you will become the sword that Elizabeth wishes to wield. The sooner you come to terms with that, the more comfortable your life will be—and the safer your friends will be."

He shifts off the wall, dusting his impeccably tailored doublet. "Now. What is it you were trying to tell us in the Queen's Privy Chamber? Walsingham confirmed that you had told him of two deaths, not one. When questioned, your fellow spies confirmed it as well." Again, he raises a hand at my riffle of outrage. "They would have done anything to prove you were not out of your mind, Miss Dee. Which you will agree was a valid concern, after your demonstration at the convocation."

I scowl at him mulishly, but he merely smiles. "And so, now you have the floor. What is it you wish to tell me?"

I blow out a long breath, tamping down my irritation. "My vision of the Queen is not as clear as what I saw of Moreland, and far more allegorical, I fear. But it's terrible nonetheless and should not be discounted. It opens with the Queen dressed in a gown of gold and black, laced with pearls."

He considers that. "I have not seen this gown, but she is ever fond of pearls. Are you certain?"

"I am—and I haven't seen the gown before either. She is on a snow-white field, in the center of a large black cross. I cannot puzzle out if the field is actually covered in snow, or how the cross is positioned so sharply and crisply upon the ground, but she is at its center. I and the other maids surround her at the field's edge, with swords of fire held aloft." I grimace, hearing my own words. "I told you, it does not hew closely to reality."

"It's a vision of the future," Cecil says, more open-minded than I would expect from such a practical man. "Those do not always come in neatly wrapped packages."

I continue, eager now for my dark tale to be done. "The Queen is crumpled on the ground, Sir William. Her crown has fallen from her head and she is dead."

Cecil just nods. "Her injuries?"

"None at all," I say. "Her mouth is closed, with no mark upon it. Her skin is unblemished. Only, her eyes remain open, staring to the sky. I have seen this vision now three times, enough that it gives me great pause. And this last time was the worst." I focus on the wall beyond Cecil, reliving the horror of that final image once more. "In the room where I saw Walsingham kill Robert Moreland, there was another watcher there. Mistress Maude from Windsortown. The Queen was at her feet, dressed in the same gown, quite dead."

"Maude!" Cecil utters the word not with wonder, but almost with validation. "Well, I can offer you some solace there, Miss Dee. Maude's role in this is not so dire as you fear."

I narrow my eyes at him. "What do you mean?"

"I mean, Maude's presence in your vision of Walsingham is to be expected." His voice rolls with satisfaction, as if he can already see the multiple uses for my Sight. "We did not only use her for the truth tonic, after all. Where do you think we got the poison that killed Robert Moreland?"

Exasperation sharpens my words. "Sir William, no. Regardless of your beliefs, Maude is not to be trusted!"

"I believe that's enough for one day," Cecil says abruptly, his voice calm as he raps on the door of the cell. "I will leave you to consider your future." The door opens, but he pauses as if a sudden thought strikes him. "One more thing," he says, holding out a hand. "Your necklace, Miss Dee."

I stiffen, feeling the weight of the obsidian stone around my neck. "My what?"

Cecil smiles triumphantly. "The bauble you wear around your neck, the black obsidian ball. Give it to me." I hesitate, and he snaps his fingers. "Give it to me or I will have the guards come in and hold you down, and I will pluck it from your neck myself."

Silently, as if in a dream, I lift the obsidian stone from my neck. I hand it over to Cecil, and feel as though something has been torn from me, as important as my hands or feet. "I cannot scry without it," I say, but Cecil merely tucks the stone into the waistband of his doublet. He shakes his head.

"Nonsense, Miss Dee. We cannot have you depending on anything but your own mind, else this stone becomes a liability." He taps his waistband happily. "Fortunately, you will have plenty of time to practice your craft as you consider what I have told you."

When he steps out into the corridor, he takes all the light with him. The door slams shut, the cover solidly fixed. Silence presses down on me once more.

CHAPTER TWENTY-SIX

The hours bleed into one another, with Cecil accosting me at odd intervals, until I do not know when is day and when is night. The cell is buried too deep within the castle for me to hear the chiming of the bells, and it appears this is one place that not even the Maids of Honor can find. I have no visitors but Cecil, no company but the silent guards. After that first day, Will Seton is not assigned to guard me, a fact that makes me fear for the stalwart man.

I am not wholly alone, however.

I lean against the cool stone wall, my knees curled beneath me in my grubby gown. For Cecil is correct. Though I do not venture far there, it has become easy enough for me to slip into the angelic realm when I am surrounded with nothing but darkness. While I sense there is something changed on the spectral plane, something different, I can still see the angels and spirits floating in the shimmering half-light.

And perhaps most important, I can see Marcus Quinn.

He is always there, his face filled with pain and anger, his mouth working, though he is never able to speak. If he is being sent by Dee to spy upon me, I cannot guess, but he stands among the angels ever vigilant. More vigilant certainly than my dark specter, whose shrouded form I have not seen since he assaulted me with the image of Walsingham and Moreland, Maude and the Queen. I cannot understand the creature—*Arc,* he said. His name is Arc. He helps me and then he vanishes. He breaks the boundaries of the spirit realm and then he flees. I find myself looking for him in the shadows, but he is never there. There is only Marcus. And Marcus is enough.

I smile at him now across the shadowed glade, and his eyes grow wide, his hand stretching out. *Reach for me,* I beg inside my mind, knowing he cannot hear me, that he is too far away. Still . . . *Reach for me.*

The sound of a crossbar grinding against wood startles me, and I straighten on my bench, swinging my legs down to plant my feet upon the floor. I wince against the sudden bright light, raising a hand to shield my eyes.

Which is why my first vision of the Queen is the hem of her gown.

"Get up, get up, let me see you," she says. The torch is affixed to the wall, and I do as she says, rising to stand straight, my shoulders back, my chin high. "They could have cleaned you up," she says peevishly. "But you are unharmed? They're feeding you?"

"Yes, Your Grace."

"Good. Cecil has given me to understand that you are ready to answer my question."

I blink at her. "Cecil has not already told you?"

"Told me what?" She scowls at my confusion "He's asked you to scry my future? For that is what I want." She folds her arms. "Walsingham says you use some rock to help you, so bring it out. Who gave you that, anyway?"

"Beatrice," I say, trying to get my bearings. "It is something she found at her house and passed on to me." Close enough to the truth.

"It's probably flawed, then. I can't see that shrew giving up anything of value otherwise." She exhales an irritated breath. "Well, come on then, girl, show it to me. I don't have all day."

"I can't." I flutter my hands helplessly. "Cecil took it from me when he put me here. He told me I needed to learn to scry without it."

"Ha!" The Queen is surprised but also pleased, I can tell. My suffering and doubt is nothing to her. "Well, let us see, then, how you do. I wish to know my future, something near. Three months out, six months. Nothing more. I'll want to verify it."

"Yes, Your Grace," I say. Without the obsidian stone to ground me, I firm my hands into fists and focus. Once again I enter the angelic realm. And once again, something seems different here, as if a vital piece is missing from the shadowy glade, but I cannot place it. Instead, from my vantage point upon the spectral plane, I look back toward the mortal plane. I can see the Queen in front of me, and the walls beyond her. I know I cannot trust her question to any angel, as I did Walsingham's future. I have to know that what I see is true, and right, and sure. And so I say the word I must.

"Arc," I whisper.

Instantly he appears at the edge of my vision, staring out from his shadowed cowl, as leaping, twisting flames surround the space where his face should be. Despite myself, I feel shame for my purpose here. This realm is not a book to be opened at my leisure. There is a price for its secrets, a price I have not yet begun to truly pay. By the same token, however, my very existence at Windsor—nay, even the safety of my friends—is dependent upon the grace of the Queen. If I am unable to serve her needs, then my status among the angels is of no merit.

"Please," I say. The Queen stiffens before me, but to her credit she does not speak. Instead she stares at me quite curiously, her eyes wide. Behind her, the dark specter tilts his head, as if to mimic the Queen. He regards me silently, his anticipation plain.

He is waiting for something more. An exchange. A promise.

Please, I say again, this time firmly in my mind. *Please tell me . . . Arc.*

The creature draws in a deep breath. Then he leans forward, and a whisper flutters across my face before—

"Sophia! Sophia, enough of this, wake up!"

My eyes pop open—when did I close them?—and I feel myself urged up to my feet, my head pounding and a moist pressure against my cheek. The Queen's delicate lace-edged handkerchief comes away from my face, and I see what I expect: the fine cloth is soaked with blood. A guard is at my side now, holding my weight, supporting me back onto the bench. I am barely seated before Elizabeth is in front me.

"I did not believe Walsingham when he told me of this. By the saints, Sophia! You were crying tears of blood!"

"I know," I begin, but she merely thrusts another linen square at me, then takes a seat next to me on the stone bench, her eyes mirror bright, her hands clasped in front of her chest like she is a girl of fifteen and not a monarch of twenty-six.

"Get out!" she says impatiently to the guard. Then she stares at me. "Tell me everything."

I take in a deep and steadying breath.

"You should live a long and fulfilling life, rich with success and challenges met," I say. In my mind's eye there are still too many images to count. "It is not easy to parse out individual events, but your reign is full and prosperous—though your enemies are many."

Elizabeth grimaces. "I don't need a seer to divine that. What else?"

I have seen too much, far more than I should ever share. I have seen men aging and dying around the Queen, and her remaining stolid, more icon than woman. I have seen her alone.

No woman wants to hear that about herself, however.

"I must take time to fully understand everything in this vision," I lie, racing through the images to find one that will serve. "The more distant the image, the less certain it is. But one thing I can share with certainty. You will be hard pressed to marry the Swedish king, Your Grace. But you must hold fast against it."

"Swedish king?" the Queen asks. "Erik, you mean? He is not yet king."

"Then he will be, in these coming months," I say. "Though his ardent passion is naught but your due, his mind is not fully whole. You must hold fast."

"Erik . . ." Elizabeth's tone is bemused, calculating. I do not tell her that the future King Erik will die in prison, a madman, within the next few decades. I also do not mention that Elizabeth's love for Robert Dudley will also receive its first devastating blow before another year passes, forever removing him as a suitable candidate for her hand—the untimely and highly suspicious death of his own wife. It is one thing to be courted by a married man . . . but quite another to be courted by a possible murderer.

The Queen's mind is far away from Dudley in this moment, however, and I am grateful for it. "Very well, then. I thank you for the warning." Her smile is radiant. "And I daresay that is enough for one day. Here." She presses her handkerchief to me again, folded over to hide the blood. "Lady Knollys will have apoplexy if she believes I have been bleeding, and you look like you're about to begin anew. Tell your angels, or whoever gives you these visions, to take better care of you." She glances around the cell. "Cecil believes you need another day in seclusion. But I am not so inclined." She frowns at me. "Still, I can't have you walking through the castle, looking as you do. Prepare yourself to leave this place, and I'll have Meg bring you down new clothes. And a hood to cover your hair."

She moves to leave, and I stand quickly, willing myself to return back to the present moment—and its present dangers.

"A moment, Your Grace," I blurt. For regardless of what

Cecil believes, I must warn Elizabeth as well. Now, when she believes what I can see. "These images I have of you, they are but one possible future. The most likely one, I'll warrant, but not the only one."

She stops, her face a mask of confusion. "What do you mean?"

"There yet remains a threat to your person, here at Windsor Castle." I cannot hesitate now, when I have her full attention. "In another vision I had, while attempting to discern Mother Shipton's prophecy, I saw you dead, Your Grace. Fallen on a field of white, a black cross etched into the ground."

Impossibly, she just shrugs. "Oh! So that is what Cecil would not tell me. Very well, then. We shall be prepared," Elizabeth says. "It is not even November; there is no snow upon the ground. And by the time there is, I shall be long gone from Windsor."

I can only stare at her. Does no one see the importance of this vision? "That's not the point, Your Grace," I try, but Elizabeth will have none of it.

"You are overwrought, Sophia, and well you should be," she says, her voice cool and patronizing, for all that she attempts to be kind. "You have worked long and hard to tell me what I should know. But come to me with visions that might play out in the next few *weeks*, not months hence. You said yourself that the further out you see, the murkier your vision becomes." She smiles confidently. "I assure you, I have no plans to be standing on a field of white anytime soon, so your warning can certainly keep."

"Your Grace, you don't understand!" I hear my voice rising against the hysteria in my heart, and the Queen hears it too. She steps back, startled, but I can no more stop my words than I can stop the roaring of the tide. "You do have enemies at Windsor, and in Windsortown. You do! You cannot afford to let yourself go lax, you cannot assume that you are safe, you cannot mingle among your people. Not when any one of them might even now be notching a bow or drawing a knife to slay you!"

"Fie! You think I don't know this already?" In my clumsy attempt to warn Elizabeth, I have instead lit the fuse of her anger, and it sparks back at me, quick and hot. The Queen lifts her chin, her back rigid, her shoulders straight, looking more like a warrior than I have ever seen her. "You think I don't understand that even my friends would easily become my foes if there were enough gold and power in the offing for them? I am no fool, Sophia. Why do you think I have sheltered you, clothed you, fed you these long months against the hope that one day you may see something of merit? I have gathered a veritable arsenal around me against the attacks of any who would challenge me, and you are not the least of my weapons." She leans forward, fixing me with a glance. "But I will not be browbeaten into some cowering wretch of a woman, either. I did not survive to become Queen at twenty-five, only to die a death born of my own fears every day of my life thereafter. You must learn to share your portents when they are useful. And not a moment before or after. Else you are no use to me."

She casts a hard gaze around the room. "Perhaps Cecil is

right," she says coldly. "Perhaps additional seclusion will do you well."

I do not speak, but merely bow. Elizabeth sweeps out of the room, secure in her cloak of outrage and indignation, her sheltering mantle of privilege and pride. And in the echo of the slamming cell door, I can almost hear the rolling, raucous laugh of Mistress Maude.

A royal house defeated,
disaster unforeseen.
Death comes to Windsor
to court the maiden Queen.

CHAPTER TWENTY-SEVEN

I have no further visitors for what seems like far too long. How many days or weeks will they keep me here, I wonder? With no one to talk to, at least on this plane, I find myself sleeping more and more, if only to have the company of angels to help me pass the hours.

The angels . . . and Marcus. With each new visit, his form seems to grow stronger in the spirit realm, as if Dee is learning how to pierce the veil more deeply. We still cannot speak, but we can see each other. And with that sight comes hope. I yearn more and more to spend every hour in slumber or in trance, for the possibility of seeing him.

My heart aches for the loneliness that Meg must have endured while locked in her watery cell, an act also sanctioned by the Queen's advisors. She had no one but herself to keep her company for days on end, and I stiffen my own resolve to wait as long as necessary.

My resolve, it turns out, needs much stiffening. Fortunately for me, I am given ample time to perfect the art. And in my silence I am forced to consider everything the angels have ever told me. All of the predictions that have not—or at least not yet—come to pass, such as the strange predictions I spoke to my fellow maids the night of Dee's arrival, during the great spectacle of stars in the Presence Chamber, or my vision of the Queen upon a white field. As I've turned these images over and around in my head, a curious sense of relief has formed there. The angels have lived a millennia, I think. What is time to them? What they have shown me could happen tomorrow, or it could happen five years from now. It is up to me to take what clues I might from the vision and prepare accordingly. And so, if I ever get out of this squalid cell, I will wait and watch for the first snowfall like everyone else, and *then* prepare to save the Queen. But until then, at least, I can rest easy, knowing she is safe.

Rest is also in great supply, here in the darkness.

At last the door opens again. Only, it's not Cecil or Walsingham or even the Queen this time. Instead, a page stands before me, a young boy not ten years old. He thrusts a bundle of clothing at me.

I straighten and squint at him, but take the fresh-smelling garments quickly enough. "Miss Sophia Dee," he cries, not looking at me, "the Queen has need of you! You are to come with me once you . . . once you . . ." He gestures at me, and I understand.

"Once I dress?"

"Yes!" He scurries back, bleating at the guards to shut the door. To their credit, they do not unlatch the cover over the grate, and I change in darkness, using what is left of the water to wash the worst of the dirt and grit from my face and hands. The new shift is a particular blessing, though the clothes are servants' garments, and the Queen has had the foresight to include a French hood to cover my hair.

When I emerge from the cell, I cannot see well at first, but I stumble after the page without speaking. I expect him to lead me to the Queen's chambers, but I am mistaken. Instead, he turns deeper into the castle, and I draw up short. "Where are we going?" I ask.

He looks back at me. "The dungeons. The Queen said to tell you that all is well, though it's an awful place." He screws up his face in thought. "Then again, where I have fetched you from is awful too."

I smile wearily, my mood buoyed by the simple fact of talking to anyone, even a page who seems to be delivering me to yet more doom. "It is at that," I say. "What day is this?"

"'Tis Friday, the feast of Samhain," he announces excitedly.

I try to hide my shock. That means I was locked up for three whole days. Three days! How could I have lost track of time so completely? The page escorts me down the long hall to where it opens onto a rocky stair, a guard on either side of the opening. He hesitates. "This is as far as I'm to go."

"Off with you, then," I say with a courage I do not feel. "You must follow the orders you've been given, and I will do the same." I hear him fleeing down the long corridor, back to hearth and safety, as I continue down the stairs. The passage is lit by torches hung upon the walls, and at length a large chamber opens up around me as I descend the last few steps. Doors line the walls, but I have no eyes for them. I see only the men who are standing there—four of them in the heavy grey robes of the Questioners. With them stands the Queen and her chief advisors.

Amidst this dour group, Cecil and Walsingham stare at me, their faces naught more than careful masks. The other men are silent as well, hidden in their robes. The Queen, for her part, waits until I am almost upon them. Then she says my name, as curt as an open slap. "Sophia."

Bowing my head, I drop into a curtsy at the edge of their circle. "Your Grace," I say, staring at the stone floor. "Is there any way I can serve?"

"It seems that word has gotten out about your seclusion. I have been asked to present you once more to the Questioners, that we may be done with their interest in you." Her words are heavy with meaning. "And I am most sincere, my lords. After today you will trouble the Crown no more on this score."

One of the men coughs discreetly. "Given the nature of the questions, I ask again, Your Grace, should we not have a *Catholic* priest in attendance?"

"No, we should *not*," Elizabeth snaps. "The pope holds no sway here, only God. Now begin, that we might have this trial done. Sophia, you may rise."

In the Questioners' semicircle of scrutiny, I stand tall, grasping for a strength that seems to be ebbing away. I know what to expect from these men, I reason. They do not frighten me.

But I am wrong on both counts.

Two of the robed men position themselves on either side of me, while the Queen stands at a short distance with Cecil and Walsingham. I try to feel Arc in this dread place, but I don't. I wonder if the dark angel even realizes I am in danger. And Marcus is yet further from me, separated by stone and the whims of the Queen.

The Questioners waste no time. One of the doors swings open along the wall, and two more hooded men approach me, carrying items as if in offering to an obscene god: a bottle and a burning brazier with a long iron rod protruding from its base. I can smell the hot metal, and my mouth goes dry in fear. What could they mean to do with that? And why does the Queen remain placid, simply watching?

"Sophia Dee, you will submit to the questioning, that we may prove your soul is blameless before God. Are you prepared to answer truthfully and without guile?" It is the tall man who speaks, and I tear my gaze away from the burning poker to gape at him. *What am I supposed to say here?*

"Yes, my lord." I gesture to the tools. "But there is no need—"

"Silence!" he thunders. "You will speak only when spoken to, and respond only to the questions we put to you. We will not be ensorcelled by any dark spirits."

My eyes widen, but not entirely out of fear. *Ensorcelled?* This assumes a great deal that simply is not true. Then the man to the right of me, slender and nearly quivering with excitement, uncaps the bottle. A noxious odor wafts up, and I can discern some of its makeup. I wonder if he's procured this little treasure from Mistress Maude, or if the good cooks of Windsor know enough to make such a terrible brew.

The man seems to revel in my confusion—a brazier to the

left, an odious draught to my right. Does he mean to give me the choice between the two?

Alas, no.

"Drink this," he growls, and I look at him in alarm.

"What is it?" The Queen's voice floats over us. She seems supremely bored.

"Naught but a mixture of wine and herbs, Your Grace," the tall man says, though I think "herbs" is a rather broad statement. Hemlock is an herb, after all. But he goes further. "Crafted to be drinkable by only the pure of heart. Anyone with secrets against God will not be able to tolerate it."

I force myself not to gasp, but in truth this is outside of enough. The vile concoction might well contain a purgative, in which case I would be forced to vomit it up whether I was "pure of heart" or not.

The Queen seems to consider this, remaining unconcerned. "And the other?"

"No witch can withstand the placement of a hot poker in her mouth." The man with the slithery voice speaks up, and I realize with dismay that he's the one holding the brazier. His fellow pulls out the poker and brandishes it for inspection. It is quite red, glowing brightly in the center of the torch-lit room.

"I rather doubt anyone can withstand that, my lord," the Queen says dryly. "And a burned mouth cannot speak God's truth, can it?"

"Or the devil's lies," the man says, clearly affronted. "You forget that we are here to protect the sanctity of your position."

"*My* sanctity is never in question," the Queen says. "But proceed. Sophia, drink."

I look at the Queen with dismay, but I cannot gainsay a direct order. Either she knows what is in the slop in the bottle, or she is not worried about what it will do to me. I do not share her confidence, but I present myself to the bulky man, holding out my hand.

Without warning, I'm grabbed hard on either side, my chin stretched up. The bottle is forced to my lips. My head is tilted back, and my mouth fills with too many tastes at once. There is wine, certainly, cheap and sweet; and at least a half dozen herbs: thyme, dragon's blood, gardenia, lavender . . . every truth-serum herb I've ever encountered, but with wormwood and devil's snare included, unless I miss my guess. I'm forced to swallow before thinking too much, and the effect is unfortunate—and nearly immediate. My vision goes blurry and my body slumps, causing the men on either side of me to hold me yet tighter. The man who stands before me looks like the devil himself, the edges of his body becoming distorted. I know better, however, and I view the scene before me as dispassionately as I can. By virtue of the fact that I have seen specters for these past many years, I can identify a real spirit. In fact, the room is filled with them as I glance around, unfamiliar angels that are leaning into the circle of the Questioners as if they have never seen anything more fascinating. They can feel the righteous zeal of these men. They are feeding on it.

"What is it you would know?" I hear myself asking.

The questions are surprisingly rote at this point. I recite

the Lord's Prayer, I decry Satan and all his works. I deny any ability to consult with spirits, despite the curious looks of the angels who press close beside me. I claim only a deep desire to worship God, and any thoughts in my head are nothing more than my own thoughts, not messages from God, the angels, or any other agency. I repeat my daily schedule, my devotion to the Queen, my work in the castle.

And on it goes. The brazier swings close to me, but the Questioners never remove the poker to wave at me a second time. They seem mollified by my abject sincerity and stoic responses. I cannot weep, though, even if I want to. With such a vile combination of herbs and spirits in my stomach, any extreme emotion is likely to make me violently ill.

At last they finish and, abruptly, stand away from me. I sway forward, but catch myself in time. "We are done?" I ask when no one speaks.

I hear the smile in the thin man's voice, for all I cannot see it. "Not quite," he says.

Another door swings open. And what I see next withers my heart into a hard and shriveled ball.

Will Seton is brought out of the chamber, his upper body stripped, his lower body clad only in loose-fitting breeches. His hands are bound before him and he stares out in wild confusion. When his head swings around and he sees me, he gapes still further. "Miss Dee!" he says, and I reflexively move forward, only to be caught in the iron grip of the closest robed man.

The man behind Seton shoves him to his knees. "Will Seton, you will submit to the questioning, that we may prove your soul to be blameless before God. Are you prepared to answer truthfully and without guile?"

"What—" At his confused response, one of the robed men strikes him, the act so abrupt and vicious I cannot stifle my scream.

"Answer the question!" the man roars, clearly relishing his role as enforcer.

Please just answer their questions! I silently beg. Will Seton has a wife and family, all of whom need his support and protection far more than I do.

"Yes!" Seton shouts as the man raises his fist again. "Yes. God's breath, what is this—"

This time the blow drives him to the ground, his bound hands unable to break his fall. The Questioners roughly pull him back up to a kneeling position. His face is bloody, and his eyes fix on me. I see for the first time a flicker of doubt.

"Do you know this woman?" the Questioner asks, and Seton frowns.

"I do! Of course I do."

"Her name?"

"Miss Sophia Dee."

"Her role within the castle?"

"She serves the Queen. She's a maid of honor, or—" He hesitates. "Lady-in-waiting. No, a maid."

"And have you ever seen this maid of honor, this servant of the Queen, engage in any acts against God or the Church?"

"What? No! Are you mad?" Seton takes the blow with a grunt, but he does not flinch this time. For his courage, the robed man picks up a short stick and cracks it across Seton's back, instantly raising a large welt. I feel tears prick at the backs of my eyes, and I bring my fists up to my mouth. I will not cry, I resolve. I will not cry!

The questions do not seem to matter from this point forward, though the violence increases with Seton's each successive refusal to betray me. And I know this refusal is a *choice* that he is making, that he could easily give me away by sharing any number of my oddities: my wild unfocused eyes; my quiet, distracted manner. My coming and going from the King's Gate at odd hours. Any one of these acts would be enough, I suspect. Enough for the Questioners to claim me a heretic and a witch. Enough for them to take me from the Queen and throw me in some jail to rot. Or, as Beatrice fears, to do far *worse* things to me. There are no good ways to die in Queen Elizabeth's realm. But some are grimmer than others.

After one particularly intense blow, I finally cry out. "Stop this!" I implore the Queen. *She* is the one allowing this horrible abuse to continue. *She* is the one who watches with only mild interest, while every lash and strike wounds my soul. "Beat me, if you must beat someone. Rip my skin and bruise my flesh. But this man has done nothing to deserve this treatment. He has served you honorably!"

The Queen's bored glance shifts to me, her cold face inscrutable. But in her eyes I see the truth. She has no desire to see me damaged. I am the vessel of her visions, the cup of her future. She would keep me whole and lovely to look upon, a bauble most precious and fine.

I have never hated anyone, in the whole of my young life. Not even Dee, though he has given me most cause to do so.

But in this moment I hate Elizabeth. Hate her for the power she holds over me, and hate her for the favor I so desperately need her to show. She alone can protect my friends from harm, and she alone will . . . but only if I give her what she wants.

Me.

"I tire of this charade." The Queen does not shift her attention from my face, but her words are no longer bored. Has she seen the emotion that burns within me? I do not care, if it means that Seton will be saved. "Finish with your questions, and let us leave this place."

Before me the Questioner leans down to Seton's ear. By now the guard can no longer kneel upright, but is held on either side by his Questioners.

"And what about the day she saved your horse, Will Seton?" the Questioner asks, savoring what is clearly his most damning accusation. "We have witnesses who would swear that she ensorcelled your mare, to save her from a poisoning that took down every other horse in the Lower Ward that day. What say you to *that*?"

The sound that fills the room is a horrible one, and I watch, mortified, as Seton moans, his voice barely a rattle in his throat. *This is it,* I think. *It has all led to this.* For not even Seton can deny that I told him how to save Ladysweet after looking into the horse's eyes. Not even Seton—poor, brave Seton—can survive a beating like this, the stone floor around his kneeling body covered in blood and gore.

The sound mounts, and it chills my blood. Seton's shoulders are now heaving with effort, his head coming up—and his bloody, cracked lips split . . . into a wild grin.

"Ensorcelled?" He almost howls the word, and I realize that the hideous sound is his laughter. "Ensorcelled, by all that's holy. Are you mad? No mere child can enchant a Queen's man. The idea is ridiculous!"

"Well stated!" The Queen's loud voice stays the Questioner's hand, which is raised to crack down the whip once more. "Release him, and gently now," she says, and the men gradually let the poor guard sag to the ground, as silent tears slip down my face at last. She stares implacably at the leader of the group. "I find I am quite satisfied with this demonstration," she says. "I presume you are as well? Excellent." Not giving him time to answer, she calls for the guards at the top of the stair. They clamber down, their faces impassive as they take in the body of the fallen Seton. "Remove him and have his wounds tended, sparing no expense. I will want a report of his care."

The men pick up Seton, whose concerned eyes turn to me even as he's carried up the stairs. I dash my tears away, and the Queen returns to her pacing, crossing back and forth between Walsingham and Cecil, and the six robed men. I don't know if my own questioning will continue, though I brace myself for it. And yet I still do not expect it when Elizabeth stops before me, her dark eyes flashing as she looks at my face.

"Who are these men, Sophia?" she asks.

I stare at her, amazed. But I do not misunderstand her. She wishes me to scry here, amidst the Questioners, and without my obsidian stone!

Just then, in this bloodstained chamber beneath Windsor

Castle, the angels surrounding us shift, their faces serene, their wings shimmering, and watch as Arc steps into their midst. He regards me from the depths of his cowl, and the entire crowd of angels turns back to me as well, their soulless eyes fixing upon me too. With him at their head, the spirits' mouths open as one. Suddenly words rush over me, through me, all around me, the breeze seeming to shift my very bones with its strength, for all that I am standing still.

And I know. I know everything.

And this time I shan't pay the angels for the knowledge with my own blood, because Seton has already made the required sacrifice. So much do I owe the man, him as well as the doves that led me to his care.

I look at the Queen, and when I speak, my voice is as cold as the blue-white fire that flares along the angels' wings. "These men approached me several days' past, at your direction. They are followers of God, and of Your Majesty."

"Indeed," the tall man says, and I sense that he, at least, has begun to pick up the scent of danger. "Miss Dee was most forthcoming during our discussion."

One of the other men—who is both fat and mean-eyed, I know now—scoffs at that, and I favor him with a gracious smile. "Lord Mallory, do you wish to say something?"

"What?" The Queen's shock is plain even as Mallory lets out a startled squawk. "Name them all," she demands.

"Of course, Your Grace," I say, and I see that Cecil has stepped forward as well, his manner intent. Behind him Walsingham watches me with frank appraisal. Surely both of them now see the value of a gift such as mine, I think grimly. Still, I follow the Queen's command. I gesture around the room and begin ticking off names like dancing partners. "Lord Crowley, Lord Magnus, Sir Jonathan, Lord Brampton, Lord Mallory. And Lord Willoughby." I end this recitation with a bow of my head, as Lord Willoughby is the leader. And as leaders do, he steps forward and directs the actions of his minions by dropping his own cowl, revealing a lined, intelligent face.

"She *is* a witch!" The hissed accusation comes from Mallory, as I'd felt it would. His face, free of his cowl, is broader and more bulbous than I expected. "There is no way that she could have identified us, she who is but a maidservant to the Crown and a child besides. Only the devil could have put such information in her head and bid her announce it so brazenly." He wheels toward me, his pig eyes bulging. "How did you do it? Do you pray to Satan at night? Do you kneel before his false image?"

Cecil stands tall. "Stand back, Lord Mallory," he barks. He observes the men with sharp eyes. "How the Crown receives its knowledge is of no concern to you, and if we choose to share it with the Queen's attendants, that is her pleasure as well. Your questions on the subject of Sophia Dee are done, however. We thank you for your pursuit of evil, and are reassured to have such men of God on the side of the Crown."

The men dare to preen, while still standing in Seton's blood. I am sickened at the sight of them. At least only Mallory still looks ready to fall upon me, fists flailing.

The Queen now takes the floor.

"I and all of England are honored to bear witness to such

stalwart men who would band together to serve the common good. Where we accepted your anonymity to ensure you felt safe in doing God's work, please understand that henceforth there is no need for cowls or hoods. You may ask your questions plainly, to any of my court. These accusations of witchcraft are not made lightly, I know, but I also would not hide them. Witchcraft is a crime against my people, and should be treated as such; for those who would do harm to others by any means, cunning or no, shall be treated first and foremost as the criminals they are, before any question of heresy may be put to them."

"But they sin against God!" Once again, Mallory cannot hold himself from comment, and the Queen beams at him beatifically—but silently—until he is moved to add, "Your Majesty."

She nods. "Whether they sin against God is a matter of their souls, Lord Mallory. And I am not charged with the care of men's souls, but with the care of the people of my realm. So I will set down laws to govern their actions, and allow God to judge their souls as He sees fit." She lifts her hand when Mallory would speak again, and instead addressees Willoughby. "Are your questions satisfied, Lord Willoughby? May we put an end to this, as regards my gentle maid?"

The request is a serious one, and she gives it its due weight. Such due weight, in fact, that I find myself holding my breath, wondering how Willoughby will respond.

He does not look at me or Elizabeth's advisors, but directly at the Queen. "They are, Your Grace. We shall remain vigilant, however, as regards the rest of your court. The plague of a soul is ever a more insidious sickness than the plague of a body, and far less easy to discern."

"And I rest easily knowing the castle's souls are in your care," the Queen says, without a trace of mockery or derision. She gestures magnanimously. "You may leave, my lords. Pray join us in but a few hours at the celebration of Samhain."

They climb the stairs silently, and Elizabeth watches them go. When they have all departed the chamber, she turns back to me. Her expression is unlike any I have ever seen on her face, a curious mix of girlish delight and hard-won vindication. It suddenly occurs to me that, as dangerous as these men were to me, perhaps they posed yet greater danger to the Queen.

"Well *done*, Sophia," she says, her eyes flashing triumph. "Well done. You should return to your fellow Maids of Honor at once, to also prepare for tonight's revel." Her smile is wide and satisfied. "You have performed all the service I need, this day."

"Thank you, Your Grace." I curtsy, hiding my face, that she might not see the emotions surging through me. Relief, that this trial is done. Outrage, that she allowed Seton to be treated with such brutality. Anger, that she tested me so callously as well. And the silent, small knowing, that she'll test me again . . . and again.

But not this night at least.

For tonight is made for dancing and for revelry, and I more than most have reason to lose myself in laughter. Amidst the raucous festival fires of Samhain, I will celebrate being alive, being free, and being once more able to see the stars.

CHAPTER TWENTY-EIGHT

I stride through the castle as quickly as I can, searching for my fellow Maids of Honor, for Marcus, for anyone that I might call a friend on this dark day. For all that I'm the one searching, Jane finds me first, stepping out of the shadows and plucking me from the corridor with a silent, firm grasp.

"Shhh," she mouths, yanking me into an antechamber. "Cecil."

I go still, and sure enough, Cecil's voice rings out down the long hallway. If I never see the man again, it will be too soon, and I willingly stand with Jane, waiting for him to pass. The moment his voice fades to a murmur, Jane turns to me. "Injuries?" she asks, pushing back my hood and peering at me. "Anything broken?"

"Only my pride," I say. "Though, that is enough." I grip her hands a bit too hard, and she suffers the contact, willing to let me be reassured by her presence. When I speak again, my voice is only slightly shaky. "Where are the others?"

She grins at me. "Waiting for you. We need to get you ready for polite company again—not to mention Marcus.

He's getting a little touched in the head, worrying over you. He's informed us that you were unharmed, said he's seen you in the angelic realm. An' to hear him tell the tale, he pushed Dee to demand your release a half dozen times, but the Queen has remained unmoved until just this morning."

I grimace, knowing that the Queen's generosity of spirit came not through a quiet word from Dee, but from the urgent summons of the Questioners. No matter, though. They will bother me no longer; I have earned my rest.

Together Jane and I slip through the castle, staying to the shadows and alcoves so that we are not caught out to do some lord's bidding or fetch some lady's hat. When we reach our chambers, I'm startled to see the other maids there—with a huge bucket of steaming water.

"A bath! But how—who?" I frown, trying to make sense of it. "We've already bathed this month."

Meg grins at me. "True enough, but it's not every day that you're released from the dungeons. And Heaven as well as I know the value of washing that place off. But still, we have to hurry. The guards will be back for the water in a half hour, and then there's the banquet and the festival after." She gestures to me when I still hesitate. "Come on, then! Beatrice is like to burst, waiting to dress you."

"This one, I think," Beatrice says, holding up a dark russet bodice in one hand, full dark skirts in the other. Then she peers at me as I pull off my French hood, allowing my hair to tumble free. "Good heavens, Sophia, your hair," she groans.

The maids commence their work upon me with the same efficiency and cheer that I have come to expect of them, and

I submit to their hands, their combs and brushes, welcoming the shock of the water, the sting of stiff bristles in my hair. Anything not to focus on the enormous swell of gratitude that surges up within me, threatening to spill over into a wash of tears.

"The Lower Ward is already lit up with bonfires." I focus on Anna's bright voice, filled with wonder. "Fully half the townspeople are in costume too. I think they know the Queen will be taking her leave soon, and things will be right boring around here when she does."

"Boring perhaps, but peaceful, too," Jane says. "You cannot deny some will be pleased not to worry about seeing a royal litter every time they turn the corner."

I wince as Meg works through a particularly rough snarl of my hair. "How goes James's *Play of Secrets*?" I ask.

"They've been working on the platform for it all day!" Meg says. "It's an enormous raised dais—not so high as the Queen's, of course, but with a half dozen sets of stairs ringed round it, so that the players can have the illusion of constantly coming and going. James is beside himself with excitement." She elbows Jane, who is still watching me with her fierce grey eyes. "There's talk of him being made the Lord of Misrule, ere we reach Londontown. Wouldn't that be fun?"

"As fun as any plague, I suspect," Jane says, her words betraying only irritation. But Anna laughs, taking up the refrain.

"We haven't had a worthy Lord of Misrule in years, what with Queen Mary so proper in all her ways," she says. "With him in charge of all the season's festivities, and allowed to commandeer the Queen's men to carry out his every whim, you cannot deny that Master James would make her first Christmas as Queen one to remember."

"Let's just hope he doesn't make it one we'd like to forget," Beatrice says wryly. "Elizabeth has already proven that her appetite for being entertained is as vast as the open sea."

We chatter on then as my fellow maids present me with a new shift, bundling away the one Elizabeth gave me, then lace me into my skirts and bodice and sleeves. Somehow Beatrice has found shoes and warm hosiery to keep off the night's chill, and by the time the guards knock on the chamber's door to fetch the water, we are all properly prepared to enjoy the evening as the Queen commands.

I cannot help but tense, however, as the guards enter the room. Neither of them look like the men who stood watch at my cell door, but they still represent the Queen, and the power she held over me—the power to lock me away in darkness and then to set me free again. Meg, at my side, puts a reassuring hand upon my shoulder. "It gets easier," she says simply. "They were just following the Queen's command—Cecil's and Walsingham's, too, I suspect."

"That doesn't necessarily make me feel better." A new thought presses down on me, and I turn to her. "What of Moreland's family?" I ask. "Are they safely away?"

"Away, yes," Beatrice says from deeper in the room, and her voice is uncharacteristically stark. "'Safe' depends a lot on the widow Moreland's new baby. If it's a girl, as the midwives predict, then she'll be safer, certainly."

"The rest of Nostradamus's prediction played out as

well, at least," Anna says, her voice equally grim. "'His blood shall turn to gold.' The Queen settled enough coin on Mary Moreland to ensure she will live comfortably when she reaches Gravesend. The woman is distraught, as you can imagine, but at least she'll not starve."

I consider this as we file out of the maids' chambers and toward the Presence Chamber, where the feast of Samhain awaits. Doubtless, the trail of the Queen's gold serves another purpose as well. If it ensures that Mary Moreland remains in Gravesend until the baby arrives, then the Queen's mind can be put to rest on the question of succession. For all that our current monarch is female, a boy with royal parentage is always considered a greater threat to one day overthrow the Crown. Accordingly, I send up a silent prayer that Mary's baby is healthy—and a girl.

Dinner is a boisterous affair, with the Queen leaving midway through the meal with her ladies to dress for the festival. Before she leaves, she commands her entire court to enjoy the evening, and her gaze rests on me long enough to make the fine hairs on my arms prickle. *I have plans for you,* her dark eyes seem to say. *But not tonight.*

For which I am heartily relieved.

Once the meal ends, we are finally able to escape the castle and step into the open air. We pause a moment at the Norman Gate, watching the lords and ladies of the Queen's court stroll through the Upper Ward as the final touches are put on Master James's enormous stage. I feel I can finally breathe, the excitement in the air crackling along with the smell of wood smoke and ale. "It's wonderful!" I say, and my voice sounds like—well, like that of the fifteen-year-old girl I am. No longer worn down with the cares of serving the Queen, at least not in this moment, but simply a young woman savoring a crisp October night.

Meg gestures to the Lower Ward with a laugh. "You must have a look at everything," she says. "We've been watching the celebration all day, but you've not seen it." She glances away, and her voice turns cagier. "Oh, but if only you had someone who could walk with you and ensure the ghosts and spirits won't distress you."

And then a deeper laugh sounds, and I turn to see Marcus Quinn before me, offering a very polite bow. His words are light as he straightens, but the intensity of his gaze can't be denied. "I would be honored to walk with you, Sophia, if you'll have me," he says.

I don't speak for a moment, my heart suddenly too full. And then a firm pair of hands between my shoulder blades sends me lurching forward, Anna's sigh of exasperation speaking volumes. "Go!" she says. "We'll meet up in the Upper Ward after *The Play of Secrets*."

With that I place my hand on Marcus's arm, and we step into the night. The Lower and Middle Wards stretch out before us as we leave the shadow of the Norman Gate, the enormous space transformed. Bonfires dot the lawn, and there are stalls of the more enterprising local vendors, selling their pastries and meat pies. Both music and ale flow freely, and there is also a keen sense of almost desperation in the air. The festival of Samhain always plucks at the nerves of the superstitious, as it opens a door between the planes, to allow the dead to walk among the living once more. For those who miss their loved ones dearly, the festival is a blessing. For those who would rather that the dead remain dead, it's a bit of a pox. Some of the revelers wear masks, to imitate or hide from the spirit walkers, though most do not.

For the children, of course, it is ever a reason to celebrate, and a burst of their laughter brings a smile to my face, despite the strain of the day. They gather around the stalls that sell the sweet pastries the festival is famed for, singing the time-worn chant.

> *"A soul cake, a soul cake!*
> *I pray thee, good missus, a soul cake!*
> *One for Peter, two for Paul,*
> *Three for Him what made us all!"*

"Sophia." Marcus's voice recalls my attention, and I turn to him fully. His face is set with equal parts worry and relief. "Tell me they haven't harmed you."

I shake my head. "They haven't, Marcus—" I try to speak more, but he pulls me roughly to him, his mouth coming down on mine. This kiss is nothing like the one we shared in Saint George's Hall, which was fresh and full of promise. This one is harder, surer, and far more desperate. Something cracks open inside me, an emotion I hadn't realized I was harboring, and it rushes through me like a spectral fire. I taste Marcus's anguish and his pain, and revel in the strength of it. When he finally releases me, however, I'm the one whose breathing is ragged. "I saw you in the angelic realm," I say. "You came for me."

"I couldn't reach you," he says, sighing. "I didn't have the strength. I think . . . I think I once *was* able to move like you do, to walk unaided through the spirit realm. The way seemed almost familiar to me when I tried to step away from Dee's carefully constructed path. But in the end I could not manage it. I could only go where Dee directed me, could only watch you as if from across a great distance."

I smile at him. "It was enough, Marcus," I say. "It was more than enough."

We make our way through the laughing crowds, bright faces reflected in the firelight, children singing for the white-sugar-and-black-currant-crossed soul cakes at the bakers' stalls, the smell of sweet spices wafting through the air. Once we again pass along the curve of the Round Tower, however, and angle into the Upper Ward, the mood shifts markedly. Throughout the Quadrangle, Elizabeth's courtiers and ladies are gathered in several small groups, also drinking and making merry, though no one sings for soul cakes here. Instead the laughter is artful and sly behind ever-more elaborate masks. I see John Dee and his companions, the men of science who revolve around him, like stars around the Earth.

I stiffen, realizing that this small constellation of learned men is the only one in the Quadrangle. "Marcus," I say slowly. "Where is Nostradamus?"

"Long gone," he says, patting my hand. "With his gold and the Queen's good favor, and a retinue of guards to ease his way. Should she ever have need of him again, he'll doubtless come running. Meanwhile, she's puffed up Dee so much that he's about to split a seam, and she's told him she hopes the two of you can work together on future projects."

I gape at him. "You cannot be serious."

"Dee, being no fool, said he would be delighted." Marcus grins. "And I, being no fool, asked for a raise."

I can't help myself; I laugh. The sound seems almost foreign on my lips, a burst of sudden, reckless joy. Marcus squeezes my hand, and for this one moment I feel like any other girl in Windsor Castle, with any other boy, our entire lives lit up with love, with hope, with breathless possibility.

Then a crackling explosion rents the air, and a cheer goes up. "Huzzah!" I hear the voice of none other than Master James McDonald, booming out over the crowd. "I bring you all *The Play of Secrets*!"

CHAPTER TWENTY-NINE

We press forward. Marcus's hand is hard on my arm, keeping me close to him. I am grateful for his presence, if only to help us work our way through the crowd. At the center of the Upper Ward, Cecil glowers at me from a raised dais where the Queen is seated in full Samhain regalia, her dress deep blue and embroidered with pearls, a dark blue cape over her shoulders also studded with pearls. Relieved beyond measure that she is not gowned in black and gold, I avoid Cecil's hard eyes for a moment to take in Gloriana. Even her crown is more pearls than gold, it seems, and she faces the stage in rapt delight, as Master James explains that the scene he has prepared for us is a gathering of courtiers at a local inn, brought together by a stranger's invitation. "As the evening and the conversation progress, and the night draws down, who knows what secrets may be revealed!" he announces, and the crowd breaks into wild applause.

But Cecil's glare draws me back before I can see who has assembled on the stage. He slides his glance between me and Marcus, and I cannot tell if there is approval or censure in his regard. Probably a bit of both. This is Cecil, after all. He seems to be trying to tell me something else, and I fight the urge to smile. I am certain that reading minds would have been Cecil's preferred psychic gift for me; alas, I can only see into the future. He will have to settle for that.

The crowd pushes and pulls at us, and I strain to see not only what is happening on the stage, but who else has gathered in the Upper Ward. Finally I step up onto a low bench, and the scene is laid out before me. Laughing, Marcus hops up as well, taking my hand in his. A quick glance round the Quadrangle reveals Walsingham watching in the crowd, and the Maids of Honor at their stations. And someone else, too.

Mistress Maude has come to watch *The Play of Secrets*.

A chill slides through me, chasing away much of my good mood. Even if she is not an immediate threat to the Queen, the woman is a menace! Nevertheless, the round and ruddy herb mistress stands quite at her ease, grinning at the edge of the crowd as she is flanked on either side by the Queen's guards. They do not push or harry her, however. If anything, they seem to be protecting her from any jostling of her fellows; her position is clearly one of honor. I resolutely force myself not to stare, and shift my gaze away. She will not ruin tonight's celebration.

Marcus tightens his hand on mine, and I frown, blinking as the scene begins to shift and roll. It's as if I were dreaming awake, and I shake my head.

"You feel it, then?" Marcus has leaned down to speak into my ear, and I shiver at his nearness. "I hoped you would, but it's not as if I've been given much chance to put my theory about our connection to the test."

"You're making me feel this way?" I ask. "But how?"

His smile is rueful. "Without Dee's incantations I cannot go with you to the other side, Sophia. I cannot do what you do. Would that I could! But since the moment I first saw you, and especially when we danced together, I suspected I could do this."

He brings his other hand round, pressing mine between his palms, and I feel the sudden shift of my senses, signaling that the angelic realm has been opened to me. Then I clasp Marcus's hands as well, reveling in his strength, his certainty.

And just like that, I fall away from this world—and into the spectral plane.

I stare around myself, trying to see everything at once. There are the crowds surrounding the stage, cheering, laughing, drinking, eating cakes. And also, ringing round the space, as plain as day to my Sighted eyes, there stand both the angels and the dead.

It is easy to tell the difference between the once- and never-living. The angels—spirits—are serene, almost smiling. Drinking in the emotions of anger, excitement, joy, lust. They shimmer with the intensity of all that is going on before their eyes, a few of them reaching out as if to feel the experience more deeply. This is what Samhain means to them. The veil has been drawn back, and they can drink their fill of mortal emotions, savoring each drop.

The dead, however, are reacting entirely differently. It is as though they were trying to burst out of their ghostly skin.

They seem to hurl themselves forward without moving, their eyes desperate and beseeching, streaming with tears, desperately wanting someone—*anyone*—to see them, to notice them. It is completely unnerving.

A movement in one of the high windows captures my attention, and I peer up into the large chamber I know to be Saint George's Hall. The very *abandoned* Saint George's Hall. But now there is someone standing in one of its tall windows, someone who stares at the chaos below. And with my Sight-aided eyes, I recognize this woman, for all that she was dead long before I was born.

It is the shade of Anne Boleyn, Queen Elizabeth's mother.

She is beautiful. Tall and straight, with jet-black hair and dark eyes, she gazes at the scene before her in rapt fascination, her wide mouth parting in soft surprise. Clearly, she sees her daughter sitting as monarch in the midst of a revel and a rout. Sees her, and must realize that she has won. Anne could not keep her crown as Queen, but by God her daughter will.

I feel Marcus's hands tightening, and I slip further away from the present world and into the angelic realm. Only, it is different. Vastly different. Where before the angels were always muted drifters, their shadowy figures fading in and out of focus, now they are sharply drawn. They look up, almost shocked to see me, as if I, too, am different to them. And in the distance, so far as to almost be indiscernible, a burst of flame shoots up in the darkness. I am smote with a wave of emotion so strong, so intense that I wrench my hands apart, jerking back. "Marcus!" I gasp, and once more we are in the Upper Ward. "How did you do that?"

He grins at me. "You have your talents, Sophia, and I have mine. I can channel for earthbound seekers, certainly, and your uncle pays me well for that skill. But I can also serve as a sort of *prism* for a true scryer's light, to focus and refine it, creating an illumination beyond compare so that they might better see what the angelic realm holds. With my touch, you cannot go too deep into the realm, but you will see farther, I swear it." His voice drops. "Your light, Sophia. You have to realize how brightly it burns."

I shake my head, lifting my hand to my right eye. There is no blood this time. I am not at all harmed from the startlingly clear vision of the angelic realm. I am not tired, nor lost upon my return—also a first for me. Marcus watches me with knowing eyes, smiling when my gaze returns to him, tracking my understanding. "I have never worked with someone with as strong a connection to the spirit realm as you, Sophia. Think of what we might find, should we search together."

Held in the momentary thrall of that vision, I see the future that we might have together, as elusive as any spirit. Marcus would help me, standing always at the gates of the plane of angels, ready to pull me back, to bring me home. *And one day we could even scry together.* Explore the spectral realm as one. That idea should excite me, and yet all I feel is fear. A warning, dark and inscrutable, and right on the edge of my understanding.

Because something horrible awaits the unwary on the spirit plane, the angels seem to whisper in the back of my mind. *Something terrible. Forbidden.*

I push those thoughts away and give his hand a squeeze,

shivering anew at the sudden prickling of my senses. "Will it always be this way when our hands meet now?" I ask Marcus. "My Sight will be sharpened, but I will feel dizzy, out of step?"

He winks at me. "I make every woman feel dizzy. You'll get used to it."

With a short laugh, I turn again to focus on *The Play of Secrets*. Upon the stage, dinner is being served to the courtiers, and they are truly a motley bunch: lords great and small, the head of the guards, and a man I suspect is one of Walsingham's spies, for all his foppish ways. At the head of the table is Master James himself, and to his right, no less than Robert Dudley. No wonder the Queen is so focused on the play. Wherever Robert Dudley goes, her eyes are sure to follow.

I turn to watch a "servant" step up onto the stage, bearing a tray heavily laden with soul cakes for all the players, and a flagon of what appears to be wine. "Well, well," I say. "I'll wager Cecil and Walsingham have drugged that wine." And three guesses on who sold them the herbs to do it. No wonder Maude feels comfortable here!

"In the middle of a theatrical production?" Marcus asks. "Isn't that unwise?"

His surprise is reasonable, but I am certain I am correct. Maude's truth tonic played so well the night of the convocation of seers, as did Walsingham's poison, that the advisors have clearly become greedy.

"Drink, drink!" James laughs from atop the stage. "To Queen and country, both so fair as to charm the dead from their very graves."

There's a murmur of nervous laughter in the crowd, and the men onstage lift their cups, then take healthy draughts. James does the same, I see, and I watch as he downs all his wine. If the Queen's advisors have indeed drugged the flagon with Mistress Maude's tincture, this could make for an interesting evening.

The production goes on, and the jokes get ever more ribald—gossiping really, about this maid or that, this Frenchman or that Spaniard, and all of the hardships that go with living in the Queen's court. "The incessant dancing!" Master James proclaims. "So much revelry, so much to celebrate! Why, you would think she is the Queen of all the world, so much attention she draws."

"And so she is!" Robert Dudley slams his cup of wine down onto the table, the shock of the sudden movement causing the audience to jump. "She is the heaven and the earth, the greatest ruler to ever grace England. She will be spoken about until time immemorial. She is our *Queen*." Dudley speaks with earnest conviction, his heart in his words, and my gaze flies to Elizabeth—as do the rest of the court's, I'm sure. For a brief, naked moment, she looks back at Dudley as if he were both her greatest joy and also her most everlasting sorrow. Then the mantle of her rule returns to settle around her shoulders, and she smiles graciously, accepting Dudley's words as if they are her due. Dudley, for his part, is panting, almost wide-eyed, but Master James merely laughs. "Indeed, as you say it, so then it is true! Would you like to propose the next toast, then?" The troupe master's words are bright and bold, shimmering in the air, but Dudley falters back, wise enough not to be drawn out as he sinks into his chair. "More wine!" he shouts instead.

"Huzzah!" James cheers, and the actors from his own troupe cheer as well, joined a half second later by the nobles, who seem to be meeting themselves coming and going at this point. One by one they all stand up, the actors playing their roles expertly, each of their fake secrets louder and more shocking than the last. The nobles begin to follow suit, seeming to forget that the secrets spilled by the actors are fabrications, whereas the secrets *they* are spilling have the uncanny ring of truth. I suspect that somewhere in this crowd, Walsingham is taking note. Somewhere in this crowd, Meg is committing to memory every statement, every chance comment. I cannot tell if Master James is playing along or if he's worked with Cecil to orchestrate the entire charade, but even he is looking a little desperate. Perhaps the play is getting out of hand?

At that moment, however, a chair topples over onstage. A young nobleman jumps to his feet, his face as flushed crimson as his doublet. "No!" he says, pointing into the crowd. "It cannot be! You are dead!"

With the benefit of my Sight, I see the shade that the courtier has spied. It is an ancient, wasp-faced man, who looks as cruel in the everafter as he doubtless did in life, his anger and belligerence so brightly obvious to me that only death could keep him on his side of the veil. And on this night, of all the nights, it seems the dead really are coming back to walk among the living.

The ladies and lords gasp and quickly spin round, looking

for the new player in their midst. I feel their apprehension swirl up as they realize no one is standing there, that the man on stage is seeing a ghost. I hear a woman cry out, a lord's nervous laugh, but as the courtier stares in growing horror, fear takes hold of the crowd. For most of the watchers, the space where the young man is staring is patently, obviously empty. Until suddenly it isn't.

"I am as dead as dead can be, Lord John, but 'tis no fault of yours indeed!"

Meg steps into the empty space where the young lord is staring. He blinks at her, shaking his head like a wounded bull.

Meg, however, continues on as if she were born to the stage—which, of course, she was. "You've cried more tears than I e'er deserved, but now I'm here your soul to serve. Look ye all!" Meg commands, and she lifts her hand in a proud flourish. "For I am Lord John's cousin if you didn't know. Prettiest girl in the village, I'm here to tell you so. Lord John urged me to have a care, but I told him I'd do as I dared."

There is a rumble of curiosity. Clearly, some of the crowd half-believe Meg's tale. As if they haven't seen her roam the halls of Windsor for lo these past six months!

Meg, for her part, is enjoying herself thoroughly. She steps into the widening space the crowd is making for her, striding for the stage. Behind her, even the pinch-faced shade looks surprised at her act.

"Then I wandered into the night, and twisting, shifting, lost my sight," Meg cries. "Fell to my death that eve, 'tis true! But again, Lord John, no fault to you!"

Accompanied by another gasp of the crowd, Meg hops up onto the stage, stepping easily toward the shocked and horrified young man. As he slumps back in his chair, Meg kneels down and grasps his hands.

I realize that Marcus is also still holding me tight. "Who did that man on the stage kill?" he asks, almost offhandedly. "Who is he looking at with such dismay?"

"His father." The words are out before I can catch myself, and Marcus grins down at me.

"You see?" he says. "We are well matched, Sophia. With me at your side, holding your hand, there is nothing you can't see, and without any harm to you."

His words unnerve me, for all that they are filled with hope and possibility, and I glance away from Marcus, pulling my hand from his and crossing my arms over my chest. Mistress Maude remains at the very edge of the crowd, smiling and laughing, but her eyes are fixed on a point far closer to me, and I turn to see what has captured her attention so.

A woman is struggling up the short steps to the Queen's dais, her head ducked in submission, her hands carrying a tray of soul cakes.

"Soul cakes! Soul cakes," bellows Mistress Maude from across the Quadrangle, in a voice loud enough to truly wake the dead. Cecil is leaning down to whisper into Elizabeth's ear, and doesn't seem to be paying a wit of attention to what's happening around them both.

Meanwhile, Master James takes up the refrain, incorporating the strange disruption into the play like the experienced troupe master he is. He snatches up one of the cakes from the plate on the stage and holds it high. "Soul cakes, soul cakes!" he echoes back in his rich baritone. "I pray thee, good missus, a soul cake!"

There is a commotion at the Norman Gate, and Marcus and I wheel around to see a line of women processing into the Upper Ward, bearing trays overladen with the round, white-frosted cakes, each surmounted with black currant crosses. The crowd cheers their delight, and over all of it, Master James calls out again. "One for Peter, two for Paul!" he cries, following the familiar chant. "Three for Him what made us all!"

I glance again at the Queen, and go rigid with shock. Suddenly I focus on the woman at her feet, offering up the tray of soul cakes. Even now, caught up in the excitement of the revel, the Queen is reaching out greedily for the sweet treats without allowing a servant to taste them first. And suddenly I see the soul cakes themselves, as if for the first time.

Everything comes together in my mind.

"Marcus!" I say urgently. "I must go!"

"But why?" He looks at me, his brows winging up. "Sophia, whatever is the—"

I don't give him a chance to finish.

CHAPTER THIRTY

I leap off the small bench and race through the crowd, the play still roaring behind me. Meg is trapped onstage, and I see Beatrice there as well, her head bent down to Robert Dudley, who appears to be crying. I don't see Anna or Jane, however. I look wildly around for them, but it's no use—I have to do this alone.

The crowd presses into me, and fear takes hold. *I'll never make it to the Queen in time!*

My heart clamoring with urgency and my need paramount, I slip into the Sight.

For a moment all is still. I realize that I am no longer in the Upper Ward, but just beyond it, in a far darker, more ethereal glade. It is heavy with shadows, and this time I realize in an instant what is missing here: there is no obsidian bench. Nothing to ground me to the outside world but a faint, almost half-remembered pressure that was once at my hands, reminding me that someone waited in the mortal realm for me. Someone true and real.

Then the words of the dark angel roar through my mind anew, vanquishing all other thoughts.

Death plays your Queen in a game without end.

The Queen is to be poisoned, in her moment of greatest triumph.

It circles and crosses, then strikes once again.

By something as sweet and simple . . . as a child's soul cake.

Can this be true? The angels' terrible vision assaults my mind once more—a white field with a black cross, the Queen at its center. And before me, on the mortal plane, the Queen is holding up her cake, the lights from the torches rendering her gown's pattern not the blue and white that I know it to be. Instead, the pearls have turned to flecks of gold, and the blue to deepest black. Just as she was dressed in my vision.

Only, in my vision she was dead.

With great effort I strain to see the world around me as it truly is. The Upper Ward! I must return to the Upper Ward! Gradually the mists clear the tiniest bit and I burst forward, but despite the speed that the Sight has granted me, I am too slow—too awkward. My legs tangle up in my skirts, and just like that, I am falling.

Strong hands yank me upright. I know without looking that it is my dark angel, and my heart surges with hope. Arc will tell me if what I fear is true! My grim specter, however, gives me no time to think. He pulls me up short, pulling me round to face him. Once more he dares to touch me with his gauntleted hands, sending the realm spinning at a frightening speed. Once more he dares to take me in his arms. As the chatter of angels around us diminishes to the sound of whirring birds and clicking insects, Arc grasps both my hands with his left, then lifts his right hand to my cheek. I force myself to hold my chin steady, to peer into the darkness where there should be a face. From the black shadows of his cowl, something stares back at me, but it is not human, exactly. It is barely discernible beneath the flames flickering around his hood.

You are afraid of me. His breathing is labored, his pain intense. *Afraid I will harm you.* Fire blazes from the edges of his cowl at what he must see in my eyes. *Never.*

His tone is full of rebuke, and I swallow, compelling myself back to my purpose here. My duty is to the Crown. Straightening my shoulders, I set aside my fear and force myself to ask the question burning in my heart.

"I believe there is a woman set upon killing the Queen," I say. Conflicting images assault me. First, the vision I saw in my cell within the castle—Elizabeth as an old woman, regal and proud, her face laden with heavy paints like some sort of precious work of art. Then, hard upon that, is the sight of Elizabeth young and beautiful, crumpled in her fine gown on a field of ghostly white, the crown toppled from her head. Which vision is true? Which will come to pass? "Does she strike tonight? Will she poison the Queen?"

A shudder passes through the dark angel. *The price is high for what you seek.* His voice is agonized, even as his gauntleted hand firms on my cheek. *It is always so high.*

"I must know, Arc," I say, and watch as he shivers again, as if even the sound of his name causes him pain. A tittering of angels surrounds us once more, and Arc scowls to the right, as much as an entity can scowl with no face. Still, a harsh wind immediately rushes through the clearing, transforming the spirits' sniggers to screams. Arc and I stand in the middle of the maelstrom, his cloak surging up and around us. He has dropped his hands away from me, and I step back, confused. And then I understand what he's doing.

He has drawn off his long leather gauntlets, and the sight of what lies beneath those heavy gloves quails my heart in my chest. Arc's hands are scored with thick white scars, his forearms as well. As if he had run through a forest of flaming swords, the blades slashing the meat from his bones. I blink up at him as he lifts his hands to his cowl, shifting it back. Then I stare as the wind howls around us.

I can see his face.

He has a *face*.

The being gazing down at me is unlike any angel I have ever imagined. He is not a fleshy child surmounted by a halo, nor a beatific mother beaming down at her children. He is a battle-hardened warrior, his face partially hidden by a large black-and-silver mask that covers his eyes and nose. The skin beneath that mask is ravaged by scars, his face brutally handsome at one time, and now—merely brutal. He is dressed like the finest courtier, in a black-and-silver-embroidered doublet and loose breeches slashed with yet more silver panels. His hosiery is black as well, and it looks like spun silk. Instead of shoes he wears riding boots that have been polished to a high shine. He has a ruff at his neck, but it is so simple that it is little more than folded cloth.

I struggle to keep myself upright as, through his mask, Arc watches me with hauntingly familiar eyes. Then his gaze shifts to something over my shoulder, and I turn. The world around me feels utterly wrong, and it takes me only a moment to realize what has changed.

No one else is moving.

They are caught, suspended almost, as if time had been ripped away for a moment, forced to hold its breath.

"What's happening?" I whisper.

Arc gestures me forward. "The feast of Samhain is a tradition older than recorded history." He speaks with a voice rough from disuse, and I realize these words are spoken *aloud*, not merely in my head.

"Now so much is lost," he continues. "The people are left only with the superstitions—these festivals, the fires." He nods at a towheaded child caught midstep, racing through the crowd with a round white cake decorated with a cross of black currant jelly, his eyes alight with mischief. "The soul cakes, I believe you call them in this time. But the one piece of the tradition everyone still recalls, if in a slightly altered form, is that of the dead being able to walk among the living."

"I see them," I say, for the dead are still here, angry and fierce, wailing and morose. They too are caught in time, their silent cries halted. In fact, no one is moving except for the angels themselves. And they are walking among the frozen bodies of mortals and shades as if they had stepped into a garden of sculptures.

"The dead cannot truly walk," Arc says. "They are but shades, even on this night. But they can be seen by those who knew them as who they once were. Seen and remembered, whether such recognition brings joy, or pain, or sorrow, or horror. They are not forgotten, in the end." He shrugs. We are steps away from the Queen. She has a cake in her hand, her eyes laughing, her mouth smiling. She is leaning forward, ready to savor the sugary confection.

"Miss Sophia." The dark angel's words draw my attention back. He is smiling down at me, and I feel something shiver inside me, an emotion I have never quite felt before, in all the years of my life.

"But—the Queen," I say, though in truth I am trapped in the spell of Arc's gaze. Not even with Marcus have I felt this unabashed wonder, as if a flower were unfurling inside me, precious and soft. "I must go to her."

"There remains a moment more," he murmurs, his haunted eyes searching mine. "I have long wished to walk with you on this night, Miss Sophia. While I have of late seen you with greater clarity, both alone and with—with the assistance of a young man."

He pauses, and I rush to supply the name. "Marcus," I say.

Arc frowns at the name, his manner almost uncertain, but there seems no judgment in him, and the warmth within me grows, suffusing my body as he smiles. "With this young man you call Marcus, it is not the same as seeing you here, like this."

I stare at him, trying to commit his ravaged face to my memory. "But how is it I can see so much of you now? And why do you wear the cowl and the cloak?"

He chooses to answer only the second question. "I wear the cloak and cowl because on every other day but this, to see so much of my face would be to cause you death," he says, his words quiet and plainly stated, but the tone beneath them heavy with a thousand years of sorrow. "You or any like you, Miss Sophia. But I should regret causing you harm, most of all."

"But you are . . ." I reach toward his face, and he reflexively shifts away.

"Nay," he says. "You must never touch my face directly, Miss Sophia. It is the one thing I dare not allow, not even when the clock strikes twelve this night." His smile is wintry soft, filled with regret. He lifts his head again, his attention shifting to the Queen. "Ah. It seems a moment's grace is all I am to be spared."

My own gaze slides past the Queen and fixes on the stage. James is there, of course, but he is not staring at the Queen at all. He is staring at Walsingham . . . only it's a Walsingham that I have never seen before. The spymaster's eyes are wide, his face white with fear, his mouth stretched tight in horror, as if he were issuing forth a silent scream. He appears to be leaping forward, bracing himself on the shoulders of two men directly in front of him, his eyes fixed on the Queen. He knows, I realize. He knows the Queen is about to eat the cake, and he recognizes the white field upon it, with its black cross. But who else fears for her?

Robert Dudley is staring at Elizabeth, his eyes glistening with unshed tears. But then, he's always staring, moony-eyed, at Elizabeth, so that's of no account. Cecil is not; he's conferring with a guard. There are maybe a half dozen other men looking at the Queen, their faces a mix of adoration, respect, interest, lust, jealousy, outrage. It is ever thus. But none of these courtiers seem to comprehend the truth of what is about to befall her. None of them but Walsingham and me.

Then, finally, I see Maude.

She is hovering at the right of the Quadrangle, as if she's edging away. But she is frozen too, staring at the Queen with earnest intensity. And there is triumph in her eyes.

She believes her work is almost finished. That the Queen will die this night.

Horror lances through me, and yet it is as if I were watching the scene the way an artist might a painting, with everything unfinished upon the canvas. With one sweep of a brush, I can change the picture entirely, I feel it in my bones. And yet . . . how?

Arc stands away from me and offers me another short bow. "Time has not stopped here, but merely has moved to a snail's pace. And we can no longer tarry, when your Queen is at such risk." He smiles sadly, nodding at my understanding of his words. "Not everything you saw in your vision will happen this night, fair Sophia. But this will, unless you stop it. This will."

Mesmerized by Arc's words, I turn back to the Queen and realize he speaks the truth. While before her smile was broad and her eyes laughing, now her gaze has shifted down, her attention focused on the small, perfectly formed cake in her hand. A field of white, surmounted by a black cross. The merest moment has passed, and yet I too feel the weight of time lurching forward.

Still, panic seizes me at the thought of leaving Arc's side. There is something more I must understand here, something I am missing! I look back at him. "We still have some moments left," I say, shocking myself at my own words. But the Queen will always need to be saved, after all. Whereas Arc . . . "Why did you find me here?" I ask him baldly. "I didn't summon you, or speak your name."

"No," he says, his tone almost self-mocking. "But here, this night—it is the closest thing to seeing you on your own plane that I may ever be granted, Miss Sophia. I wanted that, above all else." He smiles again, shaking his head. "I suppose I am a fool."

"No." I flush. His eyes are fixed on mine, and I feel dizzy to be so near to him and yet apart—so far apart—that I cannot imagine we will ever be able to cross this distance again.

"Would you . . ." I flail about for words, again wanting there to be something—anything—to bind us together, some memory strong enough to link us across the planes. "Would you kiss me?" The very idea of asking for something so brazen mortifies me, but what am I to do? I can't let Arc slip away into the shadows of the spirit realm, lost to me forever.

Arc closes his eyes briefly, as if absorbing a staggering blow. I know the answer before his eyes open again, but they do at last, holding me still. "I told you. I dare not," he whispers, and there is something in his voice . . . something almost *familiar*. "Were I to be so bold, I would steal away your breath, your life, your soul. As mine was once taken from me." He steps sharply away from me then and catches up my hand. He seems frozen for a moment, with so much anger, anguish, and an emotion I cannot name roiling off him, it is as if he were trapped in its storm. Then, so quickly

I do not have time to think, he pulls my hand to his mouth and presses his lips against the skin of my palm.

Fire jolts through me, alighting my blood and bones. I gasp but cannot pull away—*will* not pull away—even if it were to mean death itself. Arc straightens and puts my hand against his heart. "Forgive me," he rasps, but I am too shocked by what I feel beneath my fingers.

"It *beats*," I say.

"It beats." And just that quickly he pushes my hand away, as if gifting me with the very essence of his being. "Go," he orders me. "Go save your Queen, Sophia. She is worth saving."

Sound crashes all around me.

I have been thrust back into the middle of the Samhain spectacle, not five feet from the Queen. My heart pounds with urgency, all of the horror and fear and knowing I have gained this night knifing through me at once. I turn, surging forward as Elizabeth leans down to bite her pastry.

"Your Grace!" I cry.

The Queen looks up, her eyes wide and shocked as I fly up the dais and bat the cake out of her hand. "Poison!" I say, and she draws back in horror. At that moment, however, a series of fireworks lights up the night sky. It is midnight on Samhain. All the energy in the castle seems to crystallize as Walsingham bursts up the dais as well, stumbling to his knees before the Queen, mad in his urgency to reach her.

But I don't see him. I see only Arc, still standing in the crowd, lost and alone. Around him the angels remain as well, sharing space with the Queen's court on this one night a year.

Spirits and mortals, standing as one, the veil between the worlds ripped asunder. Is this why the dark angel could truly appear to me only now, in the moments before midnight? But for how long? And what is this nagging certainty I have that I cannot yet let him leave?

The thunderous chimes of the Windsor clock strike the first bell of their dolorous refrain.

What was it he said? I think desperately. "*Not even when the clock strikes twelve—*" *What is it he meant?*

One . . . two . . . The cacophony of the court musicians starts again, and I fly down the stairs, determined to reach Arc once more. My task is done, the Queen is safe. Surely I can have this moment, to see him for what he truly is! The clock is striking *three . . . four . . .*

The dark angel takes a shocked step backward, but then he stills, not trying to stop me as I race toward him. The clock strikes *five . . . six . . .* The music is wild around us, and some country dance has started, but we are not a part of it. Instead Arc opens his arms and I run into them, wanting to get as close to him as I can, knowing it is not enough, that it can never be enough. *Seven . . . eight . . .* My mind records the chimes as a death knell. I urge myself closer still. Wanting to feel his heart against my heart, his hand against my hand. I strain up to see his face, and he is looking down at me, so close to me that I can feel the heat of his lips hovering over mine. His heart is pounding in a frantic rhythm. The sound of it almost drowns out the clanging tower bells, but of course it cannot. *Nine . . . ten . . .* His eyes are haggard with pain and . . . something else, something I have never seen before in the eyes of any man.

"Who are you?" I ask, my voice broken. I am desperate, begging, but I don't care. I truly don't care.

I reach up and wrench the mask from his face, my world narrowing to a pinprick.

"No!" I scream, shocked to my core at what I see.

"I cannot . . ." Arc cries, wheeling away as the clock strikes twelve. Whatever he says next is lost in a scream of angels as he is torn away from me, pulled deep into the howling winds of the shadowy realm. I feel something else pulling at me as well, yanking me from this place even as I fight and clamor for Arc to return, to speak to me, to explain.

Instead he is thrust backward, his cloak wrapped around him once more, the shadowy hood turning as if to catch one last glimpse of me as well, until all that is left is the gleam of fire in the far-off distance, blazing around his shadowed cowl.

And then even that winks out.

I stagger back, and feel a different hand on me, a different bolstering body.

"Arc!" I shout, only it's not him. It is Marcus, strong and real and mortal, holding me up as if I weigh nothing.

"Sophia!" he says. "You disappeared! Not once, but twice. The first was but a flicker, and you went from the stage to the Queen's side in that breath. The second—" He hesitates, glancing up at the clock. "Was at about six strikes of the clock."

I let him steady me, willing myself not to loose the scream burbling up inside. "You saw nothing else?" I ask, my voice rough, intense, but Marcus only shakes his head.

"No," he says. "Whatever you saw on the other side of

the veil, I did not see. But come," he urges me. "Maude disappeared that way, toward the Visitors Apartments. There is a passage there that opens to the forest." He reaches out his hand for me, and I place mine in it. Instantly the Sight rushes over us both, rendering the riotous crowd into shadows and light.

And we are off. Where a normal man would take a stride in a breath, we take six, racing through the throng as if they were ankle deep in mud, while our feet barely touch the ground. Before we are halfway across the Upper Ward, I see Maude disappearing into the entryway to the Visitors Apartments. Just as we reach that shadowy opening, however, I see her fat form thrust back toward us. *What is this?*

Stumbling to the side, Marcus and I barely avoid crashing into Maude as she falls backward in a puddle of skirts.

"What, 'o!" she screeches into the dark passageway, even as the guards race up behind us, swooping low to yank the woman to her feet. "What manner of man are you, to treat a lady so poorly?"

John Dee steps out of the Visitors Apartments entrance in his full scholarly robes, dusting his hands off, looking quite smug.

"I knew she would try that," he says, smiling at me with fierce excitement.

For the first time in well more than a year, I want to hug the man.

CHAPTER THIRTY-ONE

The sun looms high in the sky as I linger just down the road leading from the King's Gate, Will Seton at my side. He would not allow me to escape the castle without him as protection, and nothing I said would dissuade him from his path. Along with my fellow maids, I have made my formal goodbyes to Dee and Marcus, but I find that is not nearly enough.

And so I stand in the still wood of Windsor Forest, waiting to encounter my past and future once more.

Maude did not last the night at Windsor Castle. Before Anna could arrive at her side, screeching at the guards to bind the herb mistress's hands, Maude had grabbed a pouch from her bodice and poured its contents into her own mouth. She died within minutes, mute and convulsing, bending at the waist. Her weapon of choice for her demise was a powerful dose of belladonna, according to Anna, who examined Maude after they transferred her body to the nearest empty chamber in the Visitors Apartments, away from curious eyes.

I suspect Maude wanted her tale to die with her, but that was not to be. Once I'd explained that I'd seen the shade of

Elizabeth's mother looking down upon the gathered crowd in the Upper Ward, the Queen went on a tear, demanding that I ask the angels to tell me the whole story. I complied, of course—what choice did I have? Though by the time they brought me back to consciousness, the horrible damage to my eyes gave even the Queen pause.

Still, I could tell her what I saw.

Sunlight shimmered down on Windsortown, a scene that could have happened just this morning. But the woman laboring to haul her cart of herbs and potions into the center of the town square was not Mistress Maude. At least not the Mistress Maude I knew. Instead, it was a younger, stronger version of that woman, not so round or grey. And she was not alone either. An old woman with smiling eyes and a wise laugh walked at her side. Her mother.

The scene extended in front of me, a bolt of cloth unfurled. I saw a royal litter approaching, bearing the Queen—but not my Queen. No, this woman was dressed in flame-red and gold, her hair and eyes as dark as midnight, her mouth full and her manner bold. In my mind's eye, Anne Boleyn descended from her royal perch to grace the town of Windsor, and all who greeted her bowed and stared.

And then she saw Maude and her mother, and they saw her.

Time folded on itself, and shattered.

The rest was poured into my mind as if from an overfilled cup.

Anne Boleyn, the beautiful Queen consort of King Henry, mother to the baby princess Elizabeth herself, had long fled rumors that she was a witch. The moles on her neck; her sharp, piercing gaze; even the angle of her fingers had been the cause of scandalous whispers, especially as the months wore on and she did not give birth to the longed-for male heir. During her stay at Windsor Castle, the Queen visited Maude and her mother countless times, in search of a cure to clear her complexion, to straighten her hands . . . all for naught.

But Anne Boleyn was no fool. She knew the court had turned against her, and she was desperate for someone else to draw its fickle ire.

So on that day in Windsortown, in the full and brilliant sunlight, she lifted her hand—and pointed to Maude's smiling mother, ensuring her demise.

"Witch," she cried.

With the sound of crackling fire all around me, I saw the horror play out. A questioning. A trial. A mockery of justice. The screams of a woman too quickly judged but not too quickly killed, her anguished cries washing over me—and over her still-young daughter, Maude, whose eyes were filled with horror, and with hate.

Anne Boleyn did not survive the year. Her daughter Elizabeth did, however. And so did Mistress Maude, biding her time and stoking her fury, until she could wreak her revenge. *Death plays your Queen in a game without end. It circles and crosses, then strikes once again.*

Even now, I shudder to think of Maude's terrible expression as her mother died. I can only imagine the agony she endured, to see her mother suffer such a ghastly death. I cannot help but sympathize with her fury as she saw the daughter of her greatest enemy lifted to a position of power, celebrated by all the land.

It will be ever thus for the Queen, I am certain. Consider young Robert Moreland's wife, carrying her baby, her sorrow, and the body of her fallen husband back to Gravesend. . . . If she ever learns the truth of what happened to her husband, who is to say she won't seek her revenge against Elizabeth one day as well? Being a monarch is a dark and dangerous business. But being someone who stands in the way of that monarch getting what she wants? That is more dangerous by far.

Something for me to remember.

But, for this day I am well assured of my place in Elizabeth's affections—and in her court. Even Cecil and Walsingham have begun to treat me with greater diffidence, acknowledging me as an equal among the maids, and no longer the quiet, strange girl who serves no clear purpose. The Queen, for her part, apparently seeks not only to use my gifts but to nourish them, providing me aught that I might need to increase my skills and abilities in the angelic realm. I still do not entirely know what that training will entail: audiences with masters of the arcane, certainly, learned men from across the Continent. More work with Dee as well. Even that idea no longer fills me with dismay. My uncle and I have much to overcome, yes. But there is at least the promise of a new beginning between us, and for that I am more grateful than I would have expected. My world is not so full of those who understand me, it seems, that I would push away someone I have known my whole life, as flawed as he may be.

Only the maids remain unchanged in their treatment of

me. They have always been there for me, and I do not need the Sight to know they always will be.

A small flutter of happiness unfurls within me, and I brush my hands down my skirts, once again startled by the roughness I feel on my palm. I discovered this injury shortly after we captured Maude, but it still catches me unawares. I wonder if it always will.

Two curved slashes of raised white skin scar my palm, like a burn from a long-ago fire. The slashes barely meet at the edges, and if I didn't know better, I would say I'd been burned by a set of kitchen tongs, or pincers.

But I *do* know better.

In my mind's eye I flash to Arc, flinching back from me, telling me in a haggard whisper that I dare not touch his face. Arc, who moments later kissed my hand as if he were desperate for some small remembrance of me. I run my fingers over the roughened, puckered white skin, and a thrill of awareness skates along my nerves. I have a piece of him, the barest shred.

And something more, too.

A hint. A clue. A promise for the future.

For when I pulled the mask away from Arc's face, in the moment the clock struck midnight on Samhain, when I could still see him for what he once had been, who he truly was, it was not an unknown face that stared back at me, but one I recognized very well.

What manner of magic is this? I wonder again. And what might it all entail?

"Here they are, Miss Sophia." Will Seton's gruff voice

recalls me to the bright sunshine, and I squint to see that Dee and Marcus are indeed riding toward us, their horses fresh and fine, clearly more gifts from the Queen.

Marcus sees us first, urging his horse forward into a trot. "I'll keep your uncle here," Seton says, grinning at me. "But don't take too long. You know the Queen guards her maids most jealously."

"Thank you, Will," I say, and then I am moving my horse as well, turning the young mare into line with Marcus's as he rides up. We take a well-worn trail into the forest, and I smile to think on it. How many times have I walked this way, heading for my scrying glade? And how different the forest feels today!

"Sophia." Marcus guides his horse up beside mine until our legs are touching. I look at him across the short space between us. He leans close, and I meet him halfway, our lips pressing together briefly, chastely. . .

And then not so chastely.

Suddenly Marcus's hands are at my waist, pulling me half out of my saddle as my mare shifts and stamps. My arms naturally go around him for support, and he deepens the kiss, sighing as I return his urgency.

For the face I saw when I tore away Arc's mask was no longer scarred, no longer brutalized. Instead, the dark angel's entire visage had shifted, becoming Marcus's face. Marcus, who now holds me as if I were an answer to his prayers; Marcus, who in many ways is the answer to my own—someone to walk this path with me, to venture forth both on this plane and in the angelic realm. A young man whose abilities fit with mine like a hand in a glove, and whose eyes shine with an emotion I am only now beginning to understand. An emotion that fills me up as well, until my heart is near to bursting with it, like a thousand stars all soaring across the nighttime sky at once.

"Sophia," Marcus murmurs at last. "Say that you will find me in London. Say that you will not force me to wait any longer than I must."

"You have already planted the seeds in the Queen's mind," I say, just as earnestly. "To hear Dee talk, you could serve as my honorable champion, guiding me through the spirit world under his careful eyes."

"Champion, yes," Marcus all but groans. "Honorable, I cannot promise you." He pulls away to look down at me, and again I wonder at his intensity. For so long, I have stood alone against the buffeting winds of chance and fate. Now, to imagine that I will find shelter in Marcus's embrace in the future . . . it is almost too much to consider, a gift more precious than gold.

But it is not the only gift that Marcus has brought me. The sight of his face in the angelic realm is as much a key for me to better understand that mysterious plane as my existence was a key to John Dee, I feel it in my bones. I take Marcus's hands in mine, keen to learn more, but unsure of what effect my words will have.

"Marcus, before your trouble in the spirit world, did you ever interact with the angels directly?"

He frowns at me, his expression not affronted, only curious. "I don't think so. I told you, your face is the only one

I have ever recalled after returning from that plane. I don't remember the words I speak, or the visions that I see." He smiles. "It's what makes me so good as a channel. The fact that I can tell all, but remember none of it, is highly valued by the men who wish to pierce the veil."

"But you once were stronger than you are now, on the other side, were you not?" I ask. "Before you were harmed so cruelly?"

"I don't want to speak about that," he says, his words more strained as worry haunts his face, his eyes searching mine now almost frantically. "And you shouldn't either, truly. What have you seen on the other side that you ask such questions of me?"

"Sophia! Marcus!" Will Seton's booming voice sounds from the edge of the road, and we turn in our saddles, breaking away from each other and shifting our horses farther apart. A moment later Dee rides into the clearing. "We must away, Marcus. As it is, we will barely make it by nightfall, and I've no desire to put up at an inn if we can avoid it."

He regards the two of us with interest, and I can practically see the calculations in his mind. As Marcus ably stated, Dee is no fool. If he thinks there is more to my relationship with Marcus than mere friendship, he will use that to his advantage. By his own admission, there is much about the angelic realm that he wishes to understand. "Sophia," he says, "please know that you are welcome at any time at my residence in London. I expect I will be at the Queen's bidding during the Christmas holidays, but I do hope we can spend some time in conversation while we are in the city. Marcus will be working quite closely with me. So many new experiments to try, at the Queen's command."

"Of course," I say. I smile at Marcus, but his face is still set with worry, his thoughts distracted by my questions about the terrible attack he endured in the spirit realm. I try to put him at ease about it as best I can, but his mere reaction to the topic has given me the assurance I need. "Worry not, Marcus," I say. "I didn't see anything in the angelic realm that would cause me harm. In fact, the more I see, the more I agree with you that we must strengthen your abilities as well within that plane, so that we can truly walk among the angels together, and provide my uncle with all that he might seek."

"Absolutely!" Dee says, thoroughly pleased by this line of thinking. He turns his horse around, nose toward the road. "Follow me then, Marcus," he says over his shoulder. "Don't let me get too far ahead."

Marcus's eyes widen at the second reprieve Dee is granting us, but he doesn't waste it. Urging his horse close to mine once more, he leans over and captures my face with his hands. His lips press against mine like a benediction, and once more my hand burns where it was scarred by the dark angel. There is some link between them, I am sure of it. But this is not the time to share that with Marcus. We will have opportunity enough for that, in the days and weeks and months that stretch ahead of us, filled with promise. Marcus and I were meant to walk this path together, in this world and the next, and I cannot wait to begin that journey with him.

He leans back at length. "Be safe, Sophia," he says, his worry for me returning as it ever does. "Do not attempt to enter the spectral plane without a maid to stir you to wakefulness on this side, to pull you back if the struggle grows too difficult." His expression grows wintry. "In truth, were you to stray into my domain, I would be loath to let you go."

"I'll be safe," I promise, though safety to Marcus and safety to me are perhaps two very different things. I cannot promise that I will remain on this side of the veil. There is too much that I must seek out, too much that I would know. For my Queen, for my country—and now for myself and Marcus.

And I will show them all, I think, the phrase no longer a battle cry but a simple promise. I smile again at him. "You will look for me, though? Should Dee send you to the spectral plane?"

"Every moment I am among the angels, I will search for you," he promises. "Until the day we meet again on this side of the veil."

We ride sedately back to the London Road, and Marcus takes his leave. It will be only a few weeks before I see him again, I am certain. The Queen is making noises to leave before the snow falls, the promise of Christmas banquets and revels quite enchanting her imagination.

But I will not remain idle in these weeks we have left at Windsor Castle. The Queen has already made sure of that. I am to begin studying all the books of the arcane arts that she has amassed within the royal library, so that I may be prepared for anything she asks of me, in this world or any other.

I will not fail her.

But I will not fail myself, either. Or Marcus. Or Arc.

With an affectionate farewell to Ladysweet at the King's

Gate, I leave my borrowed horse with Seton, then make my way back through the Lower Ward, pausing a moment to glance around as I reach the wooded glen beside the Round Tower. It takes only a moment for me to slip among the trees, their shadows cool and welcoming.

Tilting my head, I close my eyes, then step into the angelic realm. As usual, I search for the obsidian bench, but of course it has vanished, and so I must have a care. Without Marcus or one of the maids to guide me out, I cannot stay here long. But neither can I stay away.

I do not know where Arc has fled, across the spectral plane, nor when I will hear his roughened voice again, or sense his words inside my mind. I do not know when I'll catch another glimpse of his tortured eyes, or have the chance to gaze anew into the shadows of his cowl, warmed by its sparking fire. Or even if I'll ever again feel his lightest touch against my cheek, the brush of his fingers across my lips.

But I must try to find him.

My dark angel has some desperate link to Marcus that goes beyond what I can understand. If I am to share a future with Marcus, then it is my duty to find the truth that the dark angel has begun revealing to me. There is something on this spectral plane that ties them together, something I must know if I am ever to share a life with Marcus, to explore both this world and the next together, seeing all there is to see. It was a gift, that brief glimpse of Marcus's face, and I know that gift has opened up the greatest adventure of my life. An adventure to last as long as there are angels in the heavens and stars up in the sky.

An adventure that begins for me now.

And so I peer into the shadows, murmuring a single word into the drift of specters approaching me. My voice is soft, but it carries just the same, piercing through the angelic realm with its quiet urgency.

For love also starts as a whisper.